A Ghostly Request

THE LADIES OCCULT SOCIETY

A Ghostly Request

THE LADIES OCCULT SOCIETY

KRISTA D. BALL

ꞏ⚜ Historian's Note ⚜ꞏ

In 1800, only twenty-one percent of families in England and Wales lived off more than £100 annually. Seven percent of households had annual incomes over £200. A mere one and a quarter percent of the population earned over the £1000 mark; about 28,000 families. A household earning £150 was in the top ten percent of earners in England and Wales. *(Source: Dress in the Age of Jane Austen: Regency Fashion [2019], by Hilary Davidson)*

A family needed about £1000 per year (or "per annum") to afford a horse and carriage, and this was also the lower end of the true gentry. People like the Knights are what historian Lucy Worsley calls "pseudo-gentry" *(Source: Jane Austen at Home: A Biography [2017], by Lucy Worsley)*. The incomes listed below are averages that fluctuate annually.

Mr. Knight makes about £725. Isabella is due to inherit another £500 upon her mother's death; however, that is not likely to be anytime soon.

Miss Knight earns about £50 annually from her uncle's inheritance. She has no dowry and is due no money upon the death of her father. She has £50 in savings, as well as ownership of a book worth £3000.

Charles inherited £3100 from his mother and £1500 from the first Mrs. Knight, due to the lax marriage articles that were drawn up when she married Mr. Knight. Charles earns anywhere from £180-220, though is perpetually in debt.

The three youngest Knight girls all inherited £300 each from their mother, bringing their father a measly £36 total for their upkeep and spending money.

Mary inherited £2500 upon the death of her mother. She married Mr. James Fitzharding. His estate of Ashbrook brings in about £10,000, plus Mary's £80-100 of annual interest.

Maria Thorne's dowry was £10,000. Henry Thorne's various inheritances and properties are valued around £4000, not counting Maria's annual interest of £400.

Aunt Cass is rumoured to have £4000 per annum, but is notoriously eccentric about not letting anyone know how much she actually has. It is assumed her actual income is significantly higher.

Mr. Grant earns about £1100 as an attorney, though his recent split with the Royal Occult Society puts his future earnings in question.

Mr. Osborne makes about £2500 per annum from his bookstore and possesses significant savings. He isn't considered a part of the gentry, however, because he is in trade.

Miss Alice Thorne has a dowry of £20,000, which would produce at least £800 per annum in income. Her family controls her income, though she is allowed ready access to it for reasonable purposes.

Miss Susan Markson is penniless and solely dependent upon her aunt, Mrs. Taylor, until she is physically recovered. Mrs. Taylor receives £8 per year in pensions and annuities, as well as a recent, one-time lump sum settlement of £7.

⊰❦ Chapter 1 ❦⊱

June 4, 1810

THERE WERE PEOPLE in town who believed, truly, that there was nothing as dull as country life. Even Aunt Cass had been known to make the occasional reflection upon the supposed relaxing nature of country living as compared to town. Oh, to have all hours of the day to leisurely devote oneself to a book, she'd say. How glorious!

However, as Elizabeth examined the rectory's kitchen, now flour-dusted from floor to ceiling, she found herself also wishing for the quiet simplicity of this mythical country life. For, though she lived in a quiet village twelve hours away from London, her life was neither quiet nor simple.

Elizabeth sat down on the only chair that wasn't completely covered in flour and said to her new servant, "Perhaps, Julia, might you share what you *can* cook?"

Their regular cook, who came to the rectory early every morning, currently suffered a contagious fever. The apothecary rightfully provided the strictest of medical instructions not to stir out of doors until she was fully recovered. Therefore, she'd sent one of her daughters to assist the Knight household with the meal preparations. Unfortunately, Elizabeth now feared they would all soon starve to death in their own home if their meals were left to Julia.

The flour-covered girl, who couldn't have been more than thirteen years of age judging by her height, remained silent. Elizabeth checked her frustrations and asked, "Do you know how to prepare and boil a chicken?"

"No, miss."

"Can you boil carrots?"

"Yes, miss."

"Good. There are still a few left in the larger barn loft. Now, come. Let us see what is left in the larder. Perhaps there is some meat to be had."

Julia dutifully followed behind Elizabeth into the pantry, which was off the kitchen and away from the ovens. Elizabeth looked about at their supplies. The salt beef couldn't be used for today's meals, as it required soaking. The salt fish shared a similar issue, with the addition that Isabella could not bear the smell in her current condition.

Elizabeth frowned at the fly-covered ham left from supper the previous night. "Julia, please ensure the meat is covered with a cloth, else the flies will get at it. I do not believe we can serve this now. They have gotten everywhere. Look, they have already laid their eggs. We cannot even cut it off, they are so deep."

"Yes, Miss Knight. Sorry, miss."

If the flies hadn't completely covered the piece of ham, she'd have instructed the new maid to cut off the bad section and serve the remainder. However, the entirety was now maggoty.

"We will have to do with a piecemeal dinner tonight, with you preparing the salt beef today for tomorrow's meal. So, let us see here. I believe we should use the last of the potted shrimps. They only have a week or so left before they are no good, in any case. Let us boil up some of our garden's early potatoes along with carrots and mash them together with the butter. There are peas, for certain. Then, let us see...Ah! Use up the remainder of the pickled tongue from Monday's dinner. With your bread, that should last us all through the evening into supper." She glanced at the servant's confused expression. "Do you know how to serve pickled tongue?"

"No, miss."

"Julia, I must ask. What dishes have you prepared yourself?"

"Potatoes, miss." She looked over her shoulder at the disastrous mess in the kitchen. "And bread."

Elizabeth successfully kept her frustrations moderated. Young people were not blessed with the knowledge of adults, nor their experience. "The pickled tongue only requires thin slicing upon a plate. I shall find us eggs to boil. I will speak with Miss Cassandra. She can instruct you on making almond puddings. It appears there are enough almonds for that, provided I can procure the eggs."

"I do not know what almond pudding is, miss."

This did not come as a surprise to Elizabeth. "Miss Cassandra will show you how to prepare them. They are quite simple."

"Very well, miss. Shall I slice the tongue now?"

"No. Finish your baking first. Then, you can begin gathering the dinner items."

With her kitchen task complete, Elizabeth went in search of her younger sisters. Theodosia and Georgiana were easily found by following the loudest argument in the house. Elizabeth knocked on their shared bedroom door. However, they were too engrossed in their debate to hear beyond themselves.

Elizabeth opened the door and found both girls fighting over a bonnet. "Ladies. Shall I assume there is a problem?"

"Thea took my favourite bonnet and ruined it!" G exclaimed.

"I did nothing of the sort. You dropped it in the mud and did not clean it as soon as we returned home."

"I dropped it in the mud because you pushed me!"

Elizabeth sighed. "Girls. There is plenty of ribbon in the sewing basket. Simply replace it with another. Thea, you will do the repair."

"That is not fair, Eliza!" Thea exclaimed.

"What is not fair is being pushed into mud by one's own sister," Elizabeth countered. "Now, I required potatoes for supper, as well as some eggs gathered. Please see to it."

Both girls abandoned their argument to complain about the injustice of household chores at a country rectory. Elizabeth allowed the complaints for a few sentences, before lifting her hand to silence them.

"Girls. If you do not fetch these items, we will not have anything for dinner."

"Why don't we have a maid to do all this?" Thea whined. "Barbara Parsons has never even had to dig a potato in her life."

"Miss Barbara's father makes nearly two thousand pounds a year and can afford to hire extra help."

"Why are we so poor?" G whined.

Elizabeth smiled and said, rather cheerily, "I do not believe a family living off seven hundred pounds is considered poor. Now, come along, unless you both wish to go to bed hungry tonight."

The bonnet argument was resumed once more, taking the direction of what improvements could be made. Elizabeth went in search of her father. She found him in his study, poring over the household account books.

"Ah, good morning, Elizabeth. Have you removed the girls from the house?"

Elizabeth chuckled. "They are off to dig potatoes."

"Good. The fresh air will do them good. And how fares our replacement in the kitchen?"

Elizabeth stood in front of her father's large desk with her hands folded in front of her. Her father was looking down at his accounts book, and Elizabeth noticed not for the first time that his hair was both thinning and rapidly greying this last year. He'd had the streaks of grey and white for as long as she could remember, but what were once specks was now entire patches. His thick hair was wispier, too, to her eye.

When it was clear he was not going to look up at her, she said, "Miss Julia is very inexperienced in the kitchen, sir, but she made some excellent bread this morning. I'm going to fetch Cassandra to assist her with making almond puddings, and hopefully we shall have something edible for dinner."

Mr. Knight didn't look up from his accounts book. "Very good. There will be mutton next week, so plan your dinners accordingly, my dear."

"That will be very welcome. I wish to speak to you about the meat situation, however, until then. With Isabella unwell, we cannot use any of our fish stores currently, and we have eaten all of our bacon and smoked pork. Our hams are gone, and we will not have any salt beef after tomorrow. We'll be serving our last pickled tongue today, along with last of the potted shrimps."

Her father raised a finger to signal her silence. She ceased her speech and waited for her father to scratch out several more lines. At length, he put his pen down and looked up at her.

"I had wished to speak to you on financial matters today, so this is rather fortuitous that you, too, thought of the matter. Of course, we need meat in the house. Pray, why can we not have chicken?"

"She does not know how to prepare the bird," Elizabeth said.

"Can we not send her back? Surely, there must be a girl in the village somewhere that knows how to pluck and boil a chicken?"

"I can make inquiries, but you know the difficulties of finding help."

A displeased sound escaped her father. "I do not approve of these girls who cannot even do the most basic of tasks. They were born to serve, and yet they are shockingly lazy and stupid."

"Papa," Elizabeth said with a hint of reproof. "She is quite young. We will not starve with potatoes, potted shrimps, and tongue."

Her father made another sound. He reached into a drawer and began counting out coins. "I authorize you to spend up to eight shillings at the market. Please recall that we have the Parsons coming for dinner this coming Saturday. We need an excellent meal for them."

Elizabeth accepted the silver and copper coins and slipped them into her apron's pocket. Her father disapproved of credit; he said it was ungodly. They paid ready money for everything, no matter how small or large the purchase. "I fear Julia will not be up to the task of an elaborate meal. Upon consideration, however, I do believe two robust, if simple, courses and a helping of sweets should help out balance any lack of frills and frivolities."

"I place the success of the dinner entirely in your hands, daughter. I wish to impress Mr. Parsons, for I hope to rent some acres of his estate closest to our property. If I succeed, we shall increase our household income by one hundred pounds, perhaps even more."

"A welcome addition for sure. I wish you all the best, and I shall endeavour to offer an excellent meal at table."

"Take the donkey cart, if you wish, and one of the girls. I wish the strife above-stairs to cease."

"Of course, Papa." She waited for him to bring up the other matter he wished to discuss.

"Now, I wish to discuss your pin money."

Elizabeth remained very still as she awaited the inevitable. "Yes?"

"Now, my dear, if my recollection is accurate, you had in your possession eight pounds and two shillings. Now, I did see you purchase yet more lace for your sisters the other day, so I shall assume your personal wealth has been somewhat reduced."

Her father did not know of the fifty pounds hidden away in her writing desk and, with the Lord's assistance, he would never know. However, she did not wish to lie to him, either. So, she kept her reply as brief as possible.

"As you say. I have been assisting the girls with frivolous purchases in an attempt to keep the peace about the house. For *Isabella's* sake." Elizabeth might have put more emphasis on the last sentence than was strictly necessary.

"I am very glad to hear it. I cannot endure much more shrieking, so I approve of your lace purchases, wasteful though it is. Have you by chance received word from Mr. Thorne or Mr. Osborne? I am very curious to know what the final sum will be once your book selling business has been completed."

In this question, Elizabeth could happily tell the truth. "I have not heard from either since last Tuesday's letter, so I have no new intelligence on that score. My last note came from Maria, on Wednesday, who was instructed to inform me that Mr. Osborne has delayed the swift sale of the remaining trunk of books due to it possessing several rarer volumes. Mr. Osborne and Mr. Thorne are working together to find the best buyers. They asked my permission if I would be willing to delay the sale so that the best prices could be fetched."

"And what did you say?"

"I advised them to delay for the best price. I felt that was the sensible thing, given that I already had some money at my disposal and that a little patience could earn me more."

Mr. Knight nodded, pleased with his daughter's words. "That is better news than I'd thought. You may yet get ten or twelve pounds! What say you?"

"I would not be at all surprised if Mr. Thorne eventually returns with twenty pounds." Elizabeth smiled at her shocked father. "Indeed, Papa! In my last letter from Mrs. Thorne, she informed me that Mr. Thorne already had set aside a grand sum of thirteen pounds and that he still had several books left in his possession."

Her father glanced down at his account and nodded contentedly to himself. "This is very good news. Oh, very good news indeed. With Isabella's delicate situation, I believe we shall soon require a nurse to live amongst us. I cannot find anyone in the village, however, which means involving your aunt in London and requesting her assistance."

"I would be happy to take on that task, Papa, if you prefer."

"No, child. I have already done so. I suspect that this will cost me dearly, for both the wages, and the room and board. Oh, I did not calculate the laundry costs for a nurse, and any medicines or cures necessary." He looked down at his book before scribbling a note to himself. "Yes, this will cost me a great fortune."

She prepared herself for what was about to come. Elizabeth knew her father too well and she'd expected this conversation for some time now. To be rather honest, her only surprise had been that it had taken him so long to arrive at this place. She gave Isabella credit for his delay.

"You will be pleased to learn, I think, that I have received your uncle's paperwork regarding your inheritance. Mr. Grant has kindly offered to continue the administration of the account from London, as your uncle apparently paid him handsomely in advance for the task. Oh, to have such ready money as to make arrangements for after one's own demise! Now, Mr. Grant has written me to announce that he will be sending your first payment via Mr. Thorne when he returns to the countryside, to save us all the expense of a private courier. However, this is not the news I wish to share. Mr. Thorne will apparently be arriving with a sum of, now prepare yourself, Elizabeth, for I had to seat myself when I read the letter."

Her father's pause signalled that he wished an appropriate reaction from her. So she said, "Goodness! What amount will be arriving?"

"Twenty-eight pounds! The money was invested in the four-percents, which I shan't bother to explain..."

"I know what the four-percents are, Father."

Her father didn't appear to have heard. "Without further explanations on England's banking systems, I shall summarize by saying the four-percents performed admirably and you shall be the benefactress of that good luck. When this small fortune arrives, I assume you will wish me to manage it for you and provide a monthly payment to your purse?"

"I shall manage it, sir, if it pleases you."

Her father made one of his dissatisfied sounds, announcing that it did not please him. "It is a large sum of money and I saw the gifts you arrived with from London. I fear you will continue to be a spendthrift with this good fortune laid in your lap."

"Papa, that is unkind." Elizabeth gathered her emotions at her father's shocked expression at her disagreement. "I simply wished to purchase my sisters a few luxuries to keep them out of Isabella's way while I remained in London. Further, do not forget that Charles required a little pocket money for his own stay in London, which I provided to him so that he would not need to trouble you. I assure you, sir, I can be trusted with my own inheritance."

He waved a hand. "Large speeches are not required here, Elizabeth. If you say you can manage your own guineas, I shall trust you and will only intervene when I witness any unnecessary expenses. After all, you are not guaranteed to make this sum again in six months. The four-percents can be very volatile."

"There is little risk of me living beyond my income, sir. My needs are quite small," Elizabeth said. "I would prefer to manage my income myself."

"As you desire," her father said. "Then, I wish to discuss how I believe the care of your expenses should be distributed from now on. I shall continue to pay for your washing, which you should be aware costs me over nine pounds per annum. Your letters and parcel cost just shy of four pounds, but I shall continue to pay for those provided you exercise prudence whenever possible. Now, I wish to discuss your gowns. Your clothes cost over twelve pounds last year according to my records, and let us not forget your pin money of twenty pounds that I provide you annually. I would like you to take on your clothing expenses with your newfound wealth, and not insist upon your pin money from me. With those economies, we can afford an excellent nurse for Isabella, which is obviously for all of our sakes."

"Of course," Elizabeth said. She was relieved it was not worse. "I had already planned to speak to you on the matter."

The last part was not a lie. She had considered bringing the topic before him once her first sum of money arrived. However, she knew he would find his way there eventually, so thought it best to allow it to be his own idea.

"You are such a level-headed girl. I never understood why you were Augusta's least favourite."

Elizabeth made no reply. Her father did not understand that women had feelings and intelligence enough to be stung by such words. Or that it was in bad taste to admit one had favourites amongst their own children.

"Now, I have done the calculations for you, and your new income minus these new financial responsibilities you have taken upon yourself will still bring you a very respectable sum of just over forty-three pounds per annum, which is an excellent sum for a young lady such as yourself. To be fair, that is more money than I have to spend upon myself. You are very fortunate indeed."

"Indeed, sir," Elizabeth said flatly. She knew well enough that her dresses would not be the only expense to fall upon her purse in the coming weeks.

"And let us not forget your current coins remaining from your eight pounds..."

"A little more than seven pounds, sir," Elizabeth corrected him. "As I said, I have spread my money between my sisters to ensure the rectory's harmony."

"Money well spent," Mr. Knight said. "So, with the eventual arrival of Mr. Thorne and dare we hope for another twenty or so? My dear, that leaves you with a grand sum all together. And to think, if the funds continue to do moderately well, you might get the same income in a six-month and not have any expenses! Indeed, you are wealthier than myself at present. How fortunate you are to have had these gifts bestowed upon you. Augusta wished us to cut all ties with the Leigh family, but I will have you know that I stood up for you having contact with your London relations, no matter how poorly Augusta thought of them. Now, look at the bounty for which my Christian generosity has been rewarded. I am very pleased that I listened to my own wisdom on that score."

Elizabeth made no reply; she did not want to provoke further insults. She was not upset by the increase in her expenses. After all, she truly did believe that her good fortune was everyone's good fortune, and a nurse to assist Isabella would be a welcome relief to the entire household. However, Elizabeth was well aware that her father would not take back the expense of her dresses now, not even if he inherited twenty thousand pounds tomorrow. She would have to manage her money carefully. At least she was no longer on the marriage market and could dress simply more often than not.

"Now, about this Mr. Grant. You have met him, yes?"

"Frequently, sir. He is an excellent gentleman."

"Is he married?"

She shook her head. "No, sir. He is a widower without children."

"Lucky man! Inherited his wife's dowry without any children to share it with. What is his situation in life?"

Elizabeth was surprised by this sudden interest in a London attorney, but she could see which way this wind was blowing. She would tread carefully. "I do not know the exact details of his situation, but he was an attorney for the Royal Occult Society for some time. He had been the primary attorney for my uncle's estate, and also still works for Aunt Cass and my cousin, Mr. David Leigh. He comes highly recommended, both in his profession and his reputation as a gentleman."

Her father's face lit up with excitement. "He must be doing very well with such clients. And a widower you say?"

"Indeed. As I understand it from my aunt, he is very attached to his bachelorhood, so will most likely remain so for the foreseeable future."

He waved a dismissive hand at her. "All men say that until they meet the right young lady, of course. After all, it is God's will that we marry and have children to glorify his name."

Elizabeth could not imagine adding more children into the current mix of her problems.

"And he has been very attentive towards you."

Elizabeth gave her father a wide grin and said, "Do not forget, Papa, that he was paid to be kind towards me. It is amazing how delightful people can be when there is the promise of a paid invoice at the end of it all."

Her father let out a frustrated sound. "Are you determined to remain unmarried, Elizabeth Knight?"

"Yes, Mr. Knight, she is. What's more, I believe we must respect her wishes."

Elizabeth turned around to see her stepmother in the doorway. She looked well, all things considered, as she carefully made her way to her husband's side. She had a shawl about her shoulders, and was wearing a heavy wool gown, one normally reserved for winter.

Mr. Knight's expression darkened. "Isabella! What are you doing out of bed?"

Isabella waited until she was seated before responding. "Mrs. Green and Mr. Collins both are in an accord that it would be best for my health to take a refreshing turn about the house every hour or so. Also, I am to venture out of doors on sunny mornings for a short walk about the garden, and am authorized to sit in the sun provided I wear wool as well a shawl and promise to return inside if I feel a chill. I must also avoid the strongest heat of the day."

"But your situation!" he insisted.

"Mr. Collins believes fresh air and a small amount of exercise will do me the best good in the world." She smiled at Elizabeth. "How are you today, my dear?"

Mr. Knight did not give his daughter an opportunity to answer. "My dear, Isabella. Surely you have misunderstood the instructions. Medical matters can be difficult to follow. I am convinced that Mr. Collins has no idea of you going out of doors. Your delicate mind has created this fanciful tale."

Isabella motioned behind her. "Mr. Collins is still here, and I had supposed you would like to speak with him. I requested he wait in the drawing room while I fetched you. Forgive my interruption, Eliza."

"No apology necessary, Isabella. I am pleased to see you up and walking about."

"This new fellow knows nothing! Old Mr. Clarke would've never tolerated this. I have never heard such an instruction in my life. Sit there until I return."

Isabella dutifully remained in the chair her husband commanded her to occupy. When Mr. Knight had left the room, shutting the door behind him harder than was strictly necessary for privacy, she said, "I warned Mr. Collins that this would happen, as did Mrs. Green. But he is new here and..."

"I am simply pleased they are finally agreeing! I've seen those two argue about the weather!"

Isabella tried to laugh, but her eyes turned sad. "Alas, they both fear this will be a difficult time for me. They wish me to improve my strength, so that I will survive the process with my health preserved."

That worried Elizabeth. She understood, and indeed supported, the need to keep certain medical information away from the patient, due to the worry of the diagnosis. Even still, this did not sound encouraging nor promising. "Are you concerned?"

Isabella displayed her very best disguise of happiness, and Elizabeth allowed her the dignity of pretending. "The Lord's will be done, yes?"

"Yes." Elizabeth sighed and said, "His will be done."

There was an awkward silence between them, until Isabella found a new topic of discussion. "Pray, tell me what were you and my husband discussing when I entered."

"My inheritance and...a *slight* adjustment in my financial responsibilities." She silenced Isabella's protests. "Please, do not distress yourself. I do not object taking on the burden of my dresses and shoes so that my father can spend his money on you."

Isabella fussed with the lace of her indoor cap. "I hate these things. I look like an old maid in this, don't I?"

Elizabeth considered her words before saying, with a wicked grin, "I have never seen an old maid so large with child before."

"Elizabeth Knight!" Isabella exclaimed and reached out to slap at her stepdaughter's dress. "For shame! Don't let your father hear you speak like that, or you shall never be permitted to go to London ever again."

That sobered Elizabeth immediately, as she felt the truth of it. She decided to turn the subject to more easy topics. "Mr. Knight has given me eight shillings to feed us for the next week, until we slaughter one of the old ewes. I suppose a calf's head would not be a good choice to serve the Parsons?"

"The meat is excellent off the head, though, and so economical!" Isabella thought for a moment. "What do you think about having a head for a family dinner on Friday, and use the broth and any leftover meat to make another dish for Saturday? My mother always made a lovely hash the day after. It would be an excellent addition to the company table, and would not need to be the centrepiece of the meal."

"That is an excellent idea!"

The door swung open. "What is an excellent idea?"

Elizabeth turned her head to face her father. "We are discussing the best way to feed the Parsons with the greatest economy and simplicity. What do you think of calf's head hash? Surely, someone must have a butchered cow at this time of the year, as we will have not sold ours yet."

"Oh, I do so love it when it's, oh what is the word? When the leftovers are boiled with gravy and served with bacon and those little meat balls. It completely escapes me now. Elizabeth, you must know of what I speak."

"Are you thinking of Calf's Head Fricasseed?"

"Yes! What is wrong with my memory as of late? We have not had that since Augusta died. We should serve that, if you can find a calf's head in the village today. Surely, someone must have one. It's June now! I had planned to keep our calves to sell, or else I'd suggest we could provide one for the table."

Elizabeth glanced at Isabella, who was suspiciously picking at the frills on her sleeve's cuff. "I believe the recipe is still in the kitchen. I can look for it, provided Isabella would find it acceptable."

"Why wouldn't she be? Apparently, Isabella is to be robustly gallivanting about the countryside." Mr. Knight shook his head. "I have never heard such nonsense. How does moving about improve one's strength? Is strength not like money? Spend too much and it is all gone?"

"Perhaps it is more like investment, sir," Elizabeth said. "You must spend a little of the money to invest for the hope of greater returns later."

Mr. Knight scowled at her. "One payment of interest and I find my daughter now considers herself an expert on the funds."

"I did not say that, Father," Elizabeth said flatly.

Isabella interrupted what was about to become a quarrel between father and daughter. "I do not mind in the slightest if we begin to serve Augusta's family recipes. However, if I might make a small suggestion, perhaps you may wish to ask Thea's permission first."

Elizabeth bowed her head. "I plan to."

Mr. Knight's scowl faded into confusion. "Why would the girls care about what we serve at table?"

"Mr. Knight, we have discussed this. Thea has struggled with accepting her dear mother's death. My arrival in the household, and current situation, have not helped ease her struggles." She lowered her voice and said, "We must be sensitive to her needs for a little while longer. It is the Christian thing to do in such cases."

"I would never scoff at the notion of Christian duty, my dear, but I do not understand what any of that has to do with dinner," Mr. Knight said.

Isabella gave Elizabeth a pleading look before turning to her husband. "Mr. Knight, Elizabeth has to prepare for her trip into the village so that we do not starve to death. I believe she could ask Theodosia to accompany her so that they can discuss the matter in private."

"But it is just a dish!" Mr. Knight said, utterly perplexed. "No one would be upset over a dish."

"Mr. Knight, recall Theodosia's peculiar eating habits."

Mr. Knight looked genuinely perplexed. "What are you talking about?"

Elizabeth ignored her father and instead turned to Isabella. "Do you wish to accompany us into the village?"

"No, I believe I shall go to the kitchen and keep an eye on our new servant before she burns the house down around us." Isabella sighed. "I believe I know how to boil potatoes well enough to teach the concept."

"I cannot have you near the kitchen! The heat! The damp!" Mr. Knight protested.

As the married couple began an impassioned debate over Isabella's health and her need to be useful and not in bed all day, Elizabeth quietly removed herself from the study to fetch her sister and discuss the death of her beloved mother while they searched for eight shillings' worth of meat.

And Elizabeth still had to ensure the eggs were gathered. And find where Cassandra had gotten herself to.

So much for the blissful laziness of country living.

Chapter 2

ORGANIZING THE TRIP to the village came with an extra helping of dramatic scenes. First, the girls had only managed to dig up three potatoes in the entire time Elizabeth was with her father because they had been giggling and rushing about like children, instead of minding their task. Secondly, the disharmony returned when Elizabeth refused to allow G to accompany her and Thea.

For her part, Theodosia did not require much coaxing to go with Elizabeth into the village. G stomped and complained when Elizabeth kindly, but firmly, told her she could not come on this particular trip. The stomping continued indoors until their father was forced to intervene.

However, his assistance only fouled everyone's mood, including Elizabeth's. Her patience wore thin during his long sermon, especially as most of it was directed at herself and not the source of the issue—Georgiana and Theodosia's deteriorating relationship. Her father demanded Cassandra's presence, too, and continued his sermon of disappointment at his poorly behaved daughters. Elizabeth knew better than to interrupt him; it would only make the sermon last longer.

Cassandra was already dressed in one of her better gowns to visit the Baldwins, but she dutifully hiked up her hem enough to avoid the mud splatter while collecting eggs before escaping to her friend's house. With Elizabeth and Thea getting the donkey cart hooked up, that left G by herself in the kitchen garden with a pitchfork and heavy tears as she stabbed the new potatoes.

It was only half a mile to the village centre, so there was little opportunity for Elizabeth and her sister to speak of private matters from the heart. Elizabeth decided to first focus on the task at hand; the return trip could be at their leisure and all topics could then be broached without interruption.

Relief flooded Elizabeth when she discovered there was no calf's head to be had at either the butcher's or the market, allowing her to delay a difficult conversation for a little longer. Fresh strawberries caught Theodosia's eye and she purchased a gallon with her own money. Elizabeth supplied the ha'penny she fell short.

Old Mr. Fletcher was selling his rabbits and pigeons. Elizabeth caught her sister's attention, who was staring at the ribbons in the Thomas' shop window and snacking on her strawberries. "What is your opinion? Would pigeon pie be good enough for the Parsons' dinner?"

Theodosia shrugged, still eyeing the rolls of ribbon visible through the cloudy window. "Pears dipped in gold would not be good enough for them."

Elizabeth gave her sister a disapproving glance, but kept her silence; Thea had been scolded enough for one day. She purchased three pigeons from Mr. Fletcher and chatted with him for a few minutes before moving on. Mrs. Ash was selling her vegetables, and Elizabeth purchased cabbages and carrots, since the rectory's vegetables were late this year. From Mr. Whitby's cart, she purchased a nice leg of lamb and a small cut of bacon.

Finally, Elizabeth went inside to speak to the butcher. From Mr. Bohannon, she purchased a fresh cow's tongue and enough beef for the pigeon pies. Mr. Bohannon cut the beef into nice steaks for the pies, which was a great help. She realized she was three pennies short, however, so dug into her own reticule for the three small coins and handed them over.

"Do I have to share my strawberries?" Theodosia asked, as their cart was loaded with the supplies.

"Surely you are not planning to eat an entire gallon yourself."

Theodosia said nothing in reply.

"What if I purchase another gallon, for everyone else? Would that be acceptable?"

Theodosia sighed. "I don't care."

"Your tone suggests you do care. What will please you, dearest?"

"Not having to share things," Theodosia muttered.

She glanced about the main square at the various stalls and carts set up for the morning. "What if I purchase what is available of the cherries for the others? Would that be acceptable?"

"You have spent everything Father gave you."

Elizabeth shrugged. "I am a wealthy heiress now. I can afford all the cherries in the county."

That made Theodosia smile, and Elizabeth purchased two shillings' worth of cherries, which would keep the others very happy. Any leftovers could be dried or cooked into a nice pie, so they wouldn't go to waste.

Once their items were secured in their wooden crates, Elizabeth took the opportunity to direct the donkey the long way home. It was the first sunny day in ages, and she suspected her sister was in no hurry to return to the oppressive air of the rectory.

"Thea, I wish to speak to you privately on a small matter. May we serve one of Augusta's favourite dishes for dinner sometime soon? Our father is missing it and it would be so very nice of a treat."

Thea didn't reply. She didn't even turn to look at her sister. She merely looked out over the fields.

"Thea, dearest. Please, you must speak your mind. It is just the two of us here."

Elizabeth worried her sister would hoard her opinions. However, she eventually turned and said, "What purpose would that serve, Eliza? I am to do as I am instructed. So simply command me and I shall do as you bid."

Elizabeth frowned, but waited until her voice would have no trace of annoyance. "You speak with me now, not our father. There is no one else to overhear our conversation, excepting God, of course, and he already knows what is in your heart. So speak freely and tell me what is upon your mind. I will not tell our father, if that is your worry."

Thea went back to staring out at the wheat fields. "Everything. Everything is upon my mind."

The sisters carried on in silence for a while longer before Elizabeth said, "It is natural to still miss your mother, my dear."

There was no reply from her sister.

Elizabeth waited until they turned into the lane that would take them toward Vane Park. Then, she said, "It is understandable that reminders of her will make the grief stronger at times, but have you considered that perhaps there is no way to deal with that grief unless you confront it?"

"Is that what Papa was doing when he made me eat Melody?"

Elizabeth did not have a reply to that. Theodosia had been too attached to that old dairy cow. Elizabeth had warned her, that her delicate heart might not handle the weight of the inevitable. However, their father in his usual tact did not even think to consider Theodosia. She simply returned from the village one day to find her cow half gutted upon the worktable.

Elizabeth understood the balance that needed to exist between animal and human. Theodosia's tender heart, and her weeks-old grief for her dead mother was still raw and oozing. What their father did was cruel; Elizabeth saw it plainly. Any other father would have allowed Theodosia to say goodbye to the old beast and then sold her to another for the final end. They were not even suffering for meat or money; he could have even allowed the cow to remain until the end of its natural life. This would not be the first or last time someone had made such a decision for their beloved child. Maria Thorne's father kept a donkey far beyond its use because his darling girl deserved all happiness.

However, it had long been clear to Elizabeth that they were not beloved by their father. No father filled with human kindness would sit the head of a beloved child's own cow upon the table and then berate that child for her honest, heartbroken reaction mere weeks after that poor child buried her own mother.

"Will you not offer a defence of our father?" Theodosia turned to scowl at her sister. "Is that not your job in all of this, Elizabeth? To make excuses for his treatment of us."

"I have no excuses to make. I felt it was wrong then, and I feel it is wrong now."

"Yet, you did nothing," Thea snapped. She sucked in a breath and said, "Instead, every time I sit to the table with meat upon it, I have to endure our father's scolding, and you remain silent."

Elizabeth waited for her sister's anger to subside. She'd done nothing at the time because her father had not informed her of the decision. The fact of the situation was that she'd only found out what had happened moments after Thea, by way of the high-pitched grieving wails that had come from the girl. What Thea didn't see was how Elizabeth spoke to him after dinner, when Thea had already rushed from the room, declaring to never eat meat again because her father could not be trusted.

A vow she'd kept more often than not, much to everyone's worry.

Except Elizabeth's. She understood, and encouraged her sister to eat what she could of the other items. For the longest while, Thea had been fine with eel and salt fish, but now neither of those were allowed in the household due to Isabella's situation. The girl was, no doubt, hungry. Thea had grown thinner over the winter, too, though the spring supply of milk, cheese, butter, and more eggs than anyone knew what to do with had seen Thea's hollow cheeks puff out a touch more again.

If Elizabeth were placed in charge of the dinner table, half the dishes would be those that would nourish Thea. Alas, Elizabeth was not in charge of their dinner table, no matter how much responsibility continued to be heaped upon her shoulders. Her father's tastes alone dictated the daily menu. His preferences were the only consideration.

Finally, Elizabeth said, "I worry that you are not attaching yourself to life."

"I am very attached."

"Are you? I find that you are unhappy."

Thea did not reply.

Elizabeth pressed her point. "I see my life-loving sister sink into a despair that is laced with bitterness and disappointment. That her once fun, if frustrating, pranks have become rooted in spite and anger. You cannot be mad at your mother, for she is not here for us to berate, but we can in fact lash out at others around us to make them as unhappy as what is in your heart."

Thea remained silent, but her breathing hitched several times. "I truly know how difficult your grief is at this moment. Though I know that Mary will never admit this to you, I believe it is harder for you than it was for myself or Mary. We were so little when our own dear mother left us. We had an easier time adjusting to Augusta's replacement of our own mother. You are at the difficult age where your experience has not caught up with your understanding. So you do not have the necessary practice to accept this situation."

Thea sniffed. "I hate her."

"Hate is a sin, my love. Hate is a black tumour that will eat your soul. You, perhaps more than any of us, were not born to hate. Besides, you must direct your anger accordingly. It is not Isabella's fault that Augusta died, or that our father does not understand young ladies."

"We did not need her. We are all old enough and capable enough to care for the household ourselves. We did not need her." Thea sucked in a breath after raising her voice for the last sentence. "Now, there will be a baby in the house and we will be expected to care for it."

"Yes, we will, and we shall to the best of our abilities."

Theodosia whirled on Elizabeth, throwing her hands into the air. "How can you sit there, so calmly as if we discussed the weather, and accept this life? I did not ask for this. No one asked if this was what I wanted for myself."

"It is our plight in life. We cannot change what God has set aside for us."

"I do not believe this is the work of God."

It hurt Elizabeth to see her sister so resentful. She did not blame Theodosia. Perhaps she should, but she also could not deny that, while her sister's grief was not the fault of any one person's maliciousness, the continued pain and anguish could be laid solely at their father's boots.

"That is between you and your maker, Thea. I am not here to guide your spiritual walk with God. What I am here to do is help you through your journey as a young woman. You need to find a way to live with this reality of our lives or you shall be a very unhappy person." Elizabeth shook her head. "I want you to be happy, to eventually fall in love, to make friends, and visit new places. I wish you to find joy and happiness, and contentment."

Thea looked at Elizabeth. Her eyes were red and her nose was running. No heavy sobs came from her, though. Good. There was no point to share her feelings in the open for those to gawk and judge. "Do you not want those things for yourself?"

Elizabeth smiled. "I have those things."

"That is a lie, Elizabeth Knight."

"Thea! It is not proper to call people liars, especially not your own sister."

"Yet, you are lying to me now. You are unhappy. You have been unhappy for a very long time. You hide it and do your duty, and all of the good things that a rector's eldest daughter should do. But I know, Elizabeth. So I do not understand why you get to sit next to me and lecture me when you are just as bad."

"Oh, Thea. You misjudge me." Elizabeth took a deep breath and prepared herself for the openness and honesty she had insisted from her sister. She knew it would be difficult for someone so young to understand, but she knew her sister needed this as well. She could expose a little of her own heart for her sister's sake. "Do you believe that I remain unmarried for any other reason beyond my own choice? My dear, I have no aims for marriage. I do not wish a man to take control of my fortune, small though it is. It is enough that it must go through our father and, in time, our brother. I do not wish to go through my husband as well. He would need to be an extraordinary man, and I have not met such a creature in my life."

"What about Mr. R?"

She had not expected his name to appear in the conversation, and the laugh that escaped her was laced with surprise. "What do you know of Mr. R?"

"I overheard Mary and Cassie talking about him at Christmas."

"Ah, of course. There are very few secrets between sisters, I suppose. So armed with this information gathered from eavesdropping upon two of your sisters, you concocted an entire history based on whatever nonsense they came up with?" Elizabeth looked at her sister and knew she had to lay bare the story if there would be understanding. "I have not told the others, but I saw Mr. R in London."

"You did? What happened?"

It surprised her how little hurt there was reflecting back upon the interaction. More than anything, it was her pride that stung. She should have known he did not truly care. "He pretended he did not know me. My new friend, Miss Thorne, reintroduced us, and she was shockingly rude to him."

Thea leaned forward to whisper, though there was no one about to overhear her. "What did she say?"

Elizabeth tried to mimic Miss Thorne's attitude. "This is Miss Elizabeth Knight. From *Bryden*."

Thea laughed, even as she sniffled and dabbed her eyes. "What did he do?"

"If I must be honest, we were both unbearably rude to each other. Then Miss Thorne cut him off by saying we had shopping to do and we left him standing there in the middle of the street."

"Excellent!" Thea laughed some more. "But...did it not hurt you? To see him, I mean."

"I thought it would, and indeed I thought I would be sick from nerves when he approached." Elizabeth gave her sister a smile. "However, once it was over, I realized I did not regret a thing. He is from the past, and in the past he shall remain. I find myself without malice or bitterness. It was a rather startling revelation for me."

"But aren't you lonely?"

"I struggle to find time for my own pursuits."

Elizabeth knew there was a difference between being alone and loneliness. She did not wish to burden her sister with that knowledge. For, she was lonely, and she knew that. Oftentimes, she was at her lowest whenever she sat at a family dinner or in the drawing room as her father read sermons aloud to them.

Thea did not seem to know, or at least acknowledge, the difference. "It is my fault that you cannot pursue your studies."

"Oh, I do not blame you." At Thea's dubious expression, Elizabeth said, "No, truly. I do not blame you, nor do I hold any resentment toward you for any interruptions. Recall that I was once your age, and not that long ago. And allow me to tell you honestly, I would not wish to relive those days, not for ten thousand pounds. I do not request you be perfect. That is not possible for any person. Only, I wish you to consider your actions a little closer. I know you did not wish Papa to marry Isabella, but he did and she is now our stepmother. Regardless of our personal feelings towards our father on that score, we owe it to ourselves not to take that anger out inappropriately. Lashing out at Isabella or G does no one any good. It just makes the pain worse for it soon becomes laced with regret and guilt."

"Do not think I wish Isabella to die."

"That had not even crossed my mind, Thea." Elizabeth smiled at her sister. "In anger, we all say things we do not actually mean. And I know your heart, dearest. You do not truly wish harm to come to her."

"I become so angry at times, Elizabeth. I cannot always control it." Thea balled her fists. "I wish I were a man, so that I could join a boxing gang and then take out my anger on something other than my sisters."

Elizabeth smiled. "You are rather too thin to be a boxer, I'd think. You would get your bones broken upon the first blow."

Thea sighed. "That would be better than sitting at home, smiling, sewing..."

"Simpering?" Elizabeth offered.

Thea tried to scowl, but it came out as a smile. "I hate that I have to sew shirts for Papa and Charles, when they do not care one drop about me or my feelings."

"I know, dearest. I truly know. That is why you must work on your outbursts. It is not for their benefit or comfort, but rather for your own enjoyment of life."

"How can our very home be so oppressive? The air is a weight that wants to crush me."

Elizabeth sucked in a breath. Oh, she understood that well enough. Whenever she stepped into her family home, a weight pressed upon her chest with each and every breath she took.

Her silence was too long, though, and it prompted Thea to say, "This is why I say you are not happy. I know you feel the same as I do."

Elizabeth smiled at her sister. "I believe a change in society might do you some good. I plan to be in London in the autumn. I know, that is months away still. Nevertheless, what if I ask Aunt Cass if you can visit with me? Between myself and Miss Thorne, you can gain invitations to several balls. Isabella has been working on your father to let you and G to be out in society, and honestly, I do not see why Cassandra should be stuck with me and no one else."

"Honest?" Thea's face furrowed, as if terrified the offer would be taken away.

"I would never lie to you, unless it was strictly necessary. With your permission, I shall speak to Papa myself. I believe I know exactly how to gain his permission. Now, I caution you. You will not be having a coming out ball or anything fancy. It will simply be a quiet affair of you being allowed to attend events and the occasional dinner party at the Thornes'. So, do not expect an entirely new wardrobe and a ball in your honour, the way Miss Parsons had one."

Thea sighed. "I know. Cassie didn't have a ball, either. But she got to lead a dance at Vane Park, which I wouldn't mind. And Cassie got a couple of new dresses! And G and I have been practicing our dancing. Oh, I would love to be able to take a dance lesson, but that is impossible, I suppose, now that Charles is back at university and Isabella is so ill."

"My dear, never mind the expense. There is no one in the village you could take a lesson from! Unless you managed to convince Henry Thorne to teach you. And he's not back from town yet."

"Miss Parsons has a dance instructor staying at her house for a whole month right now!"

"Whyever for?"

"He's a relation, and he said London smells." Thea's nose was still red, but at least her features had brightened. Perhaps something to look forward to would do her some good.

"He came to Bryden to escape the smell?" Elizabeth asked dubiously. "Surely there are more exciting places that do not stink. Like Brighton."

Thea shrugged. "I only repeat what I have been told."

"Well, allow me to speak to Papa first. Do not mention this to G. I am uncertain if he will allow both of you to come out at once. Do you understand me?"

Thea shook her head. "Might I request that G not be allowed? I would like one thing that is mine, even if it is only for a ball or two."

Elizabeth thought on that and agreed readily. If she were perfectly honest with herself, she was not certain either of her younger sisters were quite ready for mixing in company. However, Thea might need it to help her grow. G, on the other hand, would only get the two of them into even more trouble, and Thea would not receive the small escapes she clearly and so desperately required.

"Allow me some time to broach the subject, but yes." She smiled at her sister. "And I will attempt to get you a new dress out of it, but I make no promises."

"I understand," Thea said, sinking back into melancholy. Elizabeth considered the fifty pounds in her desk, hidden away. No matter what, her sister was getting a new dress.

⚜ Chapter 3 ⚜

TWO DAYS PASSED before Elizabeth found an appropriate opening to speak with her father about the delicate nature of Thea's request. She had managed to carve out an hour for her occult studies. Armed with *First Forays into the Study of Occult Flora* (1805), she'd begun the task of cataloguing all of the various herbs, flowers, and weeds that grew near the rectory. The Occult Flora book included detailed information about purification, storage techniques, and uses, and she made detailed notes in her own personal occult journal. In fact, it had been Mrs. Egerton's idea to explore the occult with kitchen garden items to avoid the wrath of her father.

She was busy writing a note for herself to plant more thyme and marjoram, since they featured heavily in many workings—not to mention table dishes—and that she was concerned there would not be enough for both food and spells. Mrs. Egerton felt she was soon ready to experiment with dream occult workings; Elizabeth was less certain, but either way, it required thyme. As did her father's favourite beef stew.

"Ah, Elizabeth! The very daughter I have been searching for!" Mr. Knight called out to her, with Isabella by his side.

She closed her botany book, as well as her magical journal, and stood. She greeted them both, still holding both books in her arms tight against her chest. "Good afternoon, Papa, Isabella. What did you need?"

Her father raised an open letter in his hand. "We have a letter from your sister Mary. She is having a ball at the end of the month and requires your assistance with the organization. As well, she extends an offer for Cassandra to occupy you, if she wishes. I cannot see any harm in that, and neither does Isabella, do you, dear?"

"Not at all, Mr. Knight. Provided Elizabeth, of course, wishes to visit Ashbrook."

"My dear, I already explained this to you," Mr. Knight said, in the tone that suggested to Elizabeth this had been the source of a recent quarrel. "Mary requires Elizabeth's assistance."

Elizabeth saw Thea's chance, however, and carefully manoeuvred into position. "Actually, this is quite fortuitous!"

An expression formed on Isabella's face that could only be called confusion. "It is?"

"Indeed it is! There has been a proposal I have wished to bring to your attention, both of you, in fact, and I have been waiting for the proper opportunity."

"But, why wait? I am...but..." Her father seemed befuddled that his eldest daughter would have waited to tell him anything. "Well, what is this thing you wish to discuss? Gracious, Elizabeth. You must come forward when you have questions. I am your father and Isabella is your mother. We are here to support you, of course."

Elizabeth put on a smile and ignored the little voice in her head that sounded rather too much like Mrs. Egerton for her own comfort. She would have to work to check that voice, lest it unleash in polite conversation. "I am of the opinion that it is time for Thea to come out."

"I do not know that," Mr. Knight said. He glanced at his wife. "What are your thoughts? This is your sphere, not mine. She is rather young, don't you think?"

Elizabeth glanced at Isabella. They'd not spoken on the subject, but she had hoped her stepmother was quick enough to see her allyship was required for this scheme to be successful. "It does not need to be anything grand, if that is the worry. We aren't that sort of people in any case. However, in my opinion, this invitation to Mary's ball would be a perfect opportunity for Thea to be introduced officially to society. It would be little expense on your part, sir. Perhaps a new gown or two, some gloves and a hat. Perhaps a new pair of shoes. And since Mary so greatly needs our assistance, we would be going there in any case. I can chaperone Thea, too, so that she isn't in Mary's way."

"This is...Isabella? Pray, what is your opinion? Is she not too young? She must be too young."

"Oh, Mr. Knight, I think this is a wonderful idea."

"Truly?" Mr. Knight asked. He looked back at his daughter. "You both agree on this?"

"Indeed, sir. Elizabeth is quite right, and the thought had crossed my mind as of late. I had considered even just this last evening that I should speak with Elizabeth on the topic to discover her opinion. I imagine many of the symptoms of frustration and discord about the house lately are due to Theodosia having reached that age where a young woman needs to be out in society more. And consider, sir, that Cassandra's old friend from school has returned to the neighbourhood for a month for her cousin's lying in. It would be cruel to separate these old friends at such a time."

"But...how useful would Theodosia be to Mary?"

Elizabeth took that as her signal to speak. "Well, sir, pardon me for speaking my mind so forcefully, but young people need practice at being useful."

Isabella nodded enthusiastically. "Indeed, and there is no better way to get a young lady excited and involved than to mention the word ball around her."

"Also, Papa, we must consider what Augusta would have wanted." Elizabeth felt no shame bringing up the name of Thea's dead mother. If pressed, Elizabeth would confess that Augusta would have probably enjoyed seeing her stepdaughter scheme in such a manner. "Recall, if you will, that she allowed Cassie to come out at sixteen. I think, if she were here, this would also be her wish. I believe there is no greater...um...um..."

"What I believe your eldest daughter is saying," Isabella said, stepping in as Elizabeth faltered, "she believes it is our Christian duty to bring up Theodosia in the manner her mother would have wished if she were still here with us. If Elizabeth believes Augusta Knight would have wanted this, then, I must, in good conscience, support this scheme. I take the task of stepmother very seriously."

Mr. Knight confusedly looked between the conspiring women. "If you both feel so strongly about this, why did neither of you bring this to me before? I would have been very willing to discuss this matter. Do you not believe you can come to me with topics that involve my daughters? I do not believe I have given any indication that I am nothing if not an attentive, involved father."

Isabella glanced at Elizabeth, hoping for a rescue. Elizabeth put on a sweet smile. "It has been difficult to find the right occasion that would best benefit her. There have been a great many things happening since Thea came out of mourning for her mother. There have not been any worthwhile opportunities, except my trip to London, and that was to support my own aunt during her mourning. That would not have been an appropriate time to bring poor Thea to town."

Mr. Knight nodded, mollified. "Well...I suppose...but what about Georgiana? Would it not be easier to just release both girls into the wild and deal with the consequences of such rashness?"

"No sir, I do not agree," Elizabeth said sternly. At his startled face, she corrected her tone. "I simply believe it would be best for Thea if she had an opportunity to come out alone, just as all of us other girls had. Then, when it is G's turn, perhaps following her own birthday, she can have that same opportunity."

"I agree with Elizabeth, Mr. Knight. We must begin thinking of the girls now as their own people, each with a singular personality. We should consider how best to introduce each of them into society so that they can marry well. Thea is the age for it. Perhaps G is, too, but she is not yet sixteen. I believe she can easily wait a few months, if only so that Thea can decide if she wants her sister by her side or not."

Mr. Knight frowned. "Will this not encourage yet more distress in our home? I cannot abide more of this tomfoolery that has been plaguing our upper rooms."

"That is why, Papa, I believe I should take Thea with me, have Mary introduce her into society there, and then perhaps in the autumn, I can ask Aunt Cass to invite me and Thea—"

"Absolutely not!" Mr. Knight said, pushing his shoulders back. "The girls are not going anywhere near London. I barely trusted you going there, let alone the girls."

"But sir," Isabella said in a sweet, low voice. "Thea is more likely to meet a wider society in town and, depending upon who she meets, it would be very advantageous for her to be known as a family relation of Mrs. George Spencer."

Mr. Knight snorted. "It has done no good for Elizabeth."

"Thea and Elizabeth are very different people, Mr. Knight," Isabella said cautiously. "This would give me great comfort, sir, to see one of the girls introducing herself more into society. You do not get any younger with time, my dear husband. We must think of the girls. Mary is well married, yes, but she cannot support four unmarried sisters. We must try."

"I have no plans to go to my grave yet, my dear. And what about you, Elizabeth? I have never known you to volunteer to go to Ashbrook, for all of your fine words. What is this change about?"

"I believe it is in Thea's best interest, and I will do whatever is necessary for the happiness of my sister. Is that not my Christian duty?"

Mr. Knight's shoulders slumped and Elizabeth knew they had won the match. He shook his head, defeated. "Who am I to argue with women on the matters of women? Very well. I cannot say no with both of you conspiring against me. I assume Theodosia is out of ready money. How much expense will this cost me?"

This was the part Elizabeth feared the most. Her father would not be pleased by any expense, but she was the best person to fight for her sister. "When I came out, Augusta insisted I receive two new ball gowns, plus two everyday gowns. Also, there was my dancing shoes, a fan, gloves, and some decorations for my hair. Cassandra and Mary both received similar treatment. It would be wrong not to do the same for Thea."

Mr. Knight made a thoughtful sound. "I do not like the direction this appears to be heading. Isabella, what say you?"

"Well, Mr. Knight, I believe setting aside twelve pounds—"

"Twelve pounds!" Mr. Knight exclaimed. "For some dresses that will not get her married?"

"Sir, you do not know that," Isabella said. "Also, sir, you must consider that anything less will reflect poorly on me if she does not receive the same treatment as her elder sisters received from the former Mrs. Knight."

"Oh, the girls wouldn't blame you..."

"Sir, they will," Elizabeth said. "To speak very plainly, Thea and Georgiana will blame Isabella."

"But I am the one saying no to this foolishness," Mr. Knight said. "Isabella has no say in the affair."

"Yes, sir," Elizabeth said. "And, yet, I still believe they will blame Isabella for not explaining their situation to you."

"Twelve pounds, though."

Elizabeth considered her words carefully. "Are we not all weary of the disputes happening in our house? We must have a continuous line between Augusta and Isabella if we want any peace. If Thea gets a farthing less than Cassandra did, the conflict in our house will not improve. If we cannot afford the expense, then I shall contribute my own money towards the cause."

"That is a very good..." Mr. Knight began.

His wife cut him off. "I believe we have already asked too much of your purse, Elizabeth. Don't you think, Mr. Knight?"

Mr. Knight stumbled over what he knew was right and what his greed wished him to do. Finally, he said, "Please do not allow Theodosia to bankrupt us."

"I give you my solemn word, Papa. She shall not spend a farthing more than twelve pounds." Elizabeth smiled at her father. "In fact, sir, if you wish, I shall chaperone all spending. I will not allow Thea to so much as purchase a yard of ribbon without my permission."

"Twelve pounds," Mr. Knight said. "And not a farthing more, Miss Elizabeth Knight."

"Twelve pounds." She smiled at her father. "And not a farthing more."

"Very well. I had planned to purchase myself a new hat, but I shall have to wait on that score now." He shook his head. "Am I to assume it falls upon me to break this news to Mary?"

"If I might be so bold," Isabella said, "and, if everyone is in agreement, I would like to take that agreeable task upon myself."

"I think that's very wise," Elizabeth said.

Mr. Knight shrugged in defeat. "Well, ladies, then you know what must be done better than I so I shall take my leave. I am to Mr. Parsons' tonight. Oh, before I forget, my dear. The Parsons will not dine with us on Saturday after all. Mr. Parsons broke his hand last night!"

"Oh goodness! Is it bad?" Isabella inquired.

Mr. Knight shook his head. "Mr. Collins says it is a clean break. He won't be able to work, however, for at least a month and perhaps more, and cannot be trusted in his fields until Mr. Collins is certain the bones are set. So Mr. Parsons has called for me. I might get to rent the lands after all! Isn't this the most exciting news, my dear!"

Elizabeth smiled and said, "I am very sorry for Mr. Parsons."

"It's only a broken bone," Mr. Knight said. "Twelve pounds. Well, I shall speak to my banker in Eastmore and ask for the sum directly. I do not like you girls ringing up credit at the shops. That is where sin lays."

"Thank you, Papa."

"Well, ladies, I shall leave you to your business of planning gowns and the other silliness. I wished to go to Eastmore in any case today, so I will take my horse and ride there. Then, if you do not object, Isabella, I shall spend the day at the Parsons'. I shall make your apologies, my dear. Elizabeth, do you desire to attend in your mother's place?"

Elizabeth successfully hid the twitch. "No thank you, Papa. I have much to do today."

"As you were. Well, I shall be off. Do not keep a plate for me. I shall most likely eat dinner and supper there. I have promised to consult on a business matter pertaining to the farm in any case. Pray that I have the opportunity to bring forth my proposals for the land."

After Mr. Knight had left them for the stables, Elizabeth asked, "How are you, Isabella? What did Mrs. Green have to say today on your condition?"

"Oh, I am well enough." Her face grew sad. "Elizabeth, will you please sit? I have some distressing news, however, which I'd prefer you to hear from me and not your father."

Elizabeth took a seat next to her stepmother. "What is it?"

"Your father does not wish the girls to know this. He objected to me knowing, in fact. However, Mrs. Green insisted upon telling me, for which I am grateful. However, I ask that you keep this from your sisters, but I wished to share this information with you." She closed her eyes and released a long breath. "It is possible the babe will be stillborn."

"Oh, Isabella. I am so sorry. Is she certain?"

"Mrs. Green said it's never certain, until I enter my confinement. However, I had not felt any movement and Mrs. Green says, in her experience, these tumours that I have can often injure the child. This is why she recommends exercise now. If the child is alive, it may stir from the exercise and then we know it yet lives."

"And what benefit is there if it is already gone?" Elizabeth asked.

Isabella smiled. "Then it might speed up the process so that I do not have to endure more of this torment."

"This is very distressing. Is there anything I can do to assist?"

"There is, actually."

"Please name it. If it is in my power, I shall see it happen."

"It is distressing laying in bed all day without any employment to escape my mind's worry," Isabella said. "I know Theodosia will not wish much help from me, but if there is anything I can do. Sewing a headdress, or making a string of pearls for her hair. Anything, I beg of you. I cannot sit still any longer."

Elizabeth nodded. "I must speak to Thea, of course, but I suspect she will be very happy for any and all assistance to get her into a few gowns in time for Mary's ball. In fact, allow me to speak with her first, and then I believe we shall have to draw up a battle plan worthy of Lord Wellington himself."

"Good. Anything you need from me, even if it is mending stockings or sewing a shift, please employ me. I desire anything to distract from my worries."

"I shall do whatever I can to assist." Elizabeth grinned at her stepmother. "In fact, poor Julia, last I heard, was attempting to make boiled tongue for supper."

Isabella sighed. "I shall go supervise her, lest she burn down the house."

Elizabeth laughed. "We cannot have that!"

Elizabeth watched Isabella walk away, and an aching sadness filled her. She had already lost a mother and a stepmother to childbirth. She could not bear to lose another. She glanced at her botany book and then back at the house. She would take Mrs. Egerton for a walk and see what could be done.

⚜ Chapter 4 ⚜

ELIZABETH WALKED UP the stairs to her room and closed the door to commune with Mrs. Egerton. She tapped the book and asked, "Would you like to accompany me on a walk to Vane Park? I have an occult question that I would dearly love to discuss in private."

Mrs. Egerton sighed so much that she made Elizabeth's bedroom curtains stir. "Provided your father will not be present. That man drives me to detraction."

"My father would most likely say the same about you, if he had the pleasure of an introduction," Elizabeth said with a chuckle.

"How can such a disagreeable gentleman of dubious income and prospects attract not one, but three young wives? In my time, many deserving men struggled to find good women and your father seemingly has them throwing themselves in front of his horse to garner his attentions."

"I do not believe it is quite so dramatic as all that."

Elizabeth pulled out her thin, yellow spencer from her chest of drawers. The cropped jacket sat as high as her gown's bustline, which was rather too high for her taste and just right for current fashion. However, it turned out to be a welcomed addition to summer days when she wished to cover her arms from the sun's heat, so she kept the strange whim of fashion for another season.

As she pulled it on, she said to Mrs. Egerton, "A lady's options are limited, especially with us losing so many good young men on the continent."

"Ah, yes. The wars. Pray, is it not too warm for such a garment?" Mrs. Egerton inquired. "Even in my day, a lady was permitted to show her elbows on a hot summer's day."

"Alas, the sun is rather strong today, and I fear both my father's and my sister's wrath if I grow too brown in the sun," Elizabeth said. She tugged the garment on and fetched her parasol from her closet in hopes that it would keep some of the heat off her back. She picked out one of her simpler hats with a wide brim; Mary would be horrified if Elizabeth had any trace of tanned skin like a common labourer. With only three weeks to go before the Ashbrook ball, this was not the time to have an outbreak of the freckles.

"Tell me, how goes the herbal study? Have you determined what your next course of spell craft will be?"

Mrs. Egerton was interrupted by the high-pitched wail of a young woman downstairs. Elizabeth guessed it was G and, by the approaching wail, it was G in a state fit to be tied.

Elizabeth sighed and said, "I fear this household is not conducive to proper study and reflection."

"I believe the barn would be quieter than this place. At least the cows don't demand every waking moment of one's attention," Mrs. Egerton mused.

She debated for a moment, before deciding to take her reticule full of coins with her. Knowing Maria, once informed of Thea's coming out, Elizabeth would be dragged as far as Eastmore for shopping and planning. And, Elizabeth realized, returning home with a set of fabric samples might be just the thing to take Thea's mind off her troubles.

Elizabeth managed to pull on her gloves and wrap her reticule's dangling purse strings around her wrist before the first bellow from deep within the house.

"Eliza! It is not fair!"

Time was short. "To answer your inquiry, there was a particular problem I wished to discuss on our walk," The sound of shrieking grew closer, as did the stomping of feet upon the stairs. "Alas, I fear we may not have the opportunity."

"I had been led to believe being dead meant silence, but sadly that has turned out to be incorrect," Mrs. Egerton said with a dramatic sigh. "You require significant quiet to concentrate, which I fear does not exist in this household. I wish the Thornes would adopt some distant relation's infant so that you could be hired as a governess."

"What an interesting thing to wish for! Besides, do you think my father would allow me to earn a living when I could work for free at Mary's house?" Elizabeth said with a laugh.

Pounding at her door sounded. She opened the door and said, "Hello, G. Thea."

"Did you know about this?" her youngest sister demanded as she pushed past Elizabeth into the bedroom. She pointed at her sister. "Did you know about her?"

"Which part?" Elizabeth asked.

"Papa just said she's allowed to come out! And I'm not allowed! That's not fair!"

"Is it true, Eliza?" Thea asked.

Elizabeth wished her father had allowed her to tell Theodosia herself. He truly did not understand his daughters. Treating them like individuals with wants and wishes seemed beyond his capacity. "Yes, it is true. I spoke with our father only this morning and asked him to allow Thea to come out. He has given his consent, and has provided me, and me alone, with a spending allowance for Thea's new gowns and shoes."

G gasped and began to protest, but Elizabeth held up a hand for silence. It was respectfully obeyed. "Further, Mary is having a ball in three weeks. If she agrees, *and* if we can arrange new dresses for Thea in that time, I will be accompanying Thea there."

It was Thea's turn to gasp. "I get a new dress?"

"She gets a new dress!" G bellowed. "This is completely wrong!"

"G, you are still but fifteen. You are very capable of waiting a few more months to allow your sister some independence. I am very certain Thea will grow tired of being chaperoned by me and

Cassie soon enough and will be begging for you to show up and get her into mischief."

G collapsed on the bed. "It isn't fair though!"

"Why not?" Elizabeth asked.

G sat up and asked, "What do you mean?"

Elizabeth held up a hand to silence Thea. "G, tell me. Why is this unfair?"

"Because I want to come out, too!"

"Pray explain what that has to do with Theodosia?"

G just stared at her, slack-jawed.

Elizabeth pressed her point. "It appears to me that you are clearly not mature enough to be in the mixed company of society yet, if you cannot even handle a small disappointment like this. Even if you have to wait until your sixteenth birthday, that is only in August. It is already June, for heaven's sake! These theatrics will do nothing to convince our father to let you anywhere near polite society before you are thirty."

"This was your fault!" G shouted accusingly at her eldest sister.

Elizabeth did not flinch from the tone; she'd heard it often enough over the last year. "Our father requested my honest and truthful opinion of the situation, and I provided it. I told him that, in my estimation, it was time to allow Thea to come out. I also advised him to not allow you to come out at this time, to allow her the same opportunities as the rest of us older Knight girls have had. Were you looking to put the blame on Isabella's shoulders?"

"You betrayed me!" G shouted and kicked her feet against the side of the bed.

"Hardly, my dear. I am acting the part of an eldest sister. In this particular case, it is Thea's turn to come out. Mary is hosting a ball, which makes this the perfect time. It isn't as though Thea will have many opportunities to socialize, with us not having a carriage. However, I hope that—"

"I hate you!" G shrieked.

Elizabeth folded her hands in front of her. "Shouting horrible words at me that you do not actually feel or believe will not convince me to speak to our father on your behalf."

"I want to go to the ball, too!"

"If Thea wasn't going and getting all of this attention, you wouldn't have the slightest inclination to spend a few weeks at Mary's and you know that in your heart. Did you not complain recently that going to Mary's meant you would, oh what was the phrase you used? Ah, yes. You would have to work harder than any servant ever has worked before." Elizabeth sat upon the bed, next to her flounced sister. She gave her an affectionate pat on the thigh. "If anything, I think you should take this time to go shopping with Cassandra, making up new bonnets for yourself, and do things without Thea. I believe it would be good for both of you."

"Thea and I do everything together."

"Mary and I used to do everything together, too," Elizabeth said, and couldn't help the sadness creep into her voice. "Things change, my love. Growing up is not easy. Enjoy what is left of the world having no expectations upon you. Too soon, it will be gone."

"It's just a ball," Theodosia said.

"And it's just a ball I wish to go to!" G wailed.

"No, girls, it is not just a ball. As soon as Thea puts on her new dress, and is taken about the room for introductions, there will be expectations upon her. From that moment onward, she will be expected to find herself a husband. That will become her entire focus, as well as the intent of every other person around her. Fun and games and trivialities will be gone. She will endure people discussing her figure, her looks, the pitch of her voice, and even the lace upon her gown. She will become the property of the world, until she becomes the property of a husband. Do not wish that responsibility upon yourself so soon, G."

"You don't have a husband," G said. "Everyone knows you don't plan to marry. Not after Mr. R treated you so horribly, and Mary says I'm not allowed to talk about it, but I know all about it. Cassie told me."

Elizabeth hadn't considered how grateful she was for her encounter with Mr. Rutherford in London. There would have been a time, not too long ago, that the question would have shaken her to her very soul. Now, however, she could offer a genuine smile and a sisterly chuckle.

"Oh, G. Do not worry about myself and Mr. R. I do not regret anything on that score, so do not trouble yourself with notions of me being alone and bitter about a man. However, to answer your question, yes, you are correct. I am no husband's property. Instead, I am the property of everyone else. If Mary needs me, I am to pack my trunks no matter my interests or commitments. I do as Papa orders. There will be a time when our father is called to Heaven, and then I will be at Charles' disposal. If he remains unmarried when that unhappy event takes place, I anticipate I will be keeping house for him. Tell me, either of you, do you know what I would prefer to do this very day? Or tomorrow even? Or what any of my plans or hopes are?"

Both girls shared a guilty glance and shook their heads.

"Do not be ashamed. Why would you even think on such a matter? No one asks what I want because I am at everyone else's disposal." At her sisters' dejected expressions, she added, "I am happy to do whatever my sisters need, of course. Which often includes being here when you are angry at one another. However, remember my dearest sisters, being unmarried has not made me my own woman. I merely look after my family's needs, as opposed to a very different imaginary family I have not had, nor am likely to have."

"What do you want to do?" Thea asked. "I mean, you said no one ever asks. So, what is it that you'd want?"

Elizabeth eased G back up off the bed. She could have told the girls the truth, but that would only hurt them, and she had no wish for that. So instead, she gave them a brilliant smile and said, "I think I would like someone to die and leave me fifty thousand pounds and then take you both to London and spend it all."

That seemed to quell the argument enough by distracting the girls into a lively discussion of lace and silk. The girls invited themselves for her walk to Maria's. She picked up the ghost book anyway, which sighed with grand disapproval when the girls rushed from the room to gather gloves and parasols.

"I agree, Mrs. Egerton."

"For your sake, my dear, I hope you marry a feeble and sickly old man of ten thousand a year that will allow you to escape this house."

Elizabeth watched her sisters skip down the hallway to their room, giggling as they went. "I fear that would not be any guarantee of escape, for I suspect my father would send those two to live with me for the rest of my life."

~☙ Chapter 5 ☙~

ELIZABETH RELENTED AND said the girls could come on her walk to Vane Park, but as fate would have it, Cassandra was able to rescue her. Miss Baldwin was in Bryden visiting her relations, the Parsons, and had been an old school fellow of Cassandra's. Miss Baldwin and Cassie were out on a walk about the village, and announced they were just returned from Vane Park and were headed into the village in search of boiled sweets and ribbon for a damaged bonnet. G and Thea begged to go with them, which Elizabeth happily consented, and the party of young ladies skipped along joyously across the field, finally leaving Elizabeth alone with her thoughts.

Elizabeth walked along the lane to Vane Park in blessed solitude, with only birds and sheep as witnesses to her country ramble. She didn't speak to Mrs. Egerton about her occult question, as she wished to get herself clear of the frustrations of her situation.

Oh, but could her father show some of the Christian kindness he was so often preaching! The agreement had been for her to tell her sisters. She would have spoken to each privately and with supportive sisterly affection. Instead, her father cruelly ignored that coming out was the single most important event in a sixteen-year-old girl's life, and pitted sister against sister. Now, she would bear the brunt of his blame for the girls' behaviour come his return home that evening.

After several frustrated sighs on Elizabeth's part, Mrs. Egerton spoke up. "Upon reflection, I have amended my previous statements."

"Which ones, my dear Mrs. Egerton? You have expressed so many." Elizabeth added a small smile to her words, so that the ghost was assured there was no bitterness or mean-spiritedness meant.

"I have frequently said I could not understand why you are not married. Now, however, I understand why you are not."

Elizabeth smiled, though these words were laced with bitterness. "Mary believes no sensible man will have me."

"On the contrary. I have yet to meet a man who deserves someone as good as you. Enjoy your walk, Miss Knight. You deserve the quiet reflection. God above knows you have earned it."

"You are too kind." She fondly stroked the ghost book's spine.

Ghost and young lady walked in silence along the Vane Park lane. Elizabeth had a small regret from her talk with her sisters, for she had told a falsehood. She had not revealed her truest feelings concerning being the joint property of the Knight clan. She did not wish to, either; such young people, still so full of life and vigour, did not need to know such things. But it had been a falsehood nevertheless.

But what was she to do? It had been the continued needs of G and Thea that had allowed Elizabeth as much independence over her life as possible. They were the excuse that forced Mary to employ a governess and a nursemaid, since Elizabeth was necessary to the peace at Bryden Rectory. However, Thea would soon be out in society. G was sure to follow in August or perhaps sometime in the autumn at the latest. With those events, her freedoms would melt away. She would be summoned to the task of raising her nephews and niece, as well as a string of new siblings.

Even if this poor creature of Isabella's did not survive, she knew all too well that Isabella would probably be with child again by the new year, if not sooner. Her father was determined for another son. There would be no separate bedchambers for poor Isabella until that task was complete.

Her youngest sisters did not need to hear those thoughts. For one thing, it wasn't becoming. For another, they had expressed no true knowledge or interest in the subject, and it was not her place to force knowledge upon them. Elizabeth had puzzled out the science of families long before their age—after all, living on a farm and then watching baby after baby show up in one's household certainly helped—and she also had a married friend who was very open and eager to illuminate her on the intimate details of marriage.

What she'd not said to G or Thea, or even Maria or Cassie, and not even Mrs. Egerton, was that knowledge was the reason for her disinterest in marriage at present. Knowing what the marriage act entailed, she vowed to never marry for anything short of the deepest, most passionate affection. The thought of anything else repulsed her.

And, sadly, after years of meeting disappointing men coupled with her relative poverty meant she would die an old maid, the butt of jokes and the property of everyone but herself.

The money her uncle so kindly bestowed meant that she would never starve. She would never suffer the indignity of begging for her supper. And, if pressed, in her old age she could find a relation within their family circle to take her in for the contribution of her fifty-odd pounds per annum toward the household expenses.

Three thousand pounds.

And, if her situation was dire, she would sell that book to purchase her freedom. She would take the money and run away to America or Canada, or India or even Australia if she needed even more distance. She would run until no one could touch her. No matter what, she would never have to languish underneath a man she detested for her bread.

Her life was not her own, but she would ensure her body remained so.

"Elizabeth!"

It took Elizabeth a moment to realize her name had been called. She looked around her to find Maria walking toward her, arm entwined in Mr. Thorne's. The ladies clasped hands.

"Where was your head? We've been calling out to you!" Maria said with a laugh.

"My mind was in the excitement of telling you the news from Bryden Rectory," Elizabeth said. "Mr. Thorne, I had no idea you would be back in the country today or I would not have bothered Maria."

"Oh pish," Maria said. "I see Henry all of the time. You, my dear, I rarely see as of late."

Mr. Thorne gave Elizabeth a wink. In a rather hurt tone, he said, "It pains me to discover I am not missed when I am away from home."

Maria playfully slapped her husband's arm. "Oh, Henry. Stop your nonsense. So, Eliza, do tell us the news. What has happened?"

"First, before we begin the endless tales of young ladies shrieking at the rectory," Mr. Thorne said, "I have your money, Miss Knight. If you would walk back to the house with us, I will happily settle our accounts."

"I'd be happy to," Elizabeth said as she accepted Mr. Thorne's spare arm.

The trio walked back down the lane toward Vane Park. Elizabeth told her friend and husband about Thea's coming out and how Mary's ball would be an excellent opportunity for Thea to meet new people.

"Oh, how exciting! Henry, this gives us the perfect excuse to have a private ball. No more than sixty people. Seventy at the most. Well, we can accommodate thirty couples dancing in the ballroom, if we double up the line and move the card tables to the library. Eighty-five as the very maximum. We would need extra help for that many guests. I'd have to look as far as Eastmore for help preparing the house for so many guests. I'm certain that will be easily achieved. Yes, eighty-five guests. Easily done."

Henry Thorne dramatically sighed. "Please inform me of the date so that I can be called away on business to London."

"Oh, Henry!" Maria exclaimed in annoyance. "Three weeks is not much time to get everything for Theodosia, though. We need silk, muslin, lace...oh, she will need new shoes. Oh, and a pair of gloves or two to match her gowns. A new pelisse would not be amiss, either. There is so little time to plan. Henry, I may need to return to London tomorrow to bring back fabric samples. There is not a second to lose."

Elizabeth laughed. "I am only authorized to spend twelve pounds in total."

"Twelve pounds!" Maria gasped. "That is barely enough for one good gown."

Henry coughed. "Maria..."

Elizabeth chuckled. "It is all right, Mr. Thorne. Maria did the same thing at my coming out. She was convinced I would arrive in nothing but onion sacks stitched together since how could anyone possibly create a gown for under ten guineas."

"You mock me," Maria said, with a little hurt in her voice. It vanished before Elizabeth could apologize for her teasing, and Maria carried on with gown planning. "There is nothing stopping us, I suppose, from going to Eastmore. The fabric is slightly cheaper there than in the village, but will be very difficult to find decent silk outside of London. Poor Miss Theodosia may have to settle. Oh, and poor Miss Sims! Her eyesight isn't getting any better, so rushing the order will be difficult for her. I suppose she has her niece living with her now, but even still. This might be a challenge."

"I was considering asking Miss Sims to come stay with us for a week. With mine and Isabella's assistance, especially in the evenings when she cannot sew, we can get some of the work progressed for her to continue in the morning. If she can prepare a pattern for an everyday dress, I am certain Isabella and I can easily sew those up. Or, at least, we can sew the straight lines and leave the expert stitching to her capable hands. What is your opinion?"

Maria nodded. "Miss Sims stayed here for two weeks in April to make up my wardrobe. This year, I paid for one of the nieces in addition, to make the task easier upon her."

"What did you pay?" Elizabeth asked.

"I paid Miss Sims fifteen shillings per week, which I know is a little high, but I cannot underpay her. I've known that poor woman my entire life. I'd not be able to sleep at night knowing I'd underpaid her. I also paid the niece seven shillings a week, who turned out to be very helpful about the house with errands and such."

Elizabeth nodded. That was about what she had thought fair for Miss Sims' wages, too. "I shall see if I can strike a deal for fifteen shillings for the week for just her. I do not anticipate needing the niece with so many of us in the house. I do not plan to order that many dresses. How was her eyesight when she came to stay with you?"

Maria shrugged. "No worse than last year. She cannot sew by candlelight for any length of time, but that is where the niece can assist. Miss Sims does not trust her with a silk gown's construction, but the girl can finish a long seam as well as anyone else of their profession. Between the two of them, they produced four new ballgowns, five everyday gowns, and a very good gown for church. Miss Sims also did alterations on three of my dresses from last year to bring them up to date. Oh, and she repaired the hem of my blue pelisse."

"Depending upon the price of muslin, I am hoping to get Thea two new everyday gowns, two very nice ballgowns, shoes, gloves, a couple of new bonnets, and the like. It will depend heavily upon what the shops have available, alas."

Mr. Thorne cleared his throat. "I feel I am being asked to call for the carriage."

"A trip to Eastmore would be an excellent way to break up the tedium of this day," Maria said.

"My dear Maria, recall that I have only just arrived from London last night."

"Yes, and I am already bored," Maria said. She bumped against her husband to show she was only teasing. "Can you be spared from home for so long?" Maria asked Elizabeth.

"Isabella is alone with our poor new kitchenmaid. Cassandra and the girls are off shopping for ribbons and boiled sweets with Miss Baldwin. I suppose I cannot be away from home for long."

"I propose I pay Mrs. Knight a visit," Henry said, "and keep her company while the rest of you go off to spend my money."

"Mr. Thorne! I have no interest in spending your money," Elizabeth said.

Maria leaned around her husband and faux whispered, "If his money happens to be spent, however, I doubt Theodosia will complain."

Once inside, it was agreed that the ladies would take the carriage to Eastmore in search of fabric swatches, while Mr. Thorne would walk to Bryden and carry the news. While his wife fussed about getting ready to go shopping, Mr. Thorne summoned Elizabeth into his study.

From a desk drawer, he pulled out his leather wallet and also handed her a sealed letter. "That is from Mr. Osborne, detailing the final amounts of the book sales. He said to assure you he was quite meticulous with the accounting."

"I trust him implicitly," she said. She gave Mr. Thorne a smile. "As I do you."

"Ha! Your trust is misplaced. I was tempted to steal some of this ready cash on hand to use for the gambling tables, but alas. My honour as a gentleman held me back."

"'Tis a shame, Mr. Thorne. Perhaps you could have returned with a thousand pounds for me!"

"Or broke and facing the wrath of my wife," Mr. Thorne said. He handed her several bank notes. "First, your twenty-eight pounds from Mr. Grant. Now, those are from the Bank of London, so you will need to go to Eastmore to exchange those if you wish to spend them in the village."

She accepted the bills and placed them in her reticule. "Thank you, Mr. Thorne. I haven't decided what I should do with it yet."

"Well, don't be too hasty because I have even more for you. The final sale of your books amounts to twenty-seven pounds. Mr. Osborne decided to round it up, since it was so close."

"Twenty-seven pounds!" Elizabeth exclaimed.

"Indeed, Miss Knight." His smile disappeared. "Now, since not even Maria knows the total sum yet, what amount do you wish me to tell the others if they inquire? And, I am well aware, there will be plenty of inquires, so I must know now the details of your plan if I am to support you."

"Oh, Mr. Thorne, I can see what you are doing. I thank you; it is much appreciated. But, please do not lie on my behalf. My father is expecting twenty pounds earnings, so this is in line with those expectations. I shall not hide the sum from anyone. Thank you, however, for considering my circumstances and offering to use your good name to protect me."

He inclined his head. "You are too good sometimes, Miss Knight."

"Better to be too good than too evil, is it not?"

"Evil sounds like a lot of fun, though," Mr. Thorne said thoughtfully. "I have dabbled in it, I must confess, and it was never as horrid as the sermons suggest."

"Oh, Mr. Thorne." Elizabeth stuffed the additional bills straight into her reticule. She carried a tiny beaded sovereign purse within the small knitted pouch, but that could only handle a small selection of coins "Goodness, my purse is overflowing with money!"

"No one likes the bragging of a rich woman, Miss Knight. It's unbecoming," Mr. Thorne said.

"What is unbecoming?" Maria asked from the doorway.

"Miss Knight is bragging about her riches," Mr. Thorne said.

"Good," Maria said. "Women should brag more in my estimation. It's about time the men were put in their place."

"I will have you know this is the sphere in which the Lord himself placed me." Mr. Thorne raised his hands to encompass the room. "Who am I to argue with his divine will?"

Maria made a thoughtful sound. "Since most of the furnishings in this room were purchased with my money, I would say that you had very good fortune, indeed."

"My dear wife, it is not your money now that we are married. It is mine," Henry said, though he grinned at his wife to let her know he was teasing. "And I do believe you purchased most of the items in this room."

"That is only because you have no taste for such matters and I did not want this room to look like a poorly maintained warehouse," Maria said. "Now, James is getting the horses ready. Shall we take a cup of tea while we wait?"

ELIZABETH ARRIVED HOME with several swatches of fabrics and another stern lecture from her father, who she'd seen in Eastmore just as he was entering the bank. Elizabeth was surprised to find only Isabella and Mr. Thorne in the dining room. Apparently, the girls all ended up taking dinner at the Baldwins', and Isabella did not have the heart to refuse their request. However, that left a rather shocking amount of food on the table that required consumption, so despite her weariness and longing for silence, Elizabeth took up a chair next to Isabella.

"So all three of them are dining at the Baldwins'?" Elizabeth asked as she helped herself to a bun.

"They so rarely do anything together as a trio that I could not refuse. I know I shouldn't have allowed it, given G isn't out yet, but both of the girls have been tagging around with Cassandra for a year now to dinner invitations at friends' homes. Please do not scold me horribly."

Elizabeth spoke as she helped herself to boiled potatoes. "On the contrary, ma'am, I have no intention of scolding you. Indeed, I believe it was the only sensible thing you could do given the circumstances. This house has endured enough turmoil for one day. A little peace and quiet will do us all good."

"Have you informed Thea of your father's agreement? On her coming out?" Isabella asked.

She glanced at Mr. Thorne. "My father took that task upon himself. In *front* of Georgiana."

"Oh dear," Isabella said with a sigh.

"Is that why we found you loitering about our property this morning?" Mr. Thorne asked with a chuckle. "Desperate to escape your youngest sisters?"

"Indeed, sir," Elizabeth said with a smile. She placed a small slice of pigeon pie upon her plate. "This dinner by Julia looks quite exceptional. I am very pleased to have Mr. Thorne here to share it."

Elizabeth spoke as she helped herself to several types of pickles to go with her pie. "Oh, I saw Mrs. Collins in Eastmore, as it happens. She said that the last intelligence she'd received was that Mr. Parsons was doing well, but that the bone must be carefully monitored. There is a fear of infection."

"Poor man," Isabella said. "Mr. Thorne, would you be so kind as to pass me the turnips."

And so dinner went, with the local gossip being discussed. A servant arrived from the Baldwins with a letter from Cassandra requesting permission for all three of them to spend the night there. Isabella was not certain that would be wise, but Elizabeth successfully pleaded the case of the girls.

"My dear, Mrs. Knight," Mr. Thorne said. "Think of silence."

That quickly brought Isabella around, and Elizabeth said to shamelessly use Mr. Thorne's name if Mr. Knight was unsure of the propriety of it all. That would give Elizabeth the opportunity the following day to speak with Miss Sims and come to a business arrangement. Isabella, of course, offered her blessing as the laundry maids would not be arriving for two more weeks, offering up plenty of room for Miss Sims to stay in the attic.

They didn't normally have proper accommodations for servants to live with them permanently. However, since Mrs. Taylor's previous trip to the rectory to assist Isabella, she had taken it upon herself to arrange the cleaning out of the attic rooms as she did not wish to stay in Elizabeth's room. Under her careful eye, she arranged for the storage to be moved to the larger attic closet and back room that had the terrible drafts. From there, what was a closet was turned into a small room for a couple of male servants. Ditto the larger upper room, for the female servants.

Oftentimes, Mr. Knight just had the laundry maids stay at the currently unoccupied curate's house since it was nearby and in better condition than his attics. But now, with Mrs. Taylor's excellent assistance, they had proper housing for servants once more in the upper chamber of their house.

"Elizabeth, would it be amiss to hire Miss Sims' niece to assist in the kitchen?" Isabella inquired. "Poor Julia is trying her best, of course, but I do think a second pair of hands to assist with the cleaning and fetching of items would be of a great assistance. What is your opinion?"

"I am not certain of the wisdom of placing two twelve-year-old girls together in the kitchen," Elizabeth said cautiously.

"Julia is seventeen, dear!" Isabella said. "I am as surprised as you, I assure you."

"But she is so tiny," Elizabeth said. "I would never have guessed at her age."

"Poor nutrition," Mr. Thorne said gravely. "I've seen it often enough in town with the poor."

"Julia says she was very sickly as a baby and never fully recovered from it," Isabella said. "Poor girl. It will make working difficult for her, being as small as she is."

"Two of the nieces are apprenticing with Miss Sims, I know that. However, there are the others. Doesn't she have a cousin or some such living with her now, with her little girl?"

"I believe so," Mr. Thorne said. "The cousin's husband was a curate and he died suddenly. They were kicked from their home by the new curate with a week's notice."

Elizabeth silently listened to Mr. Thorne and Isabella talk about the poverty of the Sims' household: seven women of little fortune all huddled together in a small upper apartment over the Williams' shop, and attempting to get by in the world. She could not help reflecting upon the rectory. One day, her father would die and this, the only home she'd ever known, would be ripped from her. There would be no pension, no living set aside to care for all of the daughters. Indeed, they would be left to shift for themselves in the world.

A dark, ungracious thought fluttered through her mind: she hoped the baby did not make it. The burden of it upon their future lives would be awful. Even if a boy, all of their spare money would be going to its education, to its clothing, and investments into his income. They would sink further in an attempt to prop up this child for the hope he would one day keep them from freezing to death.

And if a girl? Well, just another mouth to feed while they slipped further into poverty with no chance of escape.

Elizabeth felt the guilt of her thoughts immediately. That was unchristian of her. She must endure the life given to her, and not complain about its unfairness. She had her fortune, though small as it was. Perhaps in time, Aunt Cass would assist her enough to keep them all from freezing in the cold. She knew her father hoped she'd inherit the bulk of Aunt Cass' estate. However, there was Mr. David Leigh to consider. And while he was an annoying young man, he would have children soon and Aunt Cass might feel differently about them.

Three thousand pounds.

As long as the book remained safe and from harm, she had options. She could invest the total sum from the sale, giving her anywhere between a hundred and twenty to even one hundred fifty pounds annually, and that would be on top of her fifty-odd pounds from her uncle's gracious gift. She also still had her savings, which she would hoard. If they lost their home, the book would keep them out of the poor house. It might not keep them in tea and sugar, but it would put a little meat upon their table and pay for school.

"Miss Knight? Are you unwell?" Mr. Thorne asked.

She looked up from her plate, realizing she'd faded into her thoughts long enough for her pie to have turned cold. "Oh, I was pondering upon a question I have about the occult's powers and how to find the answer."

"You shall have plenty of quiet tomorrow to work on the problem," Isabella said.

Elizabeth laughed. "Hardly. I still need to arrange Miss Sims' time. I shall see if she will allow me to borrow her pattern book for Thea to pick out her gowns now, as opposed to paying poor Miss Sims to listen to all of that. Then, we need to decide upon fabrics. Oh, and then I need to gather all of the sewing supplies we have about the house and arrange the purchase of anything else required so that we won't be travelling back and forth to the village all week when we should be sewing. Of course, this all relies upon Mary agreeing."

"My letter has already gone out, and I am certain she will be absolutely overjoyed with the prospect," Isabella said.

"I can tell from her expression, Mrs. Knight, that our dinner companion does not agree."

Elizabeth smiled. "Mr. Thorne, I shall not be repeating the entirety of my relationship with my sister to explain why this expression is upon my face."

Two more hours passed before the first drops of rain forced Mr. Thorne to announce he would begin his walk back to Vane Park. Isabella offered him to take one of the horses, or even their donkey cart, but Mr. Thorne laughed and said he was confident he could survive a little dampness. Isabella declared herself fatigued and took to her room to rest.

That allowed Elizabeth to finally escape to the solitude of her own bedchamber. She filled Mrs. Egerton in on all of the details that the ghost would have missed during dinner and while shopping, when her book was still in the carriage. Elizabeth did not overly concern herself with the opinions of others, but even she knew her father would hear of it if she were caught shopping with a book in hand.

"I do not understand why you have agreed so readily to visit your sister. I thought you hated her."

"Hate is a sin, Mrs. Egerton. While I am still human and am prone to mistakes, I do attempt to sin as little as possible. It makes my evening prayers easier to manage." Elizabeth sighed. "But, if you must know my reasoning, it was for Thea. She needs society. She needs to leave Bryden and meet new people and have different conversations, and…simply see more of the world. She sits here day after day, and I fear the bitterness of our situation at home had begun festering her soul. I worry for her. If we do not take extraordinary measures, we might risk her becoming prey to an unscrupulous man or even being forced into a secret arrangement that would ruin her and all of her family. All in a desperate wish to leave this life behind."

"So you risk your own happiness for a sister who has shown no signs of appreciating your work and assistance."

"Thea is young, Mrs. Egerton. Age and situation will help change that. Also, I believe working on Thea's gowns will be a welcome distraction in the household and will allow me time to think on occult matters. Thea hates all forms of sewing, so she won't even be of real use me while I work. So, I can be quiet while stitching and think."

"I remain unconvinced."

Elizabeth opened the door of her small closet and pulled down three books from the back corner. She dragged her trunk from the closet and placed it at the foot of her bed, in front of the trunk that held her bed linens. "I believe I shall take these three books, and your book, of course. But what is your opinion? Should I bring something else to study, or will this occupy me for now?"

"The ball isn't for another three weeks!" Mrs. Egerton exclaimed. "Why are you packing your trunk now?"

"I know my sister and father. I shall be in a carriage as soon as Theodosia's gowns have the final stitch in them. Upon reflection, I should bring my writing desk, too. It will make letter and journal writing significantly easier, I believe."

"Take care that your sister does not steal your money," Mrs. Egerton said.

"Oh, Mary would never steal the money. She would steal the desk, and accidentally find the money three years from now, which would incidentally be the first time she'd actually used the desk." Elizabeth raised her eyebrows at Mrs. Egerton and smiled. "However, that puts me in mind to do something with all of the money I currently have in my reticule."

Elizabeth moved her candle to the small table she'd purchased in London. She opened her writing desk, which was atop the table, and pulled out her accounts book. She carefully dug out all of the bank notes in her reticule and placed them next to her desk. Then, she began her calculations.

In total, she had £6 3s 5p left of her pin money. She set that aside in its own pile for now. There was the £27 in book sales from Mr. Osborne, and the £28 of interest from Mr. Grant.

It was a shocking amount of money, but Elizabeth was not a frivolous woman. She would need money for new gowns eventually, and she would most likely need a new warm cloak come winter. There were all the birthdays still to come. There was also Christmas, where she generally purchased a small item for each of her sisters, save Mary; she purchased sweets and a small trinket for the children instead.

She considered for a moment before deciding £6 would be an adequate savings for clothing for now. Likewise, she would add £4 for presents.

From there, she estimated her remaining expenses for the remainder of the year.

She added an additional £2 of her interest income for events in London that she wished to attend and did not have her aunt accompanying her to pay for any fees. If Thea was with her, she'd need a little extra pin money to cover for her sister's spending.

Mr. Knight currently paid the circulating library fees, which she believed was £3 for the entire family each year. She decided to also put that aside as well, as a protection against the support being withdrawn without warning. The youngest girls might not care about reading at present, but herself, Cassandra, and Isabella would suffer horribly if that escape was removed from them.

That left her with £13 until her next payment, which was still an excellent sum of money. Of course, that did not take into account her book sales, though she feared her father would soon find use for those funds. She anticipated that sum would end up going to her sisters to support them. She would leave that money for now.

She placed her £27 inside a miniature box Miss Thorne had recently sent to her from London. Elizabeth recalled the note that had been attached to the box fondly:

> *I saw this at the very curiosity shop where you'd purchased your writing desk, and the shop owner assured me it would fix your desk. I resolved to purchase it immediately and you will be pleased to know that I did not haggle, though I always do, and that I paid in ready cash, since I know how important that is to you. I hope that lessens your ire of me having purchased such a gift under no useful pretense other than I felt you simply had to have it!*

Elizabeth placed the £12 in savings underneath the small box, where it was safely hidden away from prying eyes. With her main income expenses and savings planned out, Elizabeth felt a profound sense of relief.

She started a special page in her ledger for Thea's coming out expenses. Her father had not given her the £12 yet, and knowing him it might be several days before he remembered. She had already used her own money to purchase the fabric sampler. She added that cost, as well as Miss Sims' salary of fifteen shillings and the 2s 6d for the niece to run errands and to assist in the kitchen. She hoped those figures would be readily accepted by the lady upon Elizabeth's offer of them the following day.

Elizabeth updated her recent purchases in her ledger before putting her pin money back into the tiny beaded purse she liked to carry inside her reticule. Her poor reticule was beginning to fray from carrying so much money in it. She chuckled at having such a problem! Oh, to have nothing else to worry about than worn fabric because one's purse is overflowing with coins.

Happy with the disposition of her money for the next several months, Elizabeth put away her accounts book. She carefully repacked her writing desk's money compartment, checking as she always did that the secret box was still there, and still held £50.

She swapped her accounts book for her journals. She opened her occult book to where her ribbon lay and finally asked the question that had been weighing on her heart all day.

"Mrs. Egerton? Is it possible to heal people with the occult?"

⚜ Chapter 6 ⚜

MRS. EGERTON APPEARED before Elizabeth in a cheery pink gown with brown stripes. Her bonnet was decorated with feathers. "Miracles fall under the realm of the Lord, Miss Knight. I have never seen the occult raise those from their death beds and I would be greatly opposed to such an action. That's unnatural."

"Oh, that is not my intention, I assure you. I firmly believe raising the dead belongs only to the Lord's hand and not my own," Elizabeth said. "I only wish to know if we can use the occult to fight infection or ease pain?"

Mrs. Egerton's words were deliberate and cautious. "It is somewhat possible to do those things."

Elizabeth asked very quietly, "Will you teach me?"

"Alas, I have little skill in healing spell craft. It is a rather complex area of the occult and can consume a lifetime's worth of study and dedication. I turned my interests elsewhere." At Elizabeth's disappointed expression, Mrs. Egerton sighed and said, "I shall regret this, but turn to the fourth entry in my book for a Miss Gibbs."

Elizabeth picked up the book and carefully turned the pages until she found Miss Gibbs. She read the entry.

Miss Matilda Gibbs (1722-1745)
Herbalist, Cook.
Specialties include herbal-based healing, as well as the transference of pain and ailments. Aggressively cheerful. Caution must be exercised in any summoning by inexperienced occultists.

"She was so young," Elizabeth mused. "But, aggressively cheerful? My dear Mrs. Egerton, I do believe you wrote that!"

"I did indeed, and my warning stands. However, if you promise to only consult her advice when I am summoned, then yes, I shall assist you. However, I do warn you, she is dangerous indeed and you must always be on your guard. Do not mistake cheerfulness as innocence."

"I have never heard of a person being described in such a manner. Surely, there is a misunderstanding here."

Mrs. Egerton's ghostly sigh made the curtains move. "My dear girl, I knew Miss Gibbs. You must trust my guidance on this matter. That woman could talk you into committing the most heinous of crimes with a mere smile and a feminine giggle."

"You make her sound positively evil, Mrs. Egerton!"

Mrs. Egerton's face clearly said Elizabeth would soon find out the horrors of this "aggressively cheerful" individual. For Elizabeth's part, she was more excited than ever.

June 6, 1810
Bryden Rectory

My dear Ladies of the Occult Society (London),

Forgive my momentary giddiness in the greeting. I was struck with the imaginations of our little society expanding across this fine country, and that we would need to identify which chapter or guild we are from. Since Ladies Occult Society would not be specific enough. Ah, the absurdities of a silly young woman's mind, as my father would say.

Now, be not alarmed that I have taken to writing one letter to both of you. I solemnly promise to write your individual letters tomorrow. However, I have some important—might I say formal—Society business to share and I could not rest (even though it's after eleven in the evening) until I'd written this while still fresh upon my mind.

I have been in discussion with Mrs. Egerton regarding a Miss Gibbs, the fourth entry in her ghost book. This Miss Gibbs was apparently an expert in healing that used herbs and cooking, as well as a curiosity called "transference" but Mrs. Egerton will not share the explanation until Miss Gibbs has been summoned. I am gravely concerned about Isabella's condition, and Mrs. Egerton said her old friend might be able to assist us.

However, there is a hindrance in this progress: Mrs. Egerton does not know the steps to unlocking Miss Gibbs' ghost spells. I write to beg your assistance on determining the spellworking to unlock her ghost. I have attached a very poor drawing of her autograph. I have also copied her description, in the hope that will aid you further. As well, here is a description of what my poor drawing attempts to convey:

Miss Matilda Gibbs (1722-1745)

The ink bleeds from her Christian name are decorated in common vegetables. I am certain I detect parsnips, carrots, cabbages, and I believe the leafy plant is spinach. Her family name is decorated with wheat and barley, complete with stems. The dots over her I's have been turned into spirals that resemble pea or possibly bean plants.

Mrs. Egerton calls Miss Gibbs "aggressively cheerful". I am uncertain how to take her meaning. Unless either of you feel I should have a different approach, I will be on guard for a rather happy ghost with a personal conflict with

Mrs. Egerton. Of course, if we can summon this ghost, then I shall form my own opinion on her.

I am to Mary's within three weeks (the timing of travel depends upon my sister's gowns), and I must express my disappointment that I do not think I will find the time to be in town before the autumn. I cannot even risk inviting you both to Bryden, for I am uncertain how long I am needed at my sister's house. Indeed, I fear I must say that one of us must marry very well, so that the others can come live at your estate so that we could work in peace without distraction.

Surely, there must be a wealthy man in London with two or three country estates, and a house in town, of course, who would be perfectly happy to share his wife with several young unmarried ladies of excellent reputation, eat his pheasants and drink his wine. If you find him, send him my way. I shall be at my leisure for his proposals.

I look forward to your letters,

Miss Elizabeth Knight
Ladies Occult Society – Bryden

(Sorry, my dearest friends. I could not resist one final fancy.)

✒ Chapter 7 ✒

MISS SIMS ARRIVED with her niece at Bryden Rectory on the eighth of June promptly at ten in the morning. She was very welcomed, and immediately shown to the female servants' room in the attic, which Elizabeth assured her was a very pleasant room, as the windows were only three years old and the beds were very comfortable indeed. Elizabeth detailed the work Mrs. Taylor put into it during her visit, but alas the good lady was unable to make a fireplace appear in the room. Miss Sims joked that, considering the time of the year, she would welcome a little chill in the evening.

Cassandra led Alice, the niece, to the kitchen and left Elizabeth to discuss the finer financial matters with Miss Sims. As it turned out, Alice was a very sturdy and steady girl of thirteen who already had practice in the kitchen. Contrary to Elizabeth's worries, the young girl also knew how to make several hearty family dinners at minimal costs. Miss Sims even said that, while Alice would not be hired to cook at St. James' palace anytime soon, she could feed a family on next to no money. That last part would no doubt please Mr. Knight excessively.

"Is there any word on Mrs. Cooper?" Miss Sims asked.

Elizabeth shook her head. "Sadly, there is no news to report. All of the children have been sent from the home and are staying with Mrs. Bragg. I offered Julia a bed in the attic, but she wished to stay with her siblings for now."

They continued the polite chat about the rectory's cook before Miss Sims turned matters back to the financials of the situation. "Now, Miss Knight, might I convince you to reconsider your offer of fifteen shillings. I do believe thirteen shillings for the week to be very fair, and I do not wish it to be known that I overcharged the local rector!"

Elizabeth knew the worth of the woman's skills and remained firm. "On the contrary, Miss Sims. I believe fifteen shillings with meals, tea, and lodgings is an exceedingly fair price for your expertise. Let us discuss it no more. I have a very eager sister in the drawing room who wishes to discuss several gowns in your pattern book. But, pray, we can only spend twelve pounds on Thea's entire coming out wardrobe. And, indeed, you know her love for silk and finery. I shall rely upon you directing her attentions accordingly."

That made Miss Sims chuckle. "I shall attempt to keep her within her means."

"That would be greatly appreciated."

The ladies all moved to the company drawing room, as it was next to the sewing room the ladies had set up for their various needs. Miss Sims had been too busy before now to sit with the Knight ladies; she'd had three commissions to finish first. Thea was overwhelmed with excitement to see the drawings and patterns of the latest fashions, as well as some older, but still very sensible, dresses that would be good for visiting and church. Tea was called for and, by the time it arrived in the drawing room, Miss Sims' trunks had arrived. One in particular revealed buttons, lace, ribbon, and thread, all available for purchase.

The ladies schemed over tea. It took most of the morning, and the assistance of Elizabeth and her sisters—excluding a sullen Georgiana who refused to leave her room—to help poor Theodosia decide upon her gowns. Miss Sims successfully convinced Thea to go with simpler visiting dresses for everyday, so that she could have two very fine gowns to wear at balls. Since attending balls was Thea's main focus, she readily agreed.

Thea continued her agonizing over colours and fabrics and changed her mind ten times. Maria was to arrive with her carriage at one o'clock to take Elizabeth to Eastmore to purchase the necessary fabrics, and Thea seemed determined to wait until then to make her final decision.

Mr. Knight called Elizabeth into his study to make a point about the additional expense of Miss Sims and her niece. "We cannot afford to have random servants hired without my knowledge, Elizabeth."

"Their salaries are to come out of the twelve pounds, Papa."

"Yes, you already told me Miss Sims would be paid from Theodosia's money, but what about this niece of hers? How much do I need to pay her?"

"Oh, the niece's salary will also be taken out of Theodosia's money, Papa. I apologize that I had not explained it properly. We have settled on two shillings six pence for her to stay the week. She is an excellent helper. She has already set out cold ham and fresh bread for you in the kitchen."

That seemed to mollify Mr. Knight, who preferred to take a small meal before leaving on any business in the village. "Well. I am putting all my faith in you, Miss Elizabeth Knight. You had better not disappoint me by running up debts."

"I have no intention of spending a farthing over twelve pounds, you can be assured."

Mr. Knight made a dismissive sound, that announced he did not believe his daughter. Thankfully, she was saved by the announcement that a letter had arrived for Isabella from Mary.

"My dear Eliza, pray read it aloud. Theodosia and I are attempting to choose ribbon for this gown," Isabella said. "Georgiana! There you are. Would you please assist me? You have such an eye for ribbon."

My dearest Isabella,

I am beside myself with excitement. Finally, to have another sister come out into society. I would be all too happy to assist Theodosia with her first ball. Indeed, I shall make all of the arrangements and introductions. There are several eligible young men of our acquaintance who are in the country to escape London for the summer months. I shall endeavour to have them included for her sake.

Now, we must ensure her gowns are of a very good nature. Not too high and fashionable, of course, since she is not in that class. Nevertheless, she is my sister and there will be expectations upon her on that score. I would not wish her to feel embarrassed by her new dresses when surrounded by the kind of families I dine with. Her figure is still changing, of course, but she will need gowns that display her form well. We don't need two spinsters to support in the coming years, now do we?

Elizabeth looked up at her companions and said, with a knowing smirk, "Please ignore that last sentence. It was underlined."

"Eliza!" Cassie said with a laugh.

"Did you get the lecture, Cassie, when you were young?" Thea deepened her voice, in an attempt to mimic Elizabeth. "Now, Theodosia. I am very disappointed in you. You have violated the sacred code amongst ladies. By reading aloud anything underlined and sharing it with the world, you are breaching the trust between women."

Cassie laughed. "Indeed, I did. And, Mary was on the receiving end of that lecture more than once, too, as I recall."

Elizabeth gave her sisters a smile. She would not have read aloud the underlined sentence of any other person's letter. However, as the insult was directed solely at herself, she did not feel bound by the conventions she had drilled into her younger sisters.

"I am certain Mary does not mean to be cruel," Isabella said.

"On the contrary, Isabella. I am quite certain she knows her meaning," Elizabeth said. She continued to read:

Between us ladies, I am very concerned about Elizabeth's sewing hand.

"My dear sisters, this paragraph continues with an endless onslaught of insults about my person. Shall I skip it, since it's all underlined, or should we all have a little chuckle at Mary's foolishness?"

Isabella cleared her throat and glanced at Miss Sims, who was very busy with her back turned to them and standing at the table against the back of the sewing room's wall.

Elizabeth smiled at her stepmother when Miss Sims said, "Oh, I do apologize. Were you ladies speaking to me? Why, when I am concentrating on work, it is though my ears completely stop working."

Isabella shook her head and said, "Continue the letter, Eliza. Since you are determined."

Elizabeth's work has never been what I would call quite good, and I do not think her skills merit her being able to work on even a simple everyday dress for Theodosia without constant attention. For my sake, please keep your eye upon her stitches and, pray, do not be ashamed to point out if her work requires improvement. We do not wish poor Theodosia to be embarrassed when she meets the kind of people who shall attend my private ball.

"That is very unfair," G said. "Eliza has repaired two gowns for me, and added a lovely lace trim to my pink dress that I wear to church because it was looking worn. She even changed all of the ribbon, and Miss Sims had been the one to sew that particular gown in the first place."

"I do not understand why Mary says such things," Theodosia said. "Elizabeth's work is exceptional. Even Charles commented on it, and he never notices anything we do."

"It is a wonder Mary allows me to do any work at Ashbrook," Elizabeth said.

"Did she not force you sew Mr. Fitzharding's shirts when you visited last?" Cassie asked.

"Indeed she did," Elizabeth said with a smile. "However, that was only because she was so very busy that she could not do the work herself."

"Elizabeth," Isabella said in a mildly chastising tone. "Will you please continue the letter?"

> *I cannot wait for Theodosia's arrival. There are a great many things to do and we will have to visit the shops to see if there is anything worthwhile to purchase. Elizabeth's assistance with the children will be very desirable. There is nothing here in Ashbrook for her beyond the children, and she has nothing of import to do, except that silly occult business she's fallen into, which I will forbid her from practicing in my home, let me assure you and Papa. Yes, I do believe it is best that Elizabeth do come because I shall be too busy to look after the mundane matters of my household.*

Elizabeth's pause in reading prompted her two youngest sisters to look up from their tasks to make hurried comments about how they appreciated her.

"Oh Eliza!" Theodosia said. "Ignore Mary. She only ever thinks of herself."

"We care that you have things to do," G added from her seat on the floor as she dug through Miss Sims' trunk of haberdashery. Her sulking had finally ceased when she found her way to digging through the trunk of delights.

"It has been a long time since Mary's words have cut me, girls, I can assure you."

Elizabeth gave Isabella a side glance, but offered up a smile to let her know she was not offended. How could anyone be offended by Mary? Mary was only being herself. It was forgivable or it was not, but either case, her behaviour was consistent. At least her discussion with the girls had created a lasting impression upon them. Perhaps not enough for them to understand how to change their behaviour, but enough for them to consider their actions. Elizabeth considered that a very good sign.

> *Send my love to the girls, and tell Papa that the new orchard survived the cold winter and, while we will only see*

a couple of apples this year, it is growing excessively well
and we anticipate a great yield in a year or two.

Mary

"Your sister loves any excuse to host a ball," Isabella said, breaking the lingering silence after finishing the letter.

Thankfully, they were soon rescued by Matthew, a young man of fourteen who worked for several families in the village. He arrived with his cart and announced he'd picked up a parcel from the inn for Mr. Knight, as well as brought Miss Sims' second, much larger trunk, and a cloth bag of her clothes. He also dropped off fresh fruit from the village that Mr. Knight had purchased and asked to be delivered.

Elizabeth gave him two pennies as a tip, and told him to get a piece of cake from the kitchen when he was done his deliveries about the rectory.

G immediately popped the trunk open, even over the protests of Isabella and Elizabeth, but Miss Sims only laughed and gave her ready consent. G pulled out several pieces of muslin, so fine it was nearly transparent. Expensive silk strips came next and Elizabeth recognized several cuttings from village dresses over the years. The yellow silk, in particular, was from Maria's ballgown, but then upon reflection, she realized that she'd also seen that yellow on Miss Parson's latest gown.

Miss Sims said, "Ah, you have found me out, Miss Knight! Indeed, I keep whatever scraps of fabric no one wants and I use them to embellish both new gowns and refurbished ones. It is amazing how the addition of a new ribbon and a thin line of trim across the sleeves and bodice can make a person forget they have seen a particular dress for the last two seasons."

"I am a firm supporter of thrift," Elizabeth said with a laugh.

"And, yet, Miss Sims, my eldest daughter wastes her talents by remaining unmarried," Mr. Knight called out from the hallway beyond. He poked his head in as he pulled on his black coat he favoured for walking.

"But Papa, consider," Elizabeth said, still smiling, "if I was married, then you would not benefit from my very good habits."

Her father made a slight grumble under his breath, signalling that he did not have a rebuttal at hand. "Ladies, I shall be out all day visiting the sick and then will be dining at the Baldwins' today. I will send your regards, my dear, of course."

"Might we overtake the dining room table then, sir?" Isabella asked. "It is significantly larger than the sewing table we have, and it would allow us to work swiftly."

"As you wish. Do not forget I still need my new shirts, and Charles is in a desperate way for his."

"Of course, sir," Isabella said to the back of her husband, who was already off toward the front door.

With Elizabeth and Miss Sims solely tasked with keeping Thea's expectations within her budget, Isabella decided to employ herself at the table cutting fabric for Charles' shirts. He needed three new shirts, and Mr. Knight wished to have two more for himself. They all moved to the dining room, with G helping carry Isabella's sewing items.

"Isabella, you don't need to do that right now," Elizabeth scolded when Isabella seated herself at the end of the table with the shirt linen in front of her. "My father didn't mean he wished them this very day. We need to ensure Thea does not end up commissioning forty silk dresses!"

"I am not going to do that," Thea protested.

"I assure you that you will not," Elizabeth said.

Isabella refused to stop her work. "I am useless at the moment and this is the perfect opportunity to do the work. Also consider that with Miss Sims present, if I happen to run out of fabric, she is right here to supply more. And, if I happen to have some leftover scraps, which I suspect I shall as Mr. Knight does not prefer his neck collar cut as widely as Charles' taste, there is additional fabric for sleeve linings or any mending."

Thea and G returned into the room with the smaller trunk between them. They put it down on the floor, out of the way.

"But what about my embroidery?" Thea asked shyly. "Elizabeth said you would be willing to sew some decorations for me, if there is time."

"And when we are at that stage, your brother and father will have to endure having your needs placed ahead of their own. But for the present, I believe I shall get some work done while you ladies argue about dotted or plain muslin. Oh, and I prefer the dotted." Isabella began laying her fabric out at one end of the table. "And observe that I only have a dozen yards or so of Irish linen here, and I need twice that to finish all of the shirts, so my job will be done quickly."

"If you require more, Mrs. Knight, please do not hesitate to ask. I have some superior linen at the cottage and would be happy to send Alice to fetch it."

"Thank you, Miss Sims. We shall see how this current adventure goes first, I believe," Isabella said.

The next three hours were an exhausting display of decisions. Finally, it was decided that Theodosia would have two simple everyday dresses, one very good dress, and then two ball gowns. Miss Sims felt that the ballgowns could be matched with different gloves and additional ribbon under the bodice to give the appearance of a larger variety of styles. Thea would also need neckerchiefs and the like, as well. Silk stockings, gloves, a fan, plus fabric for a new spencer and a new pelisse.

Thea picked out the fabrics she wished from the samples Elizabeth had brought from Eastmore, with Miss Sims offering guidance. She worried that the light blue silk Thea liked was not the best quality for the price, so Thea decided to go with the yellow. The final list of yardage was being written out just as Maria's carriage arrived in front of the rectory.

Elizabeth would have preferred to depart much earlier in the day, but she also did not wish to lose a full half day of work due to her own petty preferences. The two friends spent most of the afternoon shopping and stopped at the small bakery shop in Eastmore to have tea and cake.

Elizabeth showed Maria the leather-bound account book that she'd purchased for Theodosia. "I shall write in it what her expenses today cost, I believe I remember them all, or near enough. Then, she will know what items should cost, but also hopefully will get into the habit of tracking her expenses once I hand it to her. There is also the additional bonus that she can see what are good and fair prices, as they will be written out for her."

"That is rather ambitious planning of yours," Maria said. "How can you remember what any of this cost?"

Elizabeth laughed. "Poverty makes it very easy to calculate sums in one's mind while shopping for silk."

Maria gave Elizabeth a scolding glance. "I would have purchased all of the silk for Theodosia's gowns if you'd have allowed me. I would have called it my gift to her and let it be at that."

"My dear, Maria, have you not yet caught on to my scheme? I cannot take help from you now, as I do not need it. However, there may come a time when I will be desperate and living in the hedgerow with my sisters. Then, I shall depend upon you to rescue us and buy us all of the silk in England."

Maria rolled her eyes. "You are a wealthy heiress now, with your fifty pounds per annum. You do not need your old friends anymore."

Elizabeth reached across the small table to take her friend's hand. "My dear Maria, I will always need you."

"Do not be so serious or else you shall risk me becoming sappy," Maria said.

That made Elizabeth laugh hard enough to earn a withering glare from the other ladies in the establishment. She covered her mouth with her gloved hand and giggled into it, earning her even more whispers and glares.

"My dear Eliza, you are going to get us removed from this shop!"

Elizabeth's exhaustion-induced fit of the giggles continued until her tea was cold.

THERE WAS ENOUGH daylight left by the time Elizabeth arrived back at the rectory for Miss Sims to inspect the purchased items. Miss Sims held them up to Thea's face and made thoughtful sounds to herself. Occasionally, she wrote down a few notes, as opposed to merely muttering small nothings about various dressmaking techniques.

In total, Elizabeth returned home with twenty-six yards of various gown materials, including white muslin, yellow silk, two types of printed cotton, a solid cotton, and a rather lovely brown silk for a pelisse. Elizabeth also purchased Thea a rather stylish printed fan, two pairs of white silk stockings, six yards of various colours of ribbon, and a very fashionable blue velvet bonnet which inflamed Georgiana's ire to such a pitch that Elizabeth was forced to banish the girl to her bedroom until she regained control of her emotions.

Adding in the wages for Miss Sims and Alice, Elizabeth had already spent £9 4s 7d of her father's money. There were still shoes and gloves yet to purchase, but she was confident neither of those items would cost beyond ten shillings.

They all took a simple supper in the family drawing room upstairs, since the dining table was currently occupied, mostly of cold pies and cake. Elizabeth helped herself to coffee before declaring herself fatigued and wishing to retreat to her bedchamber. Elizabeth moved her candle close to her writing desk and began her letters that she could not put off, but would have no time to write during the day.

My dearest Aunt Cass,

I find myself exhausted beyond measure today. Upon my advice, my father has allowed Thea to come out. My hope being it will help break up this melancholy affliction that has settled upon her for some time now. The poor girl has struggled since the death of her mother, and the situation of the current Mrs. Knight has done nothing to ease the oppressive nature of Thea's memories. Having lost her own dear mama so recently, and now to have another in the house reminding her of her mother's last days has not been easy for any of us, but it presses upon her most of all.

Mr. Thorne presented me with the final sum of my book sales. I am still so humbled and thankful that you allowed me to inherit such a sum of money, when you could have easily kept the books for yourself. My father has, predictably, placed more financial expectations upon me, though partially that is so that we can hire a nurse for

Isabella without any reduction in the household's lifestyle. I cannot fault him for that, though I confess I know that it won't be a temporary situation for me and the reduction will be permanent.

I find myself rather without bitterness or anger. Indeed I truly find myself rather accepting of the situation. My good fortune should extend to helping my family. Is that not our motto? The good fortune of one is the good fortune of all. Therefore, I find myself willing to take over my gown and shoe expenses for the year. Though, if I am to be truthful with you – after all, if I cannot be truthful to you, my dearest aunt, with whom can I be? - that I am in no real need for new gowns anytime soon, so I do not feel the press of poverty on that score.

I am to Mary's soon and I suspect she will complain greatly about my two-year-old gowns. It occurs to me that I should ask Miss Sims, if there is time of course, to mend one of my gowns. Do you suppose Mary would notice the age of a dress if I changed the lace and ribbons? I could remove the sleeves. I am certain the shock of seeing my gloved elbow would startle Mary into not noticing the age of my gown.

Indeed, now that I write this, I believe I shall pull out my best ballgown and see if I can adjust the sleeves! That will be an extraordinary joke.

We have Miss Sims living with us for the next week. Her eyesight is not what it was, but she is still the best seamstress I have ever seen. We are paying her fifteen shillings—including her room and board, of course—to sew for the daylight hours. She can also assist myself and Isabella in the evening, as we help continue the sewing, to save her eyesight. She is making up the patterns and getting the dresses started, as well as doing the fittings. We suspect we'll be put to hard labour beginning tomorrow afternoon. That is why I write this letter by candlelight.

As predicted, Georgiana has not taken well to the news that her sister will be coming out without her own oar in the waters next to her. I have little faith that Thea will enjoy the solitude in society for very long, to be very honest, and I warned our father that G might soon need her own twelve pounds before the snow falls. However, for now, our house is a scene of much wailing and gnashing of teeth, while the rest of us attempt to pretend nothing had changed whatsoever.

I believe I finally understand now why Mary accepted the first man who proposed marriage to her. While I would not have behaved in the same manner, I do see the value in leaving the rectory as soon as possible to forge one's own establishment away from the dramatics of youth.

Our father has been spending most of his time lately away from home in the company of Mr. Parsons. He is hoping to lease several acres of farmland from Mr. Parsons, thereby adding to our annual income. It is a good scheme, if it can be managed, and I hope for all of us that he is successful. Also, Mr. Parsons broke his hand and is under strict orders to remain indoors, lest he fall or hit the hand and cause an infection. The bone has been set back into place, and there is no sign of infection at present, but I feel a person can never be too cautious with a broken bone. Too many times we have seen the patient take a bad turn overnight and there is little that can then be done for them beyond pray and hope.

Now, I feel I must broach an uncomfortable subject and inquire if you had planned to purchase Thea a shawl for her coming out. I would not have mentioned it, except she has already been discussing what she will do if you purchase her a muslin shawl similar to mine. You have started a terrible trend in our home, I fear. However, if you did not plan for that expense, I will understand and happily purchase the gift for her in your name. I can even ask Miss

> *Thorne to find an acceptable garment in the shops; she has a keen eye even if she does not show it in her own dress.*

The next part she underlined, just for safety.

> *How are Miss Thorne and Miss Susan? Are you still enjoying the company? They seem delighted with your company, though I worry that you might be growing tired of their youthful enthusiasm. Do not be alarmed; I would not betray your trust if the company was growing tedious at times for you. I love Maria with all of my heart, and I can only stay at Vane Park for a week before I miss the routine of my own life.*

> *All my love,*
> *Elizabeth*

Elizabeth yawned and blew out her candle. She would merely lie upon the bed to rest her eyes before engaging with Mrs. Egerton and the mystery of Miss Gibbs. However, Elizabeth found herself completely surprised upon waking in the morning still fully dressed in her gown and shoes.

Chapter 8

BREAKFAST DID NOT begin as a joyous occasion of the ladies of the household preparing to make gowns. In their haste of sorting the fabrics and purchases from the previous day, they had forgotten to clear the dining room table of patterns, ribbons, and Isabella's shirt pieces she'd cut. Mr. Knight arrived in the dining room before any of the ladies and began shouting.

"No man of sense and education should endure a life of such foolishness!" he bellowed, as Elizabeth and Cassandra came rushing down the stairs still in their dressing gowns. Isabella followed behind with the younger girls as quickly as she could.

"Whatever is the matter, Papa?" Elizabeth asked, out of breath from rushing to him. Though, she immediately knew upon seeing the state of the table and his expression.

"My breakfast is being disrupted by all this lace and silk!"

Thankfully, Miss Sims had decided to take her breakfast with Alice in the kitchen, and so there were no servants present for the scene. Still, Elizabeth said, "Allow me to clear a space."

Mr. Knight grumbled and berated Elizabeth as she carefully picked up the patterns Miss Sims had made, moving them gown by gown to the floor. However, Mr. Knight's anger grew watching her slow progression of moving the items away from the head of the table. Isabella, sensing this, began picking up the shirt pieces she'd cut.

"I've started the shirts for you and Charles," Isabella said, leaning over the table while Mr. Knight stood there with his plate of food and a sour expression.

Mr. Knight could not take anymore of the delay and, in a loud shout about how stupid they all were, dashed his arm across the table space nearest him. Two different dress patterns, plus the pieces for the men's shirts, all puddled to the floor in a heap.

"Papa!" Thea wailed at him. "Those were for my gown!"

Mr. Knight slammed his plate down at the head of the table and angrily flipped open his newspaper. "I wish to take my breakfast in peace, without being surrounded by such feminine nonsense. What a waste of good money this is. I am your father. I should be allowed to give you away to the nearest man of five hundred a year and be done with all of you!"

Elizabeth glanced at Isabella, whose eyes were filled with tears. She was on her hands and knees, attempting to sort through the pieces on the floor. Theodosia was wailing about the cruelty of her father, and Elizabeth felt no need to correct her younger sister about her tone.

Instead, in the calmest voice Elizabeth could manage, she said, "Cassandra, please take your sisters upstairs and dress. Then, I require eight small white buttons to repair one of my dresses, and Miss Sims does not have the appropriate size. Take both girls with you into the village."

"Of course, Elizabeth," Cassandra said. "Come, Thea. Let's get you into your gown and walk into the village."

"Pray tell me what I owe you upon your return," Elizabeth said.

"Yes, that is all the ladies of this house think about. Money," Mr. Knight said from behind his newspaper. In a mutter, he said, "Why did God curse me with only one son and three useless wives who could not properly bear children?"

Cassandra froze in her place. G gave Elizabeth an appalled look. Even Thea's tears stopped long enough for her to whisper an admonishing, "Papa!"

Elizabeth squared her shoulders and said, "Cassandra. Your sisters. Now."

"Come girls," Cassandra said. "Upstairs, both of you."

"But..." G began a protest.

"Upstairs with both of you," Cassandra instructed in an unyielding voice. "Now."

Isabella successfully held her tears in check until the door to the dressing room closed upstairs. Then, she burst into weeping and rushed from the room as quickly as her changing body would allow. That left only Elizabeth to stand in front of her father, with two opened doors on either of the room, and a temper that was rising higher than her father's.

"I suppose this is when you pretend to be the head of the house and scold me?" her father asked behind his paper.

"That was cruel, sir," Elizabeth said.

He slammed down his paper. "Was it? Tell me, Miss Elizabeth Knight who, at twenty-nine, insists upon being a burden to her father, what else should I consider a wife that will most likely not bear me sons, and my daughters who think nothing more of me than an account to dispense them money?"

Elizabeth decided not to correct him on her age; that would only make the situation worse. Her father did not like to be reminded he didn't know simple things, such as the ages of his daughters, and he would only give a cruel answer in reply.

She stared at her father, debating if she should have an argument with him. He could remove her from the household, leaving her to be stuck with Mary.

Three thousand pounds.

"I am truly sorry, sir, that you are in a foul mood this rather beautiful morning. However, in cases like these, I recommend a vigorous walk in the lane from here to Vane Park, as opposed to speaking hurtful words to your wife who cannot help her current situation."

"You are taking her side? You?" Her father laughed, and he did not hide his bitterness. "Did you not tell me it was a mistake to bring a third wife into our home?"

"I did do so, and I do not regret having advised you thus. Your youngest daughters had not stopped grieving their own mother, which you had very clearly expressed that you do not understand nor care to understand," Elizabeth said. "Be that as it may, Isabella is now your wife, she is here living with us, and she carries your child and my future brother or sister. Therefore, I will defend her and the future member of our household."

Her father lowered his newspaper so that she could more easily see his scowl. "What foolishness you speak, Elizabeth Knight. Why would I concern myself with the thoughts of a bunch of silly girls. Charles is all I have to place my hopes upon. I needed more sons to raise our fortunes. Now look at me? I am to hire a nurse, at great expense, for what? To lose a child and probably another wife and then I shall be forced to begin all over again."

Elizabeth opened her mouth to speak and closed it by the time her father had gotten to the end of his statement. Isabella was in a poor state as it was, let alone with her husband down here loudly preparing for his next wife's arrival. Finally, she gained enough command of herself to say, "Good God. Isabella is not yet dead."

Mr. Knight threw down his fork upon his plate. "What good is that to me? Mr. Collins has already explained to me her situation in greater detail than either of you ladies could possibly understand."

"On the contrary, *sir*, I can comprehend as much as a man," Elizabeth snapped, not even considering to whom she was speaking. She did not apologize, even though she felt she should. Her father was being too cruel, too heartless, and she would not dignify his behaviour with reducing herself down to apologies now.

Her father's look was full of disgust. "Ah, yes. My eldest daughter snubs her nose at everything and everyone, and yet is she punished? No, she is rewarded with fourteen hundred pounds, and the promise of even more from her aunt once she is dead in her grave. Whereas, me and Charles have to scrape by for every penny we wish to spend. My so very intelligent daughter who demands I pay for everything, and yet believes she should hoard all of her shillings in her purse. What did I do to deserve such scorn from the world?"

"This is unfair, sir," Elizabeth said. "I am truly sorry that you are unhappy about your situation in life, or that your only son is not measuring up to your expectations, but that is not my doing."

"You could share your money with Charles!" her father shouted.

Elizabeth drew her shoulders back, actually shocked that her father would shout at her in such a tone. He had been known on more than one occasion to lose control of his good sense, but it was shocking to her that he was yelling at her for no other reason than he wished her to give her money to Charles of all people.

She'd sooner give it to Mary.

Years of dealing with her father alerted her to the fact that, clearly, there was an underlying problem that had little to do with the gowns upon the table or Isabella's situation. So, in the most genteel voice she could manage, she asked, "Shall I therefore assume that Mr. Parsons will not rent you the land?"

The question satisfied some of her father's anger. "Oh, he will, and it will cost me dearly in rent and wages. I shall only be seventy pounds a year richer, at best."

Despite the temptation to the contrary, Elizabeth knew explaining to him how most of the entire country was living on that amount or less would not lighten her father's mood in the slightest. He was envious of her meager fifty-odd pounds in income, and yet sat before her angrily attacking his wife and children over a greater sum of money. She suspected Mr. Knight would never be happy when it came to money, not even if he were the richest man in England. For then, he would simply find something new to irritate his mind.

So, instead of starting yet another quarrel with her father, she announced, "I shall go speak with Isabella."

"Make her control herself. I cannot abide hysterical women." He picked up his fork again. "She is supposed to remain calm in her situation."

Elizabeth scowled but remained silent for the good of Isabella and her own sake. She went upstairs to seek her stepmother, finding her at the top of the stairs dabbing her eyes with her embroidered handkerchief. Elizabeth glanced to see the dressing room the girls used had its door firmly closed.

"Dare I ask how much you overheard?"

"Enough of it," Isabella said weakly.

"I am very sorry, Isabella." She didn't know what else to say.

"Eliza, tell me. Are his words out of anger, or does he truly mean them in his heart?"

Elizabeth was too slow with her reply.

"Ah," Isabella said. She dabbed her eyes as they overflowed once more. "You must know, I had very little choice in marrying your father. My own papa could only provide me with five hundred pounds as my dowry, and the promise of another five when my mother is dead. That was good enough for Mr. Knight at the time, as he hoped my youth would produce him several more sons. However, he has become very unhappy with his choice of wife since I will never inherit as much as his unmarried daughter. And, now that I have proven myself...unworthy as a woman." She looked down at her swollen belly and wept harder into her hand.

"That is not your fault," Elizabeth said, touching Isabella's arm to offer support. "You have no control over your body, no matter what anyone might say. This is the will of the Lord and no one else. And my father married you knowing your situation. If your five hundred pounds with a promise of more was good enough for him a year ago, then it should be good enough for him now. It is not as though we can force others to leave us their money upon their deaths."

That made Isabella smile through her tears. "If that were the case, we would all wish for a distant relation to die and leave us all ten thousand pounds."

"It would be of a great assistance, I am certain," Elizabeth said.

"Though, I suspect not even that amount would satisfy your father's love of money."

Elizabeth made no reply, but she gave Isabella's arm another squeeze of support.

"Tell me, Eliza. Is there anything in your occult studies that could help me? It appears that medicine cannot and I must rely upon God's will for my very life. However, if there is anything in the occult that could help..."

"I do not know for certain," Elizabeth said honestly. "I have found references to occult healing, but I am no expert. I have written to my friends in London, however, to ask for their assistance. I have not said anything as I did not wish to offer false hope."

"I understand," Isabella said in a tone closer to her normal one. She was mustering her emotions once more.

"Isabella! Isabella, I need to speak with you about the hiring of your nurse."

Isabella closed her eyes, and Elizabeth knew her stepmother was considering how the sudden loss of a husband might not be the worst possible thing in the world. She recognized the look of shame upon her face; she'd seen it in her own reflection more than she wished.

"I shall try to find the time to study more," Elizabeth said.

"Thank you," Isabella whispered.

"Isabella!" Mr. Knight shouted from the bottom of the stairs. He was holding a letter. "We have word from Cassandra Spencer. She has found us a nurse who is willing to move to the country."

"Of course," Isabella said. She dabbed at her eyes once more, turned to face her husband, squared her slumping shoulders, and carefully walked down the stairs to do her duty as wife.

And brood mare, Elizabeth thought bitterly.

Three thousand pounds.

She had to stop thinking about that damned book in her drawer because it was making her rebellious of spirit.

The girls soon were herded out of the house toward the shops. Miss Sims had conveniently not appeared in the dining room until Mr. Knight disappeared into his study with Isabella. Miss Sims took one look at the patterns, which were haphazardly piled at the far end of the table, not to mention still all over the floor. Her face betrayed nothing. She simply bent down to begin the task of sorting them without a word of question.

That signalled to Elizabeth that some of the servants had overheard. They did not have servants that lived in the house; they weren't of a class to really afford it and their father didn't like the expense in any case. All of their servants took the short walk from the village to begin their days. Still, it was already nine in the morning. Julia would have already arrived, plus the housemaid and the maid-of-all-work they employed. The footman was about the house somewhere, no doubt. Their groom and stable boy were most likely outside helping in the field or stables, unless they were in the kitchen having a meal.

It was a small house in a small country village. Of course, they'd all heard. Soon, all of Bryden would have heard.

Elizabeth both feared and accepted they would be the subject of village gossip once more. She suspected Sunday's sermon would be one of rebuke against the sin of idle tongues. If possible, she would develop a headache this evening and avoid church tomorrow morning. She grew tired of the hypocritical sermons.

ELIZABETH SPENT THE remainder of the morning working quietly on her occult studies in the sewing room, assisting Miss Sims as necessary. She read *First Forays into the Study of Occult Flora* and its fascinating entries on parsley, of all things. They had plenty in their kitchen garden, so it made for a useful item to collect and store. She wrote several questions for Mrs. Egerton when they had the privacy to speak. Amongst the questions included was if the inclusion of blessed parsley in a meal would boost the prosperity of the household.

She chuckled to herself at the question, for regular ol' parsley hadn't done a thing for her father. Though, she suspected that adding the occult's influence might draw upon the undercurrents of magical powers whose existence she was still only learning about.

There was both an exceeding amount of information in the book about healing, but also frustratingly little. She was uncertain if the authors of the book assumed everyone would have that inherent knowledge and would not need it explained to the reader, just as she did not need rain or clouds explained to her in a novel. Still, it was incredibly frustrating because there were small drops everywhere, hinting about the use of that herb and that tree and a sprinkle of that flower's petals to use in healing workings, but yet there was no actual recipe or direction.

According to the book, arranging a particular set of flowers on a Thursday had been known to purge a household of sore throats. However, there was no mention of the entire set of arrangements, nor what flowers were best, what—if any— incantations were needed, nothing. She made another note to ask

Mrs. Egerton, adding a small scrap of ribbon to the page mentioning the paragraph in hopes her ghostly tutor could assist.

And, Elizabeth wondered, why did it have to be a Thursday? What if the sore throat struck them on a Monday? Would they have to wait?

Elizabeth wrote her letters. A short one to Mary with the details of Thea's coming out clothing and if she could be on the lookout for an excellent pair of long, white silk gloves. Elizabeth knew that meant Mary would end up purchasing a dozen such gloves, but at least it was better than the alternative of Mary blaming Elizabeth for being negligent. Time was pressing upon Elizabeth, unfortunately, and she did not believe she would be able to arrange all that she wished to do without Mary's assistance.

She wrote two chatty letters to Miss Thorne and Miss Markson, with several apologies about the lack of occult updates this week; she had simply been too busy. However, she did include the small passage she'd read about the vase of flowers in case they could find something of merit to add to her own reading. She expected either of them would have a better time of it than her in the present circumstances.

No wonder Mrs. Egerton's group of occultists did not have husbands or children. How was there to be any time to study! She had neither herself, and yet she found her days so busy that even the simplest of tasks, such as repairing the buttons on a favourite pelisse, were well beyond her abilities at present.

Elizabeth was finishing up her letters when the girls finally returned with two shillings' worth of haberdashery and an excessive amount of boiled sweets. At least they'd remembered the buttons; those were another three shillings. Cassandra gave Elizabeth an apologetic glance, but Elizabeth dutifully handed over the funds from her reticule.

Miss Sims gave the girls a greeting and announced she had begun the cutting of the first gown for Thea. Normally, Thea wouldn't have given a fig about the intricacies of dressmaking of all things —Thea struggled to sew a straight line even at her age— but these were her special gowns and the process was more exciting now.

The wall between the sewing room and Mr. Knight's study was discovered to be rather thin when Mr. Knight's bellowing voice was heard, "I expect you to bear me sons!"

The ladies all looked at each other in uncomfortable silence, which was not lessened by Isabella's retort of, "Pray I am dead by Christmas, then, so you can find yourself another wife!"

Miss Sims raised her voice over the argument and said, "Now, Miss Georgiana, would you be so good as to dig through my trunk and see if you can find a small white button. There's several on cards of paper. Yes, just like that. There should be several more."

Elizabeth's letter to Miss Susan Markson hilariously became a distracted mess of the common mistakes in dressmaking from Miss Sims' raised voice lecture than there was anything about the occult. Several times in her letter, Elizabeth had to stop, apologize, and then attempt to go back to the occult. However, between the shouting in the study and Miss Sims' attempt to drown it out meant that her letter ended with a simple:

> As you must have noticed for yourself by now, the rectory is a lesson in distraction this morning and I find myself unable to write anything of my own accord. I shall have to end this letter now, before I risk writing you every single word uttered in this house at present.
>
> I shall write again when I am alone, or at least the house is at a normal pitch of voices as opposed to the disruption it is this morning.
>
> Your good friend,
> Elizabeth

The domestic argument in the other room was growing to a fevered pitch now, with Mr. Knight declaring that, if God had any mercy, he would strike him dead in his bed and save him from a house of useless women. Isabella retorted that it was her daily prayer.

Thankfully, the succession of slamming doors announced the end to the argument, and all of the ladies in the room let out a relieved sigh.

"Shall I call for tea?" Cassandra asked. "Miss Sims seems to have developed a slight cough from all of her chatting to Thea."

"That would be splendid, my dear girl," Miss Sims said, her voice barely a whisper now.

Cassandra caught the housemaid as she was carrying a clean chamber pot through the house. "Pray, please ask Alice to fetch us some tea. And perhaps cake?"

The maid curtsied and hurried back to the kitchen to make the request. A few moments later, a red-faced, shaken Isabella arrived in the room with a faux smile upon her face that fooled no one. She took her seat, the smile never leaving her face nor touching her eyes. Elizabeth's heart ached for her suffering.

G glanced up from the trunk on the floor and exclaimed, her own voice full of forced cheer, "Isabella! I'm so happy you are finally here to join us. Pray, look at the silk scraps Miss Sims has for sale in her trunk! Remember how you wished to have a little silk to make your sister a reticule? I am certain some of this would make an excellent purse, and we have nearly all of the proper skeins of thread to add a lovely embroidery. Do we not, Elizabeth?"

Elizabeth gave her sister a very approving smile. "Indeed, G. I believe that is an excellent idea."

"Perhaps Miss Sims would allow me to purchase some of her silk scraps for my own work," G said coyly. "Papa owes me my pin money very soon, so I shall purchase silk when I can. Unless one of my sisters can lend me the money."

Elizabeth sighed. "Do you not have any money of your own?"

"I have enough to afford the silk, let me assure you," G said confidently. She gave her eldest sister a sly smile. "Though, Miss Sims also has a rather exceptional strip of bobbin lace that would be the perfect addition to my Sunday dress, and then I wouldn't need a new Sunday dress anytime soon because the lace could cover the stain upon the bodice."

"We shall see," Elizabeth said.

"But it is only two and a half *bob*!" G wailed. She glanced at Isabella and flushed. "I only mean to say that it isn't very expensive, and that it would give me and Isabella something to do while we wait for Thea's dresses. Oh, and recall that Isabella wished to have a new fichu made because her...situation has made her...well, she has complained that her necklines are too low right now. Oh, don't give me that look, Eliza. Isabella has complained herself! I am only thinking of her. Oh! I could make it up and it be an early Christmas gift for her. You'd like that, wouldn't you, Isabella?"

"Dearest, we should wait to ensure there is enough for Thea's gowns," Elizabeth said. "We wouldn't want to run out."

Miss Sims did not look up from the work table, but said, "I am certain there is plenty to go around."

"Nevertheless," Elizabeth said, "I do believe we should wait, Georgiana. If there is any money left over at the end, which I believe there will be, I propose we use what is left to purchase enough small items from Miss Sims to employ us until judgement day."

G's shoulders slumped, but she gave Isabella another glance and said nothing.

Elizabeth sighed. She hated saying no, especially considering her father's behaviour toward the two girls lately.

Haberdashery and boiled sweets 2s 4d
1 small piece of bobbin lace 5 1/2d
A long, narrow strip of bobbin lace 10d
Small silk scraps 2 1/2d
A larger piece of silk 6d
1/4 yd of dotted muslin 10 1/2d
½ yd of white cotton 7d
a completely unnecessary number of buttons 11d

Total spent on G, who is out of pin money: 6s 8 1/2 d
Total pin money in reticule: £5 16s 8 1/2d

Elizabeth leaned back in her chair and shook her head. She knew better than to give into G's sullen sighs, but also she wanted to do something to lift the mood. G so rarely gave her stepmother any notice, that even her consideration of Isabella's feelings was something Elizabeth wished to encourage in her sister.

However, Elizabeth was also not a simpleton and was sure that, with repeated such actions, G would use those big eyes of hers to extract all of the wealth in England for lace.

At the current rate, Elizabeth would need to send Cassie into the village with a pound note to have it broken into coins because she was running rather low now, and Georgiana Knight seemed determined to purchase everything in Miss Sims' trunks. If left to her own devices, G would probably also purchase the actual trunks.

Elizabeth opened her occult journal and positioned her candle for better light. She summoned Mrs. Egerton's assistance.

"Do you know if any of the workings mentioned in the flora book are tested?"

Mrs. Egerton made a thoughtful sound. "I cannot say for certain. However, I have either done many of the spells myself, or seen others work them. They are, for the most part, simple workings that are designed for the beginner to learn about the interconnection between the occult and the physical world."

Elizabeth nodded as she wrote a summary of Mrs. Egerton's words. "I am curious, then, if the spells for improved health that involve cookery would need special tools and blessings, or would regular usage of a purified plant be enough? Or, can a plant even be purified when it is out of doors in the mud and wind?"

"Cookery spell craft is a tricky art. I never mastered it myself," Mrs. Egerton said. "Cooking is a common, everyday task. And, cookery can be a part of the occult. However, it is very difficult to combine those two elements."

"Could I smuggle blessed ingredients into the kitchen? Would that be enough?"

"I could be wrong, but I do believe you would need to do the cooking yourself."

Elizabeth sighed. "Then, I regret that I will not be able to pursue this line of learning as well as I would wish. My father would never approve me making the meals."

"I understood you girls helped in the kitchen."

"Well, yes, but my father draws a distinct line between helping the servants prepare jam and his daughters elbow-deep in flour."

Elizabeth wrote a few more lines in her journal about what she and Mrs. Egerton had spoken about. Then, Mrs. Egerton said, "Miss Knight?"

Elizabeth stopped writing in her occult journal. "Yes, Mrs. Egerton?"

"It is not a sin to dislike your father."

Elizabeth frowned, but did not reply to the ghost. She had not wanted her emotions to show, but she supposed that was impossible with the pacing back and forth outside her bedroom door.

Mr. Knight had argued that his wife be given laudanum for her discomforts, but mostly that was for his wish to have his wife asleep and little to do with her situation. However, sense prevailed when Mrs. Green and Mr. Collins were both called and entered into a pact that prevented Isabella from being given any medication at present, for fear of interfering with the natural course of things. There was little to do but allow her to pace.

Elizabeth had thought working into the wee hours of the night would help keep her mind off Isabella's situation. However, it did not as much as she'd hoped.

"Many women despise their fathers," Mrs. Egerton went on to say. "It's difficult when they are of a profession that requires them to pretend they are close to heaven. However, in my experience, they are often far from such."

Finally, Elizabeth said, "Isabella did not deserve his unkind words, especially given her health. His behaviour at breakfast was shocking and poor Miss Sims did not deserve that disrespect toward her work."

"I agree with you completely, my dear. Where else in this house were any of you supposed to cut fabrics? You are not working on refurbishing a hat, for heaven's sake. Also, I do wonder at his reaction if he'd found you all upon the drawing room floor like scullery maids scrubbing the floorboards? Yes, I am certain he would have flown into a larger rage over that."

"I am filled with so many uncharitable thoughts. This should be a joyous occasion, an event to bring all of us ladies together to work and talk and rebuild the bonds that have been fraying as of late. Instead, my father insists upon hurting as many of us as possible, and tainting the entire event with bad memories." Elizabeth put her pen down. "G is struggling enough with this. Having him withhold her pin money when Thea has twelve pounds to spend is an additional cruelty."

"Does he mean for you to support your sisters?"

"I do not know for certain, as he has not said as much. However, I have spent over six shillings of my own money today on G alone because he has yet to provide her with her quarterly installment of five pounds." Elizabeth rubbed the back of her neck. "I fear this scheme with Mr. Parsons' land rental will not make my father as rich as he'd hoped. His aim has always been to own a carriage. He'd placed all of his expectations on farming a section of Mr. Parsons' land in hopes of making that additional shortfall in his income. However..."

Mrs. Egerton cocked her head. "What is the going income for a carriage these days?"

"About a thousand pounds per annum," Elizabeth said. "My father's income is just over seven hundred. We can afford a horse for him and Charles, and a donkey cart for us ladies or the servants when necessary, though both our rectory beasts and cart are often needed in the fields. In my opinion, we do not require our own carriage, for the expense would only serve to impoverish us further. All so that my father can feel as though he has accomplished some imaginary greatness. A carriage can be easily rented from Eastmore, and even occasionally here in the village at the inn, and I do not require a carriage to make the trip to Vane Park. It is frivolous and unnecessary in my estimation."

A cry of discomfort wailed in the corridor outside Elizabeth's room. She jumped to her feet and rushed to open her door. Isabella was standing there, with her arms about her belly leaning forward. G and Cassie were also out there already, with Thea's door opening a moment later.

"Go back to bed, girls," Isabella said. Her voice was all but a whisper. "There is nothing the matter."

"I shall get Mrs. Green," Cassie said.

Isabella shook her head. "Mrs. Green left to deliver a baby. Her assistant is asleep in the attic, but I ask that you leave her be. There is nothing new. I simply must endure."

Elizabeth looked about. "Where is my father?"

Isabella drew in a fortifying breath before answering. "He has decided to sleep in his study, where there is a fireplace and solitude."

"Ah," Elizabeth said. "Would you like one of us to sit up with you?"

"I've been," G said. "What I mean to say is that Thea and I have been taking turns. Isabella has been helping me with my reticule design."

"You should go to bed," Isabella said. She forced a smile. "I do not require company."

"I cannot sleep in any case," G said through a traitorous yawn.

It pleased Elizabeth to see the worry and support coming from her youngest sister. "Isabella, I am still up working. I shall relocate to our drawing room. Or, if you prefer, I can light a fire in my bedroom and you can stay in there while I work."

"I am very willing to remain up as well," Cassie said.

"No dear, you all need your sleep tomorrow," Elizabeth said. "Go back to bed, the three of you. I shall stay up with Isabella. I promise to call you if you are needed. Now, pray, give me a moment to move my things."

Elizabeth carried her writing desk and her table into the drawing room, with Cassie's assistance. She was wearing her heavy cotton dressing gown over her own bedgown, but she pulled on a pair of stockings in case her father were to come upstairs to see her in the drawing room; he did not approve of improper displays of flesh in his daughters. She also fetched a shawl to guard against any midnight dampness in the air.

With Isabella returned to her solitary pacing in the upper drawing room, Elizabeth settled herself at her desk to begin writing in her journal. She brought Mrs. Egerton's book with her, so that the ghost could hear what was happening and also whisper any assistance as needed.

Elizabeth had been able to complete the inventory of the

various herbs, fruits, vegetables, and flowers that grew near the rectory that could be used in occult workings. She was very pleased that several of the items were necessary to the summoning of Mrs. Egerton. At present, she relied upon supplies mailed to her from London occult shops. Now, she could use the free plants in her kitchen garden. The other ladies would be very pleased to hear this in her next letter to them.

Elizabeth frowned. No letter had arrived from either Miss Susan or Miss Thorne that day, which greatly disappointed her. No doubt, they were busy with their investigations or, in the case of Miss Susan, the delights of Mr. Osborne's company.

Eventually, Isabella announced she would attempt to lay upon her bed for a quarter of an hour, so Elizabeth used the opportunity to whisper with Mrs. Egerton.

"I have not had the opportunity to ask you this, but I have read in the flora identification book that healing spellworking can affect those around the patient. Do you know what that means?"

"It is possible that the healer will drain some of the energy from those around the sick," Mrs. Egerton said. "If your sister got a sore throat before a ball, you might decide to attempt healing. But, because it's so uncertain, it's possible you will make everyone else in the household sick and your sister still wouldn't be able to go to the ball."

A dark, unchristian thought came to her mind. "Would it become worse depending upon the illness?"

"I see what you are asking. The answer is I am not certain. Very few people ever attempt real healing magic. Until we can unlock Miss Gibbs, I am without extensive answers on the subject. If you are asking for Mrs. Knight's situation, I can say this: you risk much by even considering on the matter."

"There is no sin in thoughtful consideration of one's actions," Elizabeth countered. "Do you have any direction to offer to assist further in Miss Gibb's summoning? Should we use the same template as yours?"

Mrs. Egerton paused before answering. "We were all in the same occult society, so I believe the ladies tasked with the binding work would have made similar choices. However, I do know each of us was a different spellworking, to reflect our unique characters."

"But were you not there for the actual work?" Elizabeth asked.

"Sadly, no. I did not join this particular society until after they had already agreed to bind their souls to the book."

"Forgive this question, but I had always thought the choice to bind one's soul meant your soul and your body would be parted."

"Oh, gracious no. It was simply that we all decided, when it was proper of course, that we would not be subjected to eternal peace and comforts, but rather we would remain upon this earth to help generations of women with our wisdom. For what good that apparently has done."

Elizabeth frowned at that. She considered her answer before replying. "Do you not see yourself as helpful?"

"How long have we been locked away? Decades, it seems. And the entire world of the occult has vanished from the hands of ladies and men of good sense and instead fallen to rich men who care more about rank than developing and investigating the unknown aspects of the occult that still elude us all."

"We are attempting to do as best we can, Mrs. Egerton," Elizabeth said.

Mrs. Egerton's sigh fluttered the draperies. "I do not mean to attack you and your very good ladies nor your work. Indeed, you are all doing the absolute best you can under extraordinary obstacles. My opinion of yourself and the young ladies in London is nothing but of the highest estimation. I only complain of how few of you there are, when there should be so many more of you. But, alas, I suppose all good things must eventually be destroyed by men."

"Not all men are evil, Mrs. Egerton," Elizabeth said. "Take Mr. Thorne. He is an excellent man of the best character. Also, consider my aunt's attorney, Mr. Grant. Or, Mr. Osborne, a most trustworthy individual that I hold in very high esteem."

"My good Miss Knight, out of all of the men of your entire acquaintance, you have named three. That hardly encourages me to change my opinion," Mrs. Egerton said.

Elizabeth worked all night until the servants began arriving at four that morning.

⚜ Chapter 9 ⚜

UNCHARACTERISTICALLY, THE GIRLS allowed Elizabeth to sleep until after church the next morning. In fact, she arose to find everyone in their church gowns and hard at work. A casual meal was laid upon different tables, with a third table fetched from the upstairs drawing room for the tea things. Elizabeth helped herself to coffee, though it was not as hot as the tea, and surveyed the work.

Miss Sims had clearly begun the actual dressmaking earlier that morning, and was seated upon a chair near the window for the best light. Thea was upon the sofa with an old spencer of hers in her lap. She was attempting to sew gold braiding on the front as both a sort of decoration and to cover up the fraying that was bound to happen to any favourite garment.

"Thea, I did not think that spencer fits you anymore," Elizabeth said.

"I have offered to let it out for her," Miss Sims said. "I believe there will be time at the end to finish off any small projects."

Elizabeth smiled at her sister and said, "Perhaps that is best. You have never had any patience for large sewing work."

"Indeed, I have not!" Thea declared with no shame whatsoever. "However, I must confess that my true talent, and I make no apologies for my boldness in saying so, is retrimming just about any item I lay my eyes upon."

"That is, indeed, an excellent skill to have, for the rest of us are far too busy with other work," Elizabeth said. Concerned that her words would not be taken in jest, she amended quickly, "It is an excellent way to spread the work between us. Some of us sew, while you trim and finish."

Thea didn't appear to take offence. She simply chatted on about how she would sew black braiding on G's old spencer, too, if there was time before going to Mary's. If not, she would do it upon her return. The old faded thing still fit G across the bodice, but only because Isabella had successfully let it out enough to withstand the girl's growing body. The braiding would cover up the small seam lines left behind from the repair.

After taking a small amount of food, Elizabeth had the maid bring down her writing desk. She began her letters while the girls worked. Several letters arrived for Elizabeth in the course of the day. Most were expected, but one was of a handwriting she vaguely recognized, but could not place a name to it.

My dear cousin,

I trust life in the country has been excellent and the roads exceedingly dry. Town has been so sweltering that only marriage preparations have kept me chained to London. I would share those details with you, of course, my cousin, however, my betrothed has made me promise to allow her the opportunity to write to you. Indeed, she was hopeful that you might be persuaded to make a trip to town for the happy event. Our aunt, of course, will be in attendance, and it would be a very happy affair.

However, I fear I have already said too much and now I risk her disappointment. I shall tell her, of course, for there are no secrets between us. I am the happiest of men and am determined to do everything within my power to ensure she is, at the very least, half as happy as I. For if she were, I am certain she would be more content than most of her sex could boast.

That brings me to one of the points of this letter. Might I gain your permission to allow her to write to you, at her convenience, about the wedding? She was unable to make your acquaintance during your time in town and it was of great disappointment to her.

However, this was not the only reason for writing today, though I confess this additional reason spurred me into action. Enclosed you shall find a letter that arrived here at the house only this afternoon. My dearest was visiting at the time with Mrs. Reeves, which they both called "absolutely providential" indeed, she did! She said I was now forced by duty and honour to compose this letter which I have been putting off due to the unbelievable pressures upon me now that I have a house in town.

I assure you that I have not opened the letter, in case it is a matter of privacy. My dear Charlotte informs me that a young woman must rely too often upon the unsteady natures of people, and so I inform you now that I have not so much as peeked under the seal, even though I confess the temptation was exceptionally great.

Please do write back and advise if my dear Charlotte can write to you. And if you would leave a hint about the contents of the letter, oh, my dear Charlotte leans over my shoulder now and berates me for being such a man, as she just put it. Ah, and now Mrs. Reeves has joined into the teasing. Alas, I shall end this letter before they write to our mutual aunt and ask her assistance. What would I do without my dear Charlotte, I ask you? What would I do!

Sincerely, D. Leigh

"Is anything the matter, Eliza?" Cassie asked.

"Oh, on the contrary. I have just now received a letter from my cousin David Leigh. He wishes to request my permission for his Miss Reeves to write me, which of course I shall grant. She appears to be a very sensible woman, or I suppose as sensible as any woman can be who agrees to marry someone like my cousin."

Isabella looked up from her work. "You are too hard on that young lady! A daughter of limited connections who attracted the attention of someone like Mr. David Leigh, who has his own inheritance from his father, and now your uncle's estate, and will most likely inherit something from your aunt Spencer. Indeed, Elizabeth Knight. She is a very sensible woman in my opinion."

"My opinion of her is softened somewhat by the knowledge that she did request time to consider his offer of marriage. Any woman who is willing to risk her future protection over her own happiness is a woman I hold in high regard," Elizabeth said. She smiled, "But, since she agreed to marry him, I have to confess I still think she cannot be that sensible."

"Is that letter from his Miss Reeves then?" Cassie asked.

"No, indeed! His letter's main purpose was to inform me he received a letter addressed to me at his house, which was of course my uncle's house previously. Oh! I wonder if it is from one of the many letters I sent to women rumoured to be engaged in the occult. Many did not write me back, which is no surprise given I am but a stranger to them."

"Perhaps your reputation has grown in enough circles to spur this woman to write to you," Isabella said.

Elizabeth couldn't help but laugh. "I hope only good things are being said, though I doubt the Royal Society gentlemen have spread any good word about my name!"

"Can you read it aloud?" G asked.

"Allow Elizabeth to determine if it is a private or public letter first," Isabella said.

G protested by way of sighs and groans, but said nothing of substance.

Elizabeth chuckled at her sister. "Allow me to peruse it first and then I shall read all of the parts that I can, I promise you, G. Here, read Mr. Leigh's letter in the meantime. It will provide you with appropriate entertainment, I am certain."

Dear Miss E. Knight,

First, I find myself obliged to apologize for the forwardness I have taken in writing this letter, as, to your memory, I must appear to be a complete stranger. We have a slight acquaintance, and it is upon a previous letter exchange between us that I now appeal to you. However, as you most likely do not recollect my name, indeed there is no reason to suppose you should, I will first reintroduce myself to you.

About a year ago, you had written to me from the address I have sent this letter (for which I dearly hope you are still there, or at least the new occupants know you), in which you asked if I'd had any involvement in the practice of the occult. My sister-in-law, with whom I had been living and depended upon solely for my financial situation, forbade me from speaking about the occult to a single living creature. So my letter to you was a lie, stating that I knew nothing. I know a great deal, but I was not at liberty to tell you so.

That lie has haunted me for fourteen months. My sister-in-law died shortly after I sent that letter, and my brother promptly remarried on the very day he came out of mourning. I have been very fortunate in his new choice of wife, for she does not care about my existence from one day to the next, and I am left mostly to my own devices. More importantly, my letters are now my own property, so I may write to you finally without fear of retribution.

I would not have even attempted this letter except that your reputation as a young lady attempting to work in the occult against the wishes of the Royal Occult Society has reached us all the way in our own little part of England. This knowledge has emboldened me, for I dearly hope you might wish to hear from another young lady who has attempted to dive into the self-education of the occult.

For my specific qualifications, I have collected a total of thirteen occult books from which I have been studying. They are mostly related to botany and healing magics. I have learned some of the most basic aspects of the healing properties when used in spell craft, though my abilities at present are limited to treating a sore throat. Unfortunately, it seems to infect someone else. The best I can manage is to move a sore throat to someone else. And, perhaps even more grievously, I cannot control who gains the sore throat, so if I am attempting to ensure two lovers are able to meet at a ball, I cannot guarantee that I pass the sore throat to someone wholly unconnected to either of them.

I have self-taught myself a limited amount of Latin. I cannot yet translate on sight a full page, but I can often read through a sentence or sometimes a whole paragraph without reaching for translation books for assistance.

As far as I know, there is no one else in Exeter who practices or studies the occult. I am not certain how helpful I can be to any advanced inquiry you might have into the occult. However, if there is anything I can assist with, I would be very happy to oblige. I am eager to correspond with another woman who is informed on the occult.

Miss Selina Keats

Elizabeth read the letter aloud, though she did not share the lady's full name or her location. "How extraordinary! To think, all of these women have been quietly doing their own occult study throughout the country without the permission or approval of the Royal Occult Society. Indeed, this gives me great hope for the future of ladies in the occult."

"It is most extraordinary," Isabella said. "To think of the courage this Miss Keats must have, to have written you a falsehood to protect herself and now writing again to tell you as such. I believe she will turn out to be an excellent writing companion."

"I heartily agree, Isabella. I shall write to her immediately. She must already think herself too forward or having had offended me, since the letter had to come through David first."

"Eliza? Before you begin, might I bring up something that is upon my mind?" Cassie asked. At Elizabeth's prompting, she said, "Since Miss Sims is here and assisting with any skills we ladies require, I believe it is time we opened up our mother's trunks and her closet."

Elizabeth looked about at her sisters. "Are you certain? I do not wish to give my consent if any of you will be uneasy about the task. This is an important time for Theodosia and I do not want her upset."

"It was my idea, Eliza," Thea said. "I didn't know if it was the right thing to ask, so I asked Cassie first. I didn't want to upset you, since she wasn't your mother."

"No, but she was the mother of my beloved sisters," Elizabeth said with a smile. "Miss Sims? Would you be easy with us doing such a task?"

"I have no objection at all. It would be like having Mrs. Knight here with us, because all of her beloved items are here. I knew the former Mrs. Knight well enough to know she would not have wanted her gowns and bonnets to go to waste. I'm certain we can do something with them."

Elizabeth nodded. "G? Are you certain you will be fine with this?"

G nodded. "I've wanted to do it for some time. Mama had some wonderful gowns and it's not fair to have them locked away. She had wonderful taste, didn't she?"

Elizabeth glanced at Isabella, who was pale this morning. "Isabella?"

"I find that my hands are not steady enough for shirt making today, so I would be happy to watch the girls sort and help in any way that I can."

Elizabeth nodded her consent, as she did not detect any falsehood from the ladies; she did get the feeling they'd been in quiet consultation with each other about this for some time.

Elizabeth turned her attention to her letter writing while the girls divided the chores between them. G volunteered to bring all of her mother's hat boxes into the drawing room. Cassandra fetched the footman to help bring down the trunks of gowns and personal items, while Theodosia was instructed by Miss Sims to stay in the room because she needed to pin the gown to her for fitting. Isabella's keen eye was called into assistance for this task, helping Thea make final design decisions about cut and comfort.

While all of the bustle was happening, Elizabeth wrote her letters.

Dear Miss Keats,

Imagine my extraordinary surprise—and delight, I assure you—at receiving your letter this morning! Please, do not apologize for the need for subterfuge, nor for the attempt to re-introduce yourself to me. I completely comprehend the hardships of a young lady dependent upon relations who do not appreciate an independent mind.

Now, I feel I must apologize for my delay in writing this letter and once you understand the varied path this letter took to find me, I hope I shall be acquitted of being a poor correspondent. Your letter found its way to my uncle's house. My uncle was an occultist and had tasked me with writing unmarried young ladies regarding rumours of the occult.

However, my good uncle died earlier this year, and my cousin, Mr. David Leigh, now owns the property. It was him who forwarded the letter to me rather promptly. Rest assured he exercised all propriety and care, having forwarded the letter to me without so much as opening the seal. Mr. Leigh enjoys being useful, and his own letter to me was full of excitement at being helpful. His intended, a Miss Reeves from London, I believe her to be a steady, sensible woman—we have yet to meet—and she had instructed him not to betray any information concerning your letter.

However, with your permission I would like to write to him to explain the circumstances, but only with your permission, of course. Also, may I share the contents of your letter with the other members of the Ladies Occult Society? That is what we are calling ourselves. Two of my good friends are living in London at the moment, whereas I am in the country at Bryden.

In particular, your studies into healing magic are of great interest to me. Myself, along with a Miss Markson and a Miss Thorne are, in fact, currently investigating the core of healing magic. I have some access to an expert in healing magic. I say some, because the situation is difficult to explain and fraught with complications. However, to summarize a vastly complicated history, we have a lady with several decades of experience assisting us to find a healing expert. So, in the meantime, your extraordinary abilities and knowledge will be of a great relief and excitement to all of us ladies.

Your experiences with healing a sore throat is consistent with Mrs. Egerton, our occult expert's, own understanding. She has been very cautious with us advancing healing abilities, as you can imagine she does not want one of us to accidentally injure ourselves or another. After all, to use your example, it would do no good to bring one lover back from their death bed and have it inflicted upon the other.

Oh, I am so excited by your letter that I cannot even think properly on what I should or should not share. That is typically Miss Thorne's task! Pray write as soon as possible. Does your current situation allow for a rapid increase in letters? Pray inform me if it does not so that we can moderate our correspondence accordingly.

Elizabeth Knight

Elizabeth folded and sealed her letter and then checked in with the progressing work. The girls were opening their mother's trunks and boxes, commenting on memories and stories of her.

Elizabeth sensed the heaviness in the air and called for tea and cake to sustain them through the tears and laughter that she knew was soon to follow.

Thea was still pinned up in her gown by Miss Sims, but she was staring rather intently at a black bonnet of her mother's. When prompted by Elizabeth, she said, "I am thinking what the best option for Mama's hat is. I do not believe the ribbons should be cut until I have decided upon the exact colour I wish to use. Now that I look at it, I do believe replacing the black with printed brown cotton would be the best choice. Also, the yellow silk ribbon left over from my gown would be an excellent match."

"But what about the blue ones?" G asked. "They are still so fashionable."

Thea stared at the two hats her sister held up for her to see. Thea nodded to herself, much to Elizabeth's amusement, before finally stating with full authority, "They only want for new trim about the rim and the ribbon ends resewn, since they are so frayed and dirty."

"Do you want me to begin to tear them apart then?" G asked.

Thea shook her head. "No, let us set aside everything until we've gone through it all. There are a few more bonnets."

Cassandra was busy laying out her mother's gowns on the back of the sofa. Augusta Knight had always been a fashionable woman, and all of her dresses needed only the smallest of modifications to still be very in style. Thea laughed a few times that her mother's hips had been so much bigger than everyone else's, while Miss Sims explained how a woman's body changed after having children. G declared that she would never have children, which brought a round of laughter from the assembly. However, soon tears flowed, too, at the remembrance of Augusta and how much she'd have loved to have been there with them in such an important moment in all of their lives.

"She is still here, in her own way," Elizabeth said as she gave Thea a hug. "And I do not believe she'd have wanted her gowns locked away in trunks. That was never her way. We should keep one or possibly two, to remember her by, but the remainder of her gowns should be refit as best as possible. Wearing them would be the best way to honour her, I believe."

"I agree," Cassandra said. "She was buried in her wedding dress. What a lovely blue dress that was. It was always her favourite. However, she loved this pink silk dress. Girls, would you like me to put this away?"

"I'd really like to wear it," G said.

"It would need to be pulled apart and cut to fit you," Miss Sims said cautiously. "All of the dresses will require it, which I do not mind after Miss Theodosia's gowns are done. However, you ought to know how much we'll have to cut out to fit your figure."

"I do not mind at all," Cassandra said. "I think she'd be happy if we wore her clothes."

Thea looked dubious. "Are there enough to be fair to all of us? We have Elizabeth to consider, too."

"I thank you for thinking of me, my dear, but I would never dare take a gown from your beloved mama when I do not need a dress. No, indeed, I insist the three of you work out a fair system. I will only serve as a moderating voice if there is conflict."

"How do we fairly distribute the gowns and pelisses? There is all of her jewelry yet," Cassandra said.

Elizabeth looked at Miss Sims for guidance, who quickly nodded and said, "Why not each of you choose one clothing and one jewelry or trinket that is special to you. Then, all other items are all placed into a pile. You can each take turns taking one item, or perhaps to be even more fair, can assign a coin to each of you. Then, place those coins in a purse. As they are pulled out, that person can choose. When everyone has had a turn, the coins are placed back into the purse for a second round."

"That is an excellent idea, Miss Sims," Isabella said. "I feel you have done this before."

"More than once, I can assure you," Miss Sims said with a chuckle.

"Can I finish working on the bonnets first?" Thea asked.

"Of course, my dear," Elizabeth said. "We can wait on the dresses until you are ready."

"It is not that," Thea said, eyeing the dresses. "I just want to finish the bonnets first."

"Of course," Cassie said.

Quiet settled over the girls as Miss Sims smiled at Elizabeth and went back to sewing the yellow silk before her. Elizabeth returned to her letters.

Dearest Elizabeth,

I hope the weather in the country is agreeable for it has not stopped raining in town all week. I swear we are all losing our minds from being shackled indoors. Even Mrs. Spencer is threatening to hire a carriage and take us for a visit to the country. While I would love to see you again, my dear friend, you must know how frightfully dull it is here if she is contemplating a brush with country living.

Susan sends her love, and wishes to inquire if you or your sisters need anything in town. In particular, she said there is an absolutely hideous cloth covered in strawberry print that she thinks one of your sisters might like very much indeed.

"Thea, my love? Miss Markson in London found a strawberry print fabric that she thinks you would like. Would you like her to send you some?"

"Oh yes please!" Upon reflection, she asked, "Is there enough left over from my father's allowance?"

"Absolutely." Elizabeth resolved herself that she would, most likely, be supporting her sisters' dressmaking supplies from now until their eventual marriages. So, if necessary, she would buy it for her sister, just as she purchased G's haberdashery.

"Then please! I would love that. Oh, perhaps I shall line my old spencer with it, once Miss Sim's takes it out. Just the back, so when I take it off, it'll be right there for anyone to see. How exciting!"

G sighed dramatically, to the point that Elizabeth thought it was Mrs. Egerton. "Papa has yet to give me my pin money. I only have a shilling to my name at present."

"Would you like me to bring it up to him?" Elizabeth asked.

"No, I'd rather him not kick you from the house without a farthing to your name," G said sullenly.

Elizabeth frowned at her, but couldn't offer a rebuke. Considering the scenes of the last two days, it was an honest reaction.

"My dear Georgiana, I will never be without a farthing. My uncle's will and the law are both on my side. Would you like some of the cloth yourself?"

"I would love to have enough for an apron," G said.

Elizabeth chuckled. "New cotton to use on an apron? Goodness, that is extravagant. Who would ever see it?"

G went back to sulking, and Elizabeth felt a pang of guilt for having teased her sister. "I believe it would be better as a shawl."

G's eyes lit up. "If it were a shawl, more people could see it!"

Thea opened her mouth, but Elizabeth shot her a look only an eldest sister could give. Thea gave the smallest nod and said, "There's easily enough lace in the basket to trim it, too."

"Then I shall send her detailed instructions when I reply to her letter."

Admittedly, one wonders how many reticules and shawls a young woman needs, but Susan is determined that I ask you. You might find yourself at this moment wondering why she does not simply ask you. Well, I am presently turned away from her so that she cannot easily read over my shoulder and so I shall tell you the whole story. And, my dearest friend, prepare yourself for what I have to tell you is the most delicious of news!

Miss Susan Markson is too busy to write to you at present regarding the strawberry cloth due to being engaged to write down recipes for Mrs. Osborne, the mother of our dear acquaintance and might I say friend and benefactor, Mr. Osborne. It appears Mrs. Osborne hasn't had a decent rice pudding since her cook passed away quite suddenly a year ago and she is desperate for one that reminds her of her old cook's recipe.

So, Mrs. Spencer sent over some of Cook's pudding after Mr. Osborne's last visit. Ah, Susan has left the room. Allow me to tell you that Mr. Osborne now visits every other day, and dines with us at least twice a week, and I know it is not for myself or Mrs. Spencer, though we both think him an excellent gentleman of the highest quality. Oh, she returns and demands to know why I am smiling. I have told her a falsehood that I am mocking the strawberry cloth, which isn't a true lie since I did do thusly at the beginning of this letter.

Mrs. Osborne loved the rice pudding and said it was exactly the way her old cook made and begged Mrs. Cook to provide the recipe. In payment, she sent us the most amazing custard recipe for Mrs. Cook to try. And so, my dear friend, the great recipe exchange of London has begun. There has been an endless stream of food back and forth with recipes and instructions all over the place. Amusingly, Sir William's cook next door is also getting involved and I swear neither myself nor Mrs. Spencer have seen anything like this.

I should also inform you that Mrs. Cook has been having a wonderful time, too, trying out the new recipes and experimenting within her kitchen. Though, she has been very annoyed at Susan whenever she's required to weigh and measure her ingredients; Mrs. Cook knows how to bake by sight, but as it would be rather cumbersome to draw out the instructions of a cake recipe, measuring is perhaps the best course.

Now, to the particulars of the occult and your questions in your last letter. We are still investigating the summoning of your Miss Gibbs, but have made little movement thus far. However, we have stumbled upon a manner which, if it works, may assist Mrs. Egerton to become, for lack of a more delicate means to put it, portable. Her book is too large to carry about into polite society without you being the source of idle gossip, and I felt Mrs.

Egerton would love a good ball or dinner party. The ability to bring her along in society would be excessively helpful. As well, Mrs. Spencer would also like me to convey that she still has high hopes in you finding a husband and cannot in good conscience encourage the notion of you going into ballrooms holding a book. We seem to be unable to make the spell last more than six hours, and her book still needs to be nearby to work. So, you would be able to bring Mrs. Egerton about the house in a locket, for example, but you would not be able to go to London without bringing her book.

I have enclosed the locket to use. It contains all of the proper summoning items to help with the task. Perhaps with your eyes upon our work, along with Mrs. Egerton's assistance, you might find improvements to our spellworking.

I have enclosed two sheets of our current notes. I hope you find them enlightening and can shed some of your knowledge on how to bring about Miss Gibbs.

Susan is heading this way with that knowing look of hers, so I cannot write to you more about Mr. Osborne as I had planned. However, allow me to say my hopes are increasingly high in that corner.

Your affectionate friend,
Miss Alice Thorne

"What is so entertaining in your letter?" Thea asked. She was currently having sleeves and a bodice pinned to her to ensure the fit was accurate. It was.

"My friend, Miss Susan Markson, seems to have caught the attentions of Mr. Osborne, the book seller that has been so kind to sell my books." Elizabeth smiled. "My aunt will be furious if she loses her house guest."

"Surely she would not wish to deny Miss Markson her happiness?" Isabella asked.

"She might force Mr. Osborne to move in with them!" Elizabeth said, laughing. "My dear aunt has been living alone for so long that I believe she had forgotten how comforting it is to have a houseful of considerate, and respectful, young ladies to keep her young in her heart."

"Elizabeth Knight! Your aunt is not yet fifty."

The room went silent as Mr. Knight walked into the room. He surveyed the scene and said, "If you think Cassandra Spencer is old, you must think me one foot in the grave."

Mr. Knight was in good cheer as he looked about the room. He spied his former wife's dresses and gave Cassandra a questioning look. Elizabeth answered. "The girls have decided it was time to take out Augusta's things that were in storage and see what dresses can be made up between them. There is also the trunk of jewelry, shoes, and trinkets. I will be assisting with that task."

"Good. Good. That is an excellent idea. Now, I came in search of Georgiana. Come, my child. We shall settle your accounts."

G jumped to her feet and rushed after her father. The ladies all audibly let out breaths of relief when Mr. Knight left the drawing room. His bad mood appeared faded for the time being, though perhaps maybe he'd learned how to stretch the seventy-five pounds from the rental land to eighty or ninety.

While G was off negotiating with her father why she needed more than the five pounds he normally gave her, Elizabeth finished her letters.

The quiet lasted for some time until the wailing of G startled all of them. G did not return to the drawing room. Indeed, she stormed directly up the stairs and, by the slamming of the doors, into her bedchamber to sob herself asleep. Mr. Knight returned to the drawing room, announced he was off to Mr. Parsons' with his bailiff, and together they were to strike the rental deal. He would be late for dinner, as well, so not to wait for him.

Elizabeth waited until her father was out of the house to go check on her youngest sister. As predicted, the girl was collapsed upon her bed, sobbing into her pillow. Elizabeth sat down next to her and asked what was the matter.

"Papa said we cannot afford me to come out until I am seventeen now, because he is giving Thea so much money, and you promised I would be allowed to come out sooner."

Elizabeth blew out a breath. "I think it's not worth being so upset over such a thing at present. Our father is known to change his mind."

"He said he would not be moved," G said. "And he said he cannot afford to give me more than a guinea now for my pin money."

Elizabeth had to ask her to repeat that last bit, because for certain she'd misunderstood.

"It is very true. Look, this is all he gave me." G reached across the bed for her reticule and pulled out a tarnished guinea. "That's all he said I can have until I come out, and then he said I cannot have any new dresses because Thea spent all the money."

Elizabeth remained silent while Georgiana wept some more. Finally, her tears exhausted themselves and Elizabeth could speak. "Give it a few days and I shall speak to our father. He is disappointed that his land rental from Mr. Parsons will not net him the money necessary to have a carriage."

"What do I care about a carriage? I'd never be allowed to use it in any case. The horses would be in the fields all of the time, and I prefer to walk to the village. The carriage is only so that he can show off to Mary."

Elizabeth got a sinking feeling that her father expected her to support her sisters, and here was the first step in that. Soon, she expected her entire inheritance would be going to their upkeep while she would have no money of her own.

"He said I cannot even have a new pair of boots, and I will need a new pair soon because my feet are growing and my boots already hurt dreadfully in the mud because they leak now and when I told him that, he said young ladies shouldn't be out of doors in the mud anyway, so he is doing this for my own good." G sighed and her voice began to tremble. "I hate him so much."

Elizabeth was too slow to defend her father as she so often did in the past.

"See? Not even you can defend him."

"A guinea will last you a month. Let us leave it for now. I have small coins in my own purse. I'll give those to you for the tiny purchases you wish to make. However, for now, you need to be very careful with your money until I can talk sense into our father."

"Did you get your pin money from him?"

Elizabeth shook her head. "I am to take charge of paying for my gowns and my own pin money."

G wiped at her eyes with the back of her hand. "So Papa is determined to give everything to Charles."

"Charles has very little time left to finish his ordination. He'll be done in the spring. Then, he'll hopefully get a curacy somewhere while he awaits a parsonage. And fifty pounds a year as a curate, maybe seventy-five or a hundred if he can get two close together, would give us all peace of mind without having to worry our father. So, we're almost through the worst of this."

G was very quiet when she asked, "Is Isabella going to die?"

"Whatever makes you ask that?"

"Papa said that he must put aside money in case she doesn't survive having the baby, and I know I don't like her, but I don't want her to *die*. And Papa said it will be my fault if she dies." G's sobbing grew to heavy gasps. "Was it my fault Mama died?"

Elizabeth wrapped her arms around her sister. "Listen to me very carefully, Georgiana. Are you listening to me? I need you to heed my words. No matter what happens, it is not your fault. You can only control your actions. None of us can control what happens when a woman is brought to bed, least of all a little girl. Your mother's death was not your fault."

"He says all of the fighting is making Isabella sick," she whispered.

Elizabeth said, "It is more complicated than that. Even if you were perfect, she would still be sick. Now, does the discord upset everyone in the house? Yes, it does and I will not lie to you about that. Does it make it harder for Isabella? Probably. However, there is a very large difference between you being able to make life a bit easier for everyone and you being the cause of her illness. You must learn to separate what our father says from the truthfulness of the message."

"You haven't told me it is a sin to hate him," G said.

In that moment, Elizabeth was not certain it was a sin to hate their father. However, since that was something she could not utter aloud to a living soul, she simply said, "I believe you have heard enough lectures for one day. You and God must work this out yourselves."

G went back to sobbing and said she wished to be alone. Elizabeth granted her the wish, but not before going to her own bedchamber and counting out six shillings and three and a half pence worth of her smallest coins so that G would have some spending money that didn't result in her needing to hand over a guinea. That was the last of her smallest coins.

Why on earth did her father give G a large coin and nothing else? He normally gave them a couple of large coins, yes, but then he gave them smaller ones, too. However, her father had no interest in being easy or convenient. He wanted to make life as difficult as possible now for his girls.

G meekly thanked Elizabeth for the coins, and she could only hope that it would stave off any lasting resentment between daughter and father. Or, indeed, sister and sister, for this would only serve to turn Theodosia and Georgiana's fights even more explosive.

Elizabeth attempted a smiling face and went downstairs.

☙ Chapter 10 ❧

G's DEPARTURE LEFT a sadness to the gathering. The ladies continued working until dinner, and even Isabella rallied herself a little to work on the men's shirts. Elizabeth had put down her pen and took up her needle to assist with the shirts. Thea had also repaired, mended, and refurbished three of her mother's bonnets to the point that Miss Sims said they looked as good as anything coming out of the best shops in London.

After dinner, the ladies retired upstairs to continue their work, under the eye of Miss Sims. Thea decided to fit one of her mother's lace caps to Isabella's smaller head. Isabella also did not prefer excessive frills on her caps, so Thea was pulling those off when their father arrived. He settled into the drawing room with them and complained that G wasn't with them and declared her to be sulking.

Yes, Elizabeth agreed Georgiana was sulking, but she also had a good reason in Elizabeth's eyes. Her father should not have cut off her allowance without warning or a proper explanation. He was blaming all of the cuts on Charles' schooling and Isabella's illness, but there was an aura of artfulness to the entire scheme. That this was all to hoard as much money as possible for the imaginary carriage that they could never afford, and frankly did not need.

Her father was already talking about how a carriage would allow him greater visits to Mary's and Elizabeth did not see it. They took a hired carriage anytime they wished to travel to Mary's, and indeed her father could just ride to Ashbrook on horseback, if he was so desperate to see her. Her father hated London and never went, so a carriage would never be used to convey him to town.

"You could even take the carriage to London, my dear, and wouldn't your aunt be surprised," he said to Elizabeth.

Elizabeth reminded him that her aunt did not even have a carriage of her own, since she felt it was an unnecessary expense. That darkened her father's mood, and he muttered under his breath about how wonderful it must be to be so rich that one does not need the conveniences of life the way the rest of the world did.

Elizabeth began lighting extra candles—the cost of which came out of Thea's money, since she knew her father would complain about the cost of additional lighting that wasn't for his personal benefit—and they gathered about the light as much as possible. Elizabeth began sewing the sleeves for Thea's printed day dress, which would look very good and smart when out visiting. Isabella put down the men's shirts as soon as Mr. Knight left the room for his study, and took up one of the detachable sleeves of a simple white cotton dress.

G arrived when their father's heavy steps sounded down the stairs, though she did not take up any project work of her own. The ladies chatted a bit, with Miss Sims helping guide any of the ladies who needed assistance with a particularly difficult seam or fold. However, Miss Sims had given them both the easier tasks of the gown making process, for which Elizabeth was grateful. She could use the ease of a straight seam at the moment.

Georgiana broke down crying a few times, and Thea attempted to be a good sister at first, asking whatever was the matter. That only made G snap at her, declaring she hated Thea. This upset Cassandra greatly, not in the least because Miss Sims was still there in the room for her to see this display.

"G, come now. Let me see what pattern you have cut for your reticule," Cassandra said.

"What does it signify since I am to never stir out of doors ever again and I shall be poor the rest of my life!" G exclaimed.

Miss Sims attempted to hide a smile, but Elizabeth caught the edges of her mouth tug upward. Elizabeth listened to a little more of this bickering before interceding. "Georgiana, that is an end to this jealousy."

"But..."

"No, we are now at the end. This jealousy is tiresome. You will soon have your turn at being the centre of attention. Have the good sense to realize that, if you persist, there might not be anyone willing to assist you in such a manner when your time rolls around."

"You told me Thea would want me out by Michaelmas and now Papa is saying in a couple of years! And I only get one guinea and no more because of her!" G pointed at Theodosia, who looked rather shocked. "Papa said he gave her my pin money!"

Isabella gasped and she shared a significant look with Elizabeth.

"Setting aside all that, our father can be a reasonable man. However, if you are roaming about the house throwing yourself upon the furniture and shrieking like you are possessed by demons, then no amount of kind words from me will convince our father you are ready."

G pointed at Isabella and said, "It is all her fault."

Miss Sims quietly rose from her seat and stepped from the room. Elizabeth waited until the door closed behind her before turning to her youngest sister and said, very calmly, "You will apologize to Isabella this instant."

"Eliza, there is no need..." Isabella began.

Elizabeth raised her hand. "Georgiana Knight. You will apologize to your stepmother this very moment or I swear to you that I will tell our father about your behaviour and how I believe his judgement is right in this regard."

"She is what is wrong with everything in this house!" G snarled. "It's her fault I am not allowed to come out with Thea."

Guilt crossed Thea's face, and she lowered her head. However, Elizabeth had no problem taking her own share in the responsibility. "You are mistaken, Georgiana. As I explained previously, I am the one to blame, and from your behaviour since the announcement, it is clear to me I made the right suggestion.

Now, if you had been helpful or supportive, or showed any maturity whatsoever that you were ready to be out in public, I might have gone to our father and said, I have reconsidered my position and I would like G to also come out. However, that has not happened, now, has it?"

Cassie turned to Thea and said rather loudly, "We shall need to experiment with your hair."

Thea glanced at G but gave Cassie a hesitant smile. "Oh, I love the heavy curls, like how Mrs. Thorne sometimes styles her hair."

Cassandra helped undo Thea's hair. Once it was pulled out and draped over her shoulders, Thea parted her long hair around her ears and lifted up the entire crown section that was shorter than the rest of her hair. "If we could cut a little more, we could..."

G grabbed the long tail of underneath hair, not the top hair currently dangling over Thea's face. G shoved it into the mouth of her scissors and yanked on Thea's hair. The scissors had all been sharpened to cut the fabric smoothly, and she managed to hack off a quarter of Thea's long tresses before Cassandra slapped hard against G's forearm. Thea hadn't realized what was happening until a clump of her hair collapsed on the floor next to her.

"Georgiana Knight!" Isabella roared.

Thea picked up her hair, horrified. Thea didn't scream or wail. She just stared at the hair and Elizabeth could see all of the poor girl's hopes and dreams of being the most beautiful girl at the ball dashed.

"Now you can be ugly!" G shouted.

Isabella took to her feet, unsteady, but still upright. "Georgiana, go to your room this instant."

"I don't have to listen to you!" G shouted.

Thea began sobbing, a heart-wrenching, broken sound.

Elizabeth turned to her youngest sister. "Georgiana, do as you were told and go to your room."

"Or what? You won't let me come out?" G scoffed. "What difference does that make?"

Elizabeth took a step toward G. "If you do not go to your room immediately, I will tell Father exactly what you have done here today. I will not ease the truth. I will not pretend it was an accident. I will tell him that he has raised a horrible, hate-filled daughter and that it is my recommendation that she be sent away immediately to his relations in Cornwall."

G's eyes went wide. "You wouldn't!"

"I would," Elizabeth said.

Miss Sims walked into the drawing room with her pattern book.

Miss Sims saw the hair in Thea's hands and her shoulders slumped.

"Oh dear," she whispered. "Your father approaches, Miss Knight."

"What in the devil's name is going on in here?" Mr. Knight demanded, storming past Miss Sims. "What is all of the shouting? Why is Thea on the floor...is that hair? Why is she picking up hair?"

All of the ladies were standing now, and silently waiting to see who would speak. Mr. Knight asked again, "What is going on? Ladies, I have asked a question."

"Mr. Knight," Isabella began.

"There was an accident," Thea said through broken sobs.

"An accident, you say?" He examined her closer. "Your hair is cut to your neck! Theodosia, what have you done to yourself? You look like a man!"

Thea wailed at that and Elizabeth sighed, giving her father an annoyed look. "Miss Sims? Could you take Thea to her room so that she can see for herself. I believe we can fix it, once the shock wears off."

"Indeed, Miss Knight. Come now, Miss Theodosia. I swear to you, it appears worse than it is. Come, let us go see for ourselves."

Miss Sims helped Thea to her feet, and she wrapped an arm around the weeping girl, and led her from the room. Miss Sims pointedly closed the door.

Elizabeth closed her eyes at that in an attempt to regain her composure. If her father found out what just transpired, there would be a reckoning in their house that all of the women would suffer under, including Isabella. His anger would be directed at herself and Isabella and neither of them would have a moment's freedom or comfort again.

"Well?" Mr. Knight demanded. "What has happened here?"

"I...accidentally...cut Thea's hair," G stammered out. She looked at Elizabeth pleadingly.

"How could you cut anyone's hair accidentally? Did you fall and trip and catch her hair in your scissors?" Mr. Knight's voice was rising now. He looked at Isabella. "How could you let this happen?"

"Indeed, Papa, it was an accident," Elizabeth said, regaining her voice. Her heart pounded from the lie.

"Isabella? Is this true?" He glared at her. "Would my wife lie to me?"

"Indeed, I would not lie to you, sir," Isabella said. She looked at Georgiana, straight in the face, and said, "Cassandra had asked Thea how best to style her hair. G was attempting to show Cassandra where braids could be added. However, G's hand slipped and she accidentally cut the hair she'd been using the scissors to display."

"Cassandra Knight, is this true?"

Cassandra nodded. "Yes, Papa."

"And so you ladies all allowed G to cut Theodosia's hair? We might as well dress her up as either a man or a harlot, since she no longer looks like a respectful young woman," her father declared.

"Mr. Knight, this is not helpful," Isabella snapped. She sucked in a deep breath and said, "It is only a small cut from underneath her hair. If you had not seen the evidence before you, I do not believe you would have ever noticed her hair was shorter on one side."

"I will not—"

"And, considering that you are the reason G has not been careful all day today, I do not see how your input into this is welcome or appreciated or even helpful."

Elizabeth stared at Isabella. Cassandra looked a bit wild about the eyes, like a rabbit who'd been cornered. G didn't appear to be breathing.

"How dare you speak to me in such a way before my daughters, Isabella," Mr. Knight said.

"You cut Georgiana's pin money and blamed it on Theodosia's coming out. Yet, you had the money already set aside. Augusta's will clearly stated her gold locket and her ruby-set ring was to be sold to pay for the younger girls' coming out. I know that because my brother assisted you with the sale and that you received twenty-eight guineas for them," Isabella said. "There was no need to steal from Georgiana."

"That money went to Charles," Mr. Knight said. He lowered his voice almost to a whisper. "I told you that in confidence as my wife."

"And now the girls know it," Isabella said. "Shall we finally stop holding secrets from one another in this home and tell the whole truth."

"I cut Georgiana's pin money because she is a spendthrift and it would do her good to experience poverty," Mr. Knight said.

"You cut it so that Elizabeth would give her money," Isabella said. She pressed her hand against her stomach and grimaced. "If you cannot even attempt fairness between your children, sir, then frankly you do not get to complain when they are upsetting the household. And you shall apologize to Thea for calling her a boy. She does not look like one, and it was wrong of you to say so."

"I will do nothing of the sort," Mr. Knight said. "And I will not have some young wife of mine speak to me in such a manner."

"Then perhaps you should not have married a young wife again," Isabella snarled.

Mr. Knight's eyes widened. He lifted his chin and said, "Clearly, your condition is making you hysterical. You do not know what you are saying. I shall send for Mr. Collins so that he can sedate you. Clearly, you are out of your mind."

"Sir," Elizabeth said sternly. "We do not need Mr. Collins. We simply need to deal with this accident in a calm, ladylike manner."

"If you are so bothered by Georgiana's pin money situation, pray why not share some of your wealth with her?" Mr. Knight asked.

"I did, sir," Elizabeth said. "I gave her over six shillings in small coins so that she would not have to break the guinea you so kindly bestowed upon her."

Three thousand pounds.

He gave her a sneer before saying, "I find that you have changed since you have become involved in the occult, Miss

Elizabeth Knight. You are brazen and opinionated. Those are not traits that appeal to a man."

She said nothing. She didn't dare speak for fear she would end up being kicked from the house. She was tempted, though.

"There is too much discord in this house, and I wish it to cease immediately," Mr. Knight said.

"Your daughters are not dogs, sir," Isabella said. She was leaning one hand against the chair now. "You must treat them as people if you are to get the results you seek."

Mr. Knight looked genuinely confused. "I do not understand."

"They are individual people, sir," Isabella said. "It is time to treat them as such, and not as a collection of one."

"What difference does that make?" Mr. Knight asked.

"You, sir, are the cause of all that you complain of," Elizabeth shouted. She had not meant to shout the words, but she did. Her heart thudded in her chest. She looked at G and Cassandra and said, "Leave. Both of you."

"But..." G said.

"Get out," Elizabeth ordered.

Cassandra grabbed G's arm and escorted her out of the room. Once that was done, Elizabeth turned to her father, took a breath to moderate her tone, and said, "Sir, allow me to speak freely."

"Oh, please feel free to continue. It is not like you have not done so already. Indeed, I do not know who is the head of the household here anymore, for surely it is not I."

"Sir, I asked you to allow me to speak to Thea about her coming out. You purposely disregarded that and told G and Thea at the same time, in the most shocking manner. Then, you cut G's pin money and said she could not come out for a couple years because you could not afford the expense. Then, most grievously, you said it would be her fault if Isabella dies."

"Mr. Knight!" Isabella whispered in horror.

"That was only to make the yelling stop. Come now, Elizabeth, surely you agree the shrieking has been out of control. I am surprised the servants haven't told the entire village that we are possessed by banshees."

"I agree, sir, and it has been very difficult. I have been attempting to read and study and work on my occult skills." Elizabeth paused for Mr. Knight's scoff. "However, I have spent the majority of my time caring for my sisters and attempting to fix the errors you have been making."

"I am not the one yelling," Mr. Knight said.

"No, sir. You are the one purposely pitting sister against sister," Elizabeth said. "I am very sorry, Father, that you are jealous of my inheritance."

Mr. Knight stared at her. Finally, he said, "Jealousy is a sin."

"Indeed it is," Elizabeth said and did not break his gaze.

"If you wish G to come out early, you are very welcome to give her twelve pounds of that money Mr. Thorne arrived with."

Isabella clawed at her neck until she untied the ribbon. She handed Elizabeth a locket. "That is made of gold. It will fetch you at least eight pounds. Use that to pay for G's coming out."

"My dear," Mr. Knight said.

"I will not have Elizabeth paying for her sister's coming out when there is more than enough money in this household to pay for it."

"That was from me upon our marriage," Mr. Knight said aghast.

"Yes, it was," Isabella said.

Elizabeth fondled the locket before placing it upon the table. She shook her head and announced, "I have to tend to my sisters."

She turned her back on her father, and walked out of the room. She never longed to be at Mary's so much in her life. She knew she'd be treated poorly, but at least there would be no surprises on that score.

IN TIME, ELIZABETH returned to the upper drawing room and worked on sewing sleeves. The emotions of the household needed time to settle, as did her own. The sewing gave her a welcome distraction. So much so that she started, and finished, the other sleeve. If they did not finish Thea's dresses, Mary's assistant would be required to browbeat some poor seamstress near Ashbrook into finishing them.

Elizabeth wished to avoid that fate for any woman.

Putting aside her work, she picked up her candle and went into the hallway. She found G slumped on the floor across from her bedroom. Elizabeth carefully eased herself down the wall to join her sister. Elizabeth could hear whispers and sobbing from beyond the closed door.

"Are you going to lecture me next?" G asked.

Elizabeth ignored the question. "Thea still won't let you in?"

"No," G said sullenly. "I wish to apologize, but she won't let me."

"Can you blame her?"

"No," G said. "I regret it all."

"Good."

They sat in silence for a moment before G spoke again. "She is never going to forgive me, is she?"

"I do not know, Georgiana. I wish I could say it would all be better, but what you did might be unforgivable, for at least a while."

G looked around before whispering, "Papa made it worse by saying she looked like a boy. She doesn't! I didn't even cut that much of her hair. With some pins, no one would even have noticed. Then you and Papa and Isabella had that big argument... Thank you for lying for me."

Elizabeth was silent for a moment. She needed to choose her next words very carefully. "Georgiana, I need you to reflect upon your actions this day. What you have done has been inexcusable. I do not mean only Thea's hair, either. Your actions caused your sisters, and Isabella, to all lie for you. I want you to remember that the next time you feel the urge to attack Isabella for nothing more than living in this house. After all of the abuse you have dished out to that poor woman, she lied to her very husband to protect you. I recommend you spend time in deep reflection upon that fact. You are not a little girl anymore, Georgiana Knight. You wish to come out into society. To do so early, you will have to prove that you are capable of trust and responsibility. Thus far, you have used up a significant amount of good will."

"Is he going to send me away?" G asked. "I don't want to go live with my aunt and uncle in Cornwall. They are very strict."

Their father's sister and her husband were so strict that her father had a falling out with them for being too lax with the girls. Once, his sister suggested the belt be taken to Mary, who was fifteen at the time. An inappropriate age to have a young lady's bare backside spread across her father's knee, and even her father was horrified by the suggestion. Mary's crime? Having a second helping of pudding after dinner without asking the adults if they wished to be served first.

They would beat G within a sliver of her life, and Elizabeth regretted even giving the threat. G would need to turn to housebreaking before Elizabeth would actually have followed through with that recommendation.

However, Elizabeth also felt G needed to understand, truly, where her behaviour was taking her. There was precious little patience in the Knight household for female discord. If G was not honestly told the end consequences of her behaviour, she might very well end up in Cornwall, and God help her if that happened.

The door cracked open and Cassandra stepped into the hallway. She looked down at G and said, "Thea says you can come in *if* you are willing to apologize."

G rushed inside and the door slammed behind her. Cassandra helped Elizabeth to her feet. "Shall we go back downstairs?"

Elizabeth followed Cassandra to the sewing room. They lit the candles and decided to work on their father's shirts so that Isabella would not incur more of Mr. Knight's wrath.

⁓⊶ Chapter 11 ⊷⁓

A CALMNESS DESCENDED upon the rectory the next morning that it had not experienced in some time. As they gathered about the dining table for breakfast, Elizabeth found herself staring at Thea's hair and unable to see any visible cut lines. The girl gave a nervous smile and asked, "Well?"

The plan was soon revealed. Thea's recovered strands of hair had been braided into her own hair, with the join tightly wrapped with dark brown thread.

"With the addition of decorative pins," Isabella said, "I do not believe anyone will be any wiser. It is not as though she wears her hair down except at home before breakfast, and even then, Thea often wears it in a thick braid."

"I must be careful when I brush it," Thea said. "I do not wish to hook it and lose more of the strands. I wonder how long it will take for my hair to grow out."

"Several months," Isabella said. "But, I suspect it won't bother you nearly as much come the winter. Who knows? Perhaps short hair will come into fashion for people of our class, and then you can be the most fashionable young lady in Bryden."

Thea blushed and said, "I only care about getting through my first ball at Ashbrook."

The real test, however, came when their father walked in the room, took one look at Thea, and said, "I thought your hair had been cut. It looks no different than before."

Elizabeth got the hint that Isabella had prompted her husband to speak kindly about his daughter's hair, though he appeared genuinely surprised that it had been fixed with such ingenuity. "I would never have thought to braid it back in. And the thread, ah yes, I see it now that I look for it, is to serve what? To hold the ends in place?" He nodded to himself, seemingly pleased with the fix. "Then little harm was done. The girls will need to be careful with their hair, of course, but this is not the catastrophe it appeared yesterday. See, my daughters, this is why I believe calmness and reflection are the order of the day. We cannot rush about indulging our feelings. If Georgiana had indeed meant to ruin poor Theodosia's hair and make her ugly, I would have been obliged to send her to Cornwall to stay with my sister for a stern level of correction than I am not capable of giving. Now, none of us would wish that, now would we girls? But, now I see that we are all getting along this morning over a lovely meal."

Elizabeth and the other girls shared significant looks and all looked down to quietly eat their hot and cold rolls. G spilled the coffee as she attempted to pour it, her poor hands shaking excessively.

"Careful now, the pot is hot," Isabella said. She helped G pour it.

"Thank you, Isabella," G said very quietly.

Tears filled the woman's eyes. In that moment, Elizabeth realized she had never heard G or Thea thank Isabella for anything. How awful it must be for her; to live in a house where the most basic civilities were not extended to her. Elizabeth would do better. Isabella deserved that kindness.

"Isabella helped me with my hair," Thea announced. "It was all her idea."

Isabella smiled away the glistening in her eyes and dabbed at the tablecloth to prevent the spill from hitting G's dress. "Indeed, there was such a hair emergency when I was a girl. One of my friends and her sister had a similar...accident. That is how her mother repaired the damage. After several months, her hair had grown to such a length that the remaining hair could be cut into a usable style."

"It was very quick thinking," Elizabeth said. "I am pleased, too, that I have finished my own work on one of Thea's gowns last night, and Miss Sims is in the drawing room putting the final fixes to it. Then, Thea can try it on for any last adjustments."

"Are you excited, my child?" Mr. Knight asked.

"It is very exciting, indeed," Thea said in a very quiet voice. Everyone was very quiet that morning. They walked upon barrels of gunpowder and could not risk the slightest slip.

Elizabeth helped herself to coffee and pound cake. "Miss Sims has been up since the first light sewing one of the silk gowns. I swear she'll have the entire bodice done by the time we go back with her to work."

"This is very good news, girls," Mr. Knight said. "This is what I require in my household. Calm, sensible girls behaving themselves. Yes, this is most excellent."

"What are your plans for the day, sir?" Isabella asked her husband.

Elizabeth noticed her stepmother had only torn apart her cold roll, and had not taken more than a bite. There was no other food upon her plate.

"I am to Eastmore today to settle with my banker." A smile spread across his face. "Mr. Parsons and I have struck upon a deal. I shall rent three hundred acres from him for the next two years. The rent will make things difficult to start, but I believe it will add to our accounts in the positive by the end of next year. With Charles to be ordained in the spring, God willing, we shall be in a very comfortable way. Perhaps not well enough to have a carriage, but you never know the small quirks of life that allow for blessings to come in one's path. Look at Elizabeth. No matter what happens to me, I know two of my daughters are now cared for. There is comfort in that."

Elizabeth dropped her knife.

At everyone's glances, she gave a shaky smile. "My hands are not used to so much sewing. I find them cramped this morning. But, yes, Papa. My uncle was very kind."

"Do not forget Mr. David Leigh and Mrs. Spencer, too," Mr. Knight said, shaking his fork. "She could have kept those books, or indeed Mr. Leigh could have. He has a wedding to prepare for and setting up a new house for a woman is never a cheap prospect. However, neither did so. Instead, aunt and nephew conspired to ensure you were at the receiving end of good things. Now, look at you with twenty-seven pounds from your book sales no doubt locked away in your writing desk and another six or seven in your purse. Keep your eye on that money, my dear. You may need it to support yourself soon."

"My dear papa," Elizabeth said with worry in her voice. "Are you ill?"

"Whatever would make you ask a question like that? I feel perfectly fine."

"Then why hint about life after your death, sir! That is hardly the topic for the breakfast table." Elizabeth smiled to let him know she was teasing. Though, part of her actually did worry that he was dying and he was making amends before meeting his maker. It would explain all of this. "Nine in the morning is too early for such seriousness."

"Oh, my dear girl, I have no intention of dying anytime soon, you can be assured. However, one never knows what tomorrow may bring, and there is comfort in knowing yourself and Mary are safe." Mr. Knight took out his pocket watch and frowned. "Well, ladies, I must be off. There is much to do today and I wish to be in Eastmore and back by dinner. Pray, do not wait for me, however. If the meal is ready, then seat yourselves and I shall have whatever is left at supper."

With that, their father bid them an excellent day and left the house. The ladies quietly shared glances, but did not speak. Isabella's strength mustered a little with Cassandra's encouragement to try a boiled duck's egg and a little slice of cake.

Elizabeth asked the footman to put together a lovely plate for Miss Sims, as she feared the woman had not yet eaten. She also ordered tea for the drawing room, with an appropriate amount of cake for all of the girls to enjoy throughout the morning before any visitors arrived.

By the time they finished breakfast, Miss Sims had completed Thea's first ball gown and had begun work on the second. Thea rushed upstairs to try it on to have it appropriately fitted. G assumed she would go to help, but Cassandra requested that she remain. At G's downcast spirits, Cassandra assured her it was only because she was due to walk with Miss Baldwin and the various Miss Parsons later that morning and she wanted help getting into her own dress.

That mollified Georgiana, who decided it was time to work on her reticule. However, she had to interrupt Miss Sims several times for assistance on how to stop pinching the material when she did a particular back stitch. Miss Sims, with all of the patience of her trade, showed G the same steps each time, going so far as to hold her hands and do the stitch that way, as if she were a child.

G's assistance was soon needed upstairs for Cassie's hair, and G rushed off up the stairs with much noise and exuberance. Elizabeth sighed and said to Miss Sims, "Augusta Knight could not have departed at a worse time. The girls had just entered that age where only their own mother could teach them further, but they are too full of spirit and life to learn on their own."

Miss Sims laughed heartily at that. "Why else would God make ladies young if not for them to enjoy themselves?"

And on went the day. Dinner was another quiet affair, with a well-dressed boiled mutton neck. Thea avoided it, of course, but she helped herself to two hearty slices of the herb pie, which was made mostly of eggs and cream along with a nice selection of their kitchen garden's herbs. There were a few new potatoes on the table, nicely boiled, as well as turnip greens and turnip, which were both a welcome addition to their diets. Elizabeth encouraged her sister to eat as much as those as possible.

"There is nothing bad in the rice pudding," Elizabeth coaxed. "I assure you, I checked with Alice and Julia, and it is only rice, eggs, milk, and a lovely pastry that's only made from butter."

Thea took a small helping, declared it to be exceptionally delicious, and took another, larger, portion. While her sister ate, their father joined them, still in excellent spirits. As he helped himself to his own meal, he asked the table what they had been discussing when he'd arrived. With the silence lingering, Elizabeth found herself prattling on about the healthful properties of several of the dishes upon the table.

"Indeed, Papa, I had no idea that the study of the occult would come with a thorough education on the healthful benefits of the very things we grow in our garden. For example, the turnip greens strengthen a young lady's spirit and body to get through the tasks of the day."

"I had no idea," her father said. He was helping himself to a significant amount. "Though, it does not surprise me. They are an excellent vegetable."

Elizabeth glanced at Thea, who was eyeing the last of the greens and said, "Papa? Might Thea be allowed to have the remaining amount. There are some of the kidney beans from the garden mixed in there, and they would be very beneficial to her."

"Oh, yes, of course. My, we do not need to stand upon such ceremony here at our own dinner table with no visitors!" Mr. Knight exclaimed.

Mr. Knight's good mood continued past dinner, when he retired to his study to work on both his next sermon and his plans for the newly leased lands. Cassandra was once again spending the evening with Miss Baldwin, leaving the bulk of the sewing to Elizabeth and Isabella.

"Should I have not given Cassandra my blessing then?" Mr. Knight asked as the ladies departed the dining room to retired upstairs.

"Not at all, Papa," Elizabeth said. "Miss Phoebe Baldwin is only in this part of the country for five weeks. There is no telling when Cassie will be able to see her again. Of course, she should go to visit as much as possible."

Mr. Knight called out that he would most likely take supper in his study as he had a great many things to accomplish. That left the ladies to work in peace and quiet, without his interference.

Elizabeth and Isabella successfully finished the bulk of a second day gown for Thea, and Miss Sims had finished both the minute fitting details of the first gown and was nearly completed sewing the second. Elizabeth and Isabella both finished those as darkness fell. Thea also finished all of the household bonnet refurbishments, and Georgiana finished her reticule, including embroidering a small pineapple motif.

Miss Sims declared herself exhausted and asked permission to retire early so that she could be up as soon as the dawn light came. Isabella gave the seamstress her blessing, and suggested that Elizabeth go work on her occult studies while she did more work upon the men's shirts.

Unsurprisingly, Elizabeth spent the first while waiting for the knocking at her door to cease. Finally, Isabella took to the pianoforte for the girls to practice dancing and Elizabeth could finally set to work.

Elizabeth laid the locket upon her bed and knelt down as if she were to say her prayers. She read the incantation provided by Alice and Susan;

Forever young, body, soul, and mind
Here to teach, to show, to inspire
Let this locket hold your soul steadfast
For the good of all who know of you

Elizabeth stared at the locket and glanced over at the still very visible Mrs. Egerton, who'd transformed into a lovely pink and brown striped dress for the occasion, sporting a hat that would have made Georgiana swoon.

"I recommend placing my book next to the locket. Perhaps we are missing a step in the process."

Elizabeth did so and repeated the spellworking. The attempt failed, though Mrs. Egerton's ghost flickered twice before solidifying.

"Shall I attempt with you returned to your book?" Elizabeth asked.

"I believe we should try all approaches."

Elizabeth broke the spellworking that would keep Mrs. Egerton's soul bound awake for the day. She attempted the spellworking again, and this time a breeze blew through the room and Elizabeth's arm hair stood on edge.

Elizabeth attempted to resummon Mrs. Egerton from her book, but could not. Hopeful the spell worked, she tied the locket about her neck, carried her book in her hand, and walked into the family drawing room. She took a turn upon the piano to allow

Isabella's back a rest, and also took a turn dancing with each of her two sisters.

"I thought you would have been working," Isabella said.

"Indeed, I am. I have merely taken a rest in hopes to see if my work has come to some benefit."

The girls soon collapsed on the worn settee and declared themselves exhausted. Thea asked if G would like to finish trimming their hats, and both girls ran off to fetch their supplies.

"It appears that Thea has forgiven G at least," Isabella said.

"It was fine thinking repairing her hair as you did. I am certain that helped their sisterly affection. Will Cassie be returning home tomorrow? We must spend the day going through Augusta's things, I believe. The hats are all well and good, but I believe a firmer hand is needed now or we shall never have the work done."

"I believe Miss Phoebe Baldwin goes to London tomorrow to see her relations for a short visit. Did you wish me to step in to organize the girls?"

"No, I shall do it. I do not wish any of their grief to be taken out upon you." Elizabeth smiled. "Besides, I am the eldest. They expect me to herd them about like the sheep they too often resemble. Well, I should return back to my studies, if you are agreeable to that. Do you need anything? I can have it brought up."

"Oh, I am very well. My appetite has returned a little this evening, so I have had a small bowl of custard which did my spirits a world of good."

"Excellent. Please send one of the girls to fetch me if you require anything. Including a moderating voice if war should break out once again."

Elizabeth returned to her bedchamber as the girls were clambering up the stairs with baskets, ribbons, and enough frills and lace to repair a dozen hats. They disappeared beyond into the drawing room and Elizabeth closed her door. She attempted the spellworking reversal three times before getting the steps correct. She made careful note of each failure before attempting again, even though her heart pounded with worry for Mrs. Egerton.

However, on the third attempt, Mrs. Egerton appeared into focus with a wide smile and said, "Oh, well done!"

"Then, it worked?"

"Indeed. It was a very odd experience. Within my book, but summoned, I can see everything that is in view of my book from all sides and directions. However, in this case, I could only see in the direction the locket faced. A few times, your locket flipped around and I was reduced to only seeing your décolletage."

Elizabeth felt her cheeks heat. "Oh dear. That was not my intention at all!"

"I should hope not. I believe, for now, let us test this spell on the locket for the next day or so, and then we shall attempt a more robust spellworking. I do not wish you to bring a book to a ballroom, so we must work on range."

Elizabeth nodded, pleased that she'd done the working herself, though with significant help from her friends.

"I shall write to the ladies this instant, while all of the details are fresh in my mind."

June 10, 1810
Bryden Rectory

My dearest friends,

What extraordinary results have occurred from your excellent advice! I have successfully transferred Mrs. Egerton's essence to the locket you have so kindly provided. There are some concerns, however, so Mrs. Egerton and I are to work on them. However, as the current situation here at Bryden is not conducive to thinking at present (I shall detail all of that tomorrow morning as an appendage to this letter), I hope that you can both provide me some guidance.

First, the spellworking still requires the sight of Mrs. Egerton's book. We attempted me walking around the corner, and her essence was returned to the book via a strong breeze. That was rather shocking and my heart skipped a beat before pounding rapidly, for I had feared I'd lost her. However, true to her word, she was not affected by the spellworking failure, and only was inconvenienced for but a moment.

One curious side effect of the spellworking is that Mrs. Egerton could only see forward, in the direction she faced. Therefore, as I assisted my sisters with their dancing, at times Mrs. Egerton could see nothing but the inside of my bodice, which I am certain that was not the intention! She has made much sport on that score.

She wishes to know if one of you are able to draw her likeness from memory? If so, we might be able to use that as a more solid anchor, since there will be no uncertainty. I realized this is an impossibly tall order, and we are both accepting that this task may have to wait until after Michaelmas, which we understand, of course.

The hour grows late and my father will soon scowl at me for wasting a candle at this hour of the night to write letters, so I must bid you adieu for now.

E

❧ Chapter 12 ❧

THE NEXT FEW days began with the usual letters arriving and leaving, and the quiet comfort of their father's overall demeanour smoothed out once the real plans began in earnest with regards to the new land lease. Visitors came and went, and dresses were sewn.

Thea's gowns were ready a day early, thanks in part to the extra work by Elizabeth and Isabella. Therefore, that allowed Miss Sims to spend all of Thursday assisting the younger Knight girls with the repairs and refurbishments to Augusta Knight's dresses.

"This ugly thing should go to Eliza," G said. "She's always cold."

Elizabeth laughed when G tossed her the rather boring dress. The woollen brown dress with red leaves would never be worn into society by any woman of fashion, but it was thick, warm, and comfortable. Augusta had worn it frequently on chilly mornings before breakfast when working about the house. The easy bodice style allowed for quick dressing without any assistance. She slipped it over her dress for Miss Sims to mark a new hemline and where the sleeves required shortening. Miss Sims pinned adjustments to the bust and shoulders, as well as a small tuck to the hips, and Elizabeth slipped out of the gown for the expert to begin her work.

"The dress was designed to wear pockets underneath," Miss Sims said. "However, I do not see any pockets about with her things. Do you wish the seams sewn or do you have a pattern to make your own pockets? They are a little out of style, I grant you, but we older ladies all have a pair under our gowns!"

"I have a pair, but they are long since too small about the waist and I had not bothered to make another set, since the fashions have changed so much. I shall make a new set. I wonder, will there be enough fabric left from removing the train to sew a matching set?"

Miss Sims eyed the dress and nodded. "For the pockets, yes. However, you may need to use a different fabric for the waist tie. The dress is dark, so it will not matter what colour you use."

Elizabeth nodded, pleased to have gotten a dress to wear for everyday with so little work or expense.

Poor G wanted her mother's pink and white dress, but Miss Sims managed to reason with the girl. She warned G that she'd have to cut clear a full quarter of the material from the bust and hips just for it to fit G. Then, the alterations would only allow the dress to fit for a few months, perhaps a year at best, due to her still growing body.

"My dear, this silk is simply timeless. With only the smallest modifications for fashion's sake, be it sleeves or a ruffle or a line of lace, this can be remade into a stunning new gown for your own coming out that no one will know was once your mother's," Miss Sims said. "Now, we must take care, however, to store the dress properly so that it is not ruined in the damp or by moths."

Cassandra received her mother's lovely ballgown made out of blue silk that Augusta hadn't worn in several years. The dress also had to be hemmed significantly, for Cassandra was the shortest of the Knight girls and hemlines were much higher these days than when Augusta wore trains on her gowns, but the excess fabric meant that a damaged sleeve could be repaired.

Thea decided upon her mother's light blue summer pelisse. Miss Sims helped pin the proper sizing and Isabella began working on it. She said it would take her a couple of days on her own to make the repairs; she was not nearly as fast of a seamstress as experienced Miss Sims.

"That is perfectly acceptable, Mrs. Knight," Miss Sims said. "Better to go slow and right the first time, then pull it apart five times and ruin the edge. I will attempt to assist with the shoulders and back as soon as I finish with Miss Knight's gown."

"Oh, you can leave my dress," Elizabeth said.

"Do not fret, Miss Knight, for the delicate repairs about the shoulders will only take this morning, and then we have all afternoon yet. And still tomorrow if needs be."

To mollify G, she was given two of her mother's neckerchiefs, which required no work whatsoever, and her mother's best muslin shawl that had been a wedding present from Aunt Cass. Stockings, shifts, and the like were easily distributed and anything requiring mending or adjustment was placed into the work basket for later.

Elizabeth decided that she would not divide up the jewelry with Miss Sims in the house, as that was a private, intimate affair and she would leave that for later.

All told, they spent another seven shillings four pence on Miss Sims' haberdashery and fabric scraps, which Elizabeth handed over out of her own pocket. Thankfully, Miss Sims had enough coins in her own reticule to provide change for a pound note, or else Elizabeth would have been leaving an extraordinarily generous tip to the seamstress.

Isabella commissioned Miss Sims to let out one of her gowns for her growing belly, but that would be done at a later point and for a reasonable cost of six shillings.

Finally, Miss Sims' wages were paid, along with the niece's. Once Miss Sims finally left them, Elizabeth teased her sisters that they'd purchased nearly two pounds of various haberdashery from Miss Sim's personal supply.

"She could use the money, Elizabeth," Isabella said.

"Oh, I am not upset at Miss Sims for earning her way in the world. Only that my sisters are trying to impoverish me one strand of ribbon at a time!"

The girls protested their innocence, and Elizabeth laughed at their silly justifications for why they needed eight different shades of yellow silk ribbon.

Of course, Elizabeth would never complain about a single woman attempting to earn her way in the world, especially one that stole her eyesight far too early for doing nothing more than working to feed herself and a growing horde of female mouths who were unable to find husbands.

It was a problem, indeed, in these days. There were simply too many women in the world and not nearly enough men to marry them.

Elizabeth was pleased to find herself with the ability to surprise her father with nine shillings and ten pence. He looked at her offered coins, sighed, and said, "Please give those to Georgiana so that we might have peace in this house."

Elizabeth placed the coins back in her reticule. "I am certain that will make G very happy. With your blessing, I wish to divide Augusta's jewelry between the girls, and Charles. We gave away all of the items that were in her will, but there is much still left. I believe it is time."

He nodded. "Yes, of course. I shall leave that to your good sense. You did well with the dresses, it appears. There was not even one argument that I could hear."

Elizabeth smiled. "Miss Sims managed to convince G to wait until she's out to alter one of the dresses. She does not require a pink silk gown at present, and it would be silly to adjust such an expensive gown for it not to fit her in a six-month."

"Very wise, my dear. Very wise. I say, though, I shall be very sorry to see that niece of Miss Sims gone. The food has been excellent since she arrived. Both girls together, it seems, was what we needed to replace Mrs. Cooper."

"How is she? I have not heard word in two days."

Mr. Knight shook his head. "The news is grave, my dear. Mr. Collins told me this very morning that the infection is now very much upon her and that she might not recover the full use of her lungs again, even if God decides to spare her, which is not likely."

"Oh, how horrible," Elizabeth said. "Pray, what is to happen to poor Julia? Should we not offer to allow her to stay here? We have plenty of room in the attic now that Mrs. Taylor has done all of that work. It bothers me greatly that she is displaced as she is, with her mother so ill."

Mr. Knight waved a hand. "Unnecessary, my dear, but very good thinking. She insists now upon staying at Vane Park in the servants' quarters there. Her sister is employed there as a maid, so Mr. Thorne has graciously allowed her to remain there while the sickness is contagious."

"That is good news, but I am uneasy with Julia walking from Vane Park here and back in the dark. If I had known, I would have immediately spoken to you about it, sir."

Mr. Knight frowned. "Do you think it is improper? She is but a maid. There is nothing wrong with that class walking about alone. You make the journey on your own often enough. Are you saying it is not safe for you?"

"I do not mind the walk during the day, but she is here before dawn and it is so dark in the lane. She could fall and not be found for hours. I believe the Christian thing to do would be to extend her the offer of her room and board, at least as long as she is employed here."

Mr. Knight frowned, but nodded. "I suppose a girl of her size would not be much of an expense upon our food stores. What is your opinion on the other Sims girl?"

"I believe we should take her on, at least for a month. She does not need to stay, living so close as she does. If the Lord wills it, Mrs. Cooper will recover and we won't need two cooks. Until then, however, I do believe employing both girls will only improve our table for little expense."

He nodded. "I shall visit Miss Sims tomorrow and request to engage her niece's assistance. For a month, you say?"

Elizabeth nodded. "This is such a distressing news, all the same."

"Indeed it is, my dear. However, we must put our faith in the Lord that his plan is being acted upon. I assure you, Mr. Collins is doing all that he can." Mr. Knight motioned at her reticule. "Now, run along. I wish to get the ritual shrieking out of the way."

"Yes, Papa," Elizabeth said.

"Elizabeth?" Mr. Knight waited for her to turn back to face him. "You did very well managing the girls this last week. This is the exact type of behaviour I expect from all of my girls, and it was good to see my instruction had not fallen completely by the wayside."

Elizabeth drew in a breath and inclined her head. "Thank you, Father."

She left him to seek out G and present her with her new pin money. The excited shrieking began and Thea and G asked for permission to walk to the village to see what was in the shops for sweets that day. Elizabeth sighed, but gave her permission for them to go, provided they walked with Cassandra. They asked her to join them, but she declined, wishing to finally turn her attentions back to her studies.

However, a knock came at the door. Before she could look out the window to spy who it was, G rushed into the study and said, "Papa! Elizabeth! Hurry. A Mr. Grant from London is here."

ELIZABETH HURRIED OUT of her father's study to find Mr. Grant standing at their front door. She curtsied and said, "My dear Mr. Grant! What on earth are you doing here? Please, come in. My father will be…ah! Here is my father now."

Elizabeth did introductions and there was much excitement over a new visitor. Mr. Grant was ushered into the drawing room, where profound apologies were made for all of the dresses upon the furniture. Mr. Grant laughed when the explanations were given and said he did not mind in the slightest.

"Finery does not bother me, my dear Miss Knight. I have been known to admire a piece of lace on occasion," Mr. Grant said, which sent the youngest Miss Knights into giggles.

Details of his accommodations at the village inn were interrogated out of him (he'd taken their best room for two nights), as well as how he'd managed to arrive so early (he'd arrived late the previous night, but did not want to bother the family). Soon, a dinner invitation was issued and readily accepted.

He looked at the girls and said, "Now, which of you is Miss Theodosia Knight?"

"I am," Thea said.

He presented her with a brown paper parcel. "This is for you, from Mrs. Spencer. She says to tell you that she could not find a shawl with pineapple embroidery but hopes this will be to your tastes."

Thea tore into the parcel, despite the protestations of her father and eldest sister, and made delighted sounds when a gauzy shawl appeared. Thea held it up and let out a little gasp. "Strawberries!"

The muslin shawl was perfect for summer visiting. It was wide enough that Thea could wrap it around herself to keep some of the sun off her arms, but also thin enough to not be an encumbrance to simply wear around her neck and left to drape down to her knees.

Best of all, to Thea's tastes, the entire white shawl's edge was embroidered with the tiniest little strawberry plants—flowers, leaves, and fruit.

"Oh, please tell Mrs. Spencer I send my heartfelt thanks. Oh, this is wonderful. How on earth did she manage to find this and so quickly! Oh, Eliza, look at it!"

"That is a lot of fruit," Isabella said.

"I shall never understand ladies' fashion," Mr. Knight said. "Well, Mr. Grant, while my daughter goes upstairs to be vain in front of a mirror for a quarter of an hour, what news is there from London? How fares my daughter's relations?"

"Mr. Leigh plans his wedding, of course. And Mrs. Spencer is always in the most excellent of health. She's been enjoying the company of her two young companions for some months now."

"I had written to my aunt to ask if she was still appreciating the youthful vigour of two ladies living with her after she'd had the house to herself for so long," Elizabeth said. "But she has yet to reply to my letter."

"Oh, do not worry about your aunt. She is quite content." Isabella asked, "Was not one of the girls ill? Mrs. Taylor's niece, yes?"

"And how is Mrs. Taylor?" Mr. Knight asked.

"Mrs. Taylor is in excellent health for a woman her age, let me assure you," Mr. Grant said. "Mrs. Spencer will not let the woman have so much as a slight sniffle without calling for a physician to consult upon the matter. As for Miss Markson, the young lady in question, well! She has been in her full health for nearly a month now! Miss Markson has been hinting that it is time for her to move on to a position. You might recall, madam, that she was a governess before her illness." That last bit he said to Isabella. Then he turned to Elizabeth and said, "But your aunt will hear none of it!"

That made Elizabeth laugh. "Is she enjoying being dragged to every opera in London still?"

"I would not go so far as that, I admit, however, she cannot bear to be parted with them. Miss Thorne's relations have tried to retrieve her twice now, but Mrs. Spencer always manages to develop a malady that only Miss Thorne's attentions can cure. And, if I might be so bold, as Miss Thorne vastly prefers life at Mrs. Spencer's over raising her niece and nephews, this is a better arrangement all around. Though, I suppose not for the mother of all those niece and nephews!"

"A young, unmarried woman should be at the disposal of her married family members," Mr. Knight said.

Mr. Grant laughed and said, "My dear Mr. Knight. Living with so many young ladies, you surely must know that what society thinks is right and what the young ladies *will* do are often opposite actions."

"You do not need to tell me that, Mr. Grant," Mr. Knight muttered.

"Now, Miss Knight, do not mention this bit of news to either of the ladies in your letters, but Mrs. Spencer has been in discussion with me about whether or not she should hire Miss Markson to be her lady's companion. That way, she could keep the young lady's company, and the young lady could receive wages to allow her independence."

Elizabeth chuckled at the idea of her aunt taking on a lady's companion. "And what was your advice on the matter?"

"Well," Mr. Grant said, giving Isabella a faux whisper. "I recommended bringing Mr. Osborne's opinion into the mix."

Isabella laughed and said, "Mr. Grant! You are worse than any woman I know."

"My dear Mrs. Knight," Mr. Grant said. "I am a lonely widower from London. As my marriage days are behind me, I wish to see every young person in the kingdom married off."

"Mr. Grant, you cannot be more than thirty, I am certain. You are a little young to swear off marriage," Mr. Knight said, not even bothering to hide his astonishment.

"My dear sir, I am thirty-seven now, and very entrenched in my bachelorhood."

Mr. Knight shook his head gravely. "I do not understand what is becoming of this country. We have sensible young men and young women who are very compatible and all refusing to marry."

Mr. Grant laughed. "If it brings you some comfort, sir, Mrs. Spencer frequently makes similar comments."

"Mrs. Spencer has always had the reputation of a sensible woman here at Bryden Rectory," Mr. Knight said. "This is just another example why."

Elizabeth cleared her throat to gain the attention of the room. She smiled and said, "Mr. Grant. My sisters were preparing to leave for the village in search of sweets. And it seems now that no one amongst my London friends is giving me full intelligence about the situation there, and now I must rely upon the good luck of your arrival. Indeed, I have barely heard a word from Mr. Henry Thorne on the subject of Miss Markson and Mr. Osborne, and that man gossips more than any woman I have ever known."

"Elizabeth Knight!" her father exclaimed. "Let us not insult our very illustrious neighbour to our guest."

"On the contrary, sir, I have met the *illustrious* Mr. Thorne and I confess I had said the exact same words to Miss Knight," Mr. Grant said. "Well, ladies. I have a carriage outside and I would be very happy to escort you wherever you wish to go. Mr. Knight, might I be so bold as to request if I can escort your entire household of ladies as far as Eastmore's shops if they wish it?"

Mr. Knight bristled at G's shriek of excitement. "Mr. Grant, I beg you, please take them and do not return them for hours. I have a sermon to write."

"I shall keep them away as long as Miss Knight allows," Mr. Grant said with a bow. "Until dinner. Oh, I should ask. When is dinner in the country?"

"We take our meal at five o'clock," Mr. Knight said. "We used to take it at four, but our neighbours continued to drop by during the meal and I have had enough of that. Soon, Bryden will be just as bad as town for dinner hours."

Mr. Grant laughed. "Do not fret on that score, sir. Just the other day, I was invited to a dinner party that did not start until seven in the evening."

"Seven!" Mr. Knight exclaimed. "Think of the candles in winter!"

Mr. Grant said, "How better to spend frivolously than a seven o'clock dinner? Ah, the young ladies beckon me and I am at their service. Until five o'clock sharp."

"I shall be right along, Mr. Grant," Elizabeth called out.

"At your leisure, Miss Knight. At your leisure!"

Once Mr. Grant was out of hearing, Mr. Knight sighed. "He is a very delightful man."

"I am pleased to hear you say that, Father," Elizabeth said. "I have often said to my aunt that you and Mr. Grant would be excellent acquaintances. Are you very comfortable now with him handling my inheritance?"

"Oh, very much indeed. How I wish he would be my son-in-law. With Theodosia now coming out, I suppose there is hope he'll take a fancy to her."

"Oh, Papa. Mr. Grant does not want a silly wife," Elizabeth said with a smile. "And, as much as I love my sister, Theodosia would make him a very silly wife indeed."

Mr. Knight sighed. "I suppose we could attempt to push Cassandra on him. She is still not too old to think unmarriable."

"Papa! She is only eighteen! Give her a chance," Elizabeth exclaimed with a laugh.

Her father only sighed. "She could attract a man, if she had the opportunity. We must call her back from the Baldwins' today so that she can dine with Mr. Grant. We cannot waste this opportunity."

"It is perhaps best we allow things to progress naturally, sir," Isabella said.

Mr. Knight gave her an annoyed look. "If we allow things to progress naturally, we shall be stuck with another Elizabeth."

"Sir! I protest this abuse," Elizabeth said, and she laughed harder at the annoyed expression her father gave her.

Elizabeth glanced out of the drawing room window at the sight of Mr. Grant attempting to stuff the two younger Knight girls into his carriage. "Would it be proper to excuse myself from the party by developing a sudden headache?"

"I thought you liked Mr. Grant," Isabella said.

"Oh, indeed, he is an excellent gentleman. I fear there is not enough room in the carriage for me at present." She glanced at her father and smiled. "Also, my father has planned for Mr. Grant to marry one of his daughters and I should only confuse the poor man if I am there."

"Elizabeth Knight!" Her father scolded her, which only made Elizabeth chuckle. She offered her apologies for being free with her words and went to join the crowded carriage, where now Mr. Grant was evicted by the giggling girls and was good-naturedly sitting with the coachman.

✑ Chapter 13 ✑

ALAS, MR. GRANT did not propose to one of Mr. Knights' daughters during his rather brief visit to the country. He returned to London the next day, leaving the girls excited by a new acquaintance and Mr. Knight lamenting that he still had too many unmarried daughters who would do nothing to attract the men.

With Thea's dresses ready, they were destined to leave for Mary's on the Tuesday. Thea's gowns were packed, her new shoes purchased and delivery to Ashbrook arranged, and her new gloves were safely stuffed into her trunk. Elizabeth continued her work on Mrs. Egerton's locket and was rewarded with adding some distance before the spellworking faded.

On the morning of leaving for Ashbrook, Georgiana was more sullen than Mr. Knight would have preferred and less sullen than Elizabeth had expected. Their father travelled with them in the hired hackney chaise from the Trap and Gully Inn in Eastmore. Elizabeth had attempted to sell her cause, stating she was now old enough to both travel by herself and also escort her younger sister six miles in a hired carriage.

Her father agreed that she was approaching the age where such independence could be afforded to a single young lady, especially with her sister under her wing. However, as her father wished to see Mary, and could return back to the rectory in the same carriage with no additional expense, he wished to come along for the journey.

What should have been a joyous affair became a two-hour sermon about feminine deportment, the volume of one's voice, and the evils of men and their designs to ruin young ladies. His attentions were surprisingly turned upon Elizabeth more than once, letting her know that her newfound wealth would make her a prime target for unscrupulous young men wishing to seduce her for her one thousand pounds.

Elizabeth offered her father only the base politeness of replies. She understood that Theodosia would need the lectures. However, she was to be twenty-nine in September and well past needing such instruction. She knew all too well the evils of men's hearts and had no ambition to entertain any man simply because he had a nice smile.

However, she also knew that there were not roving bands of men ready to seduce every young lady who so much as turned in their direction. Perhaps in London, or even Bath, but Ashbrook House? Or the surrounding countryside? Or the local village of Ashbrook with its dozen shops? It always surprised her to what a low degree her father held his own sex.

In Elizabeth's' mind, Mrs. Egerton's dislike of men was grounded in sense and experience. The poor woman had died seeing a world of change and uncertainty. When she was summoned back to the world of the living, she was faced with the realization that men had stolen the occult from the hands of women and hidden their accomplishments from the world. The ghost's resentment towards men made sense to Elizabeth. Her father's mistrust had always perplexed her.

Of course, with a third young wife in the house, Elizabeth found herself wondering if perhaps the reason for his dislike was that he assumed all young men were as him, and that the apple did not fall far from the tree of men.

"What are you thinking about so intently?" Mr. Knight demanded. "I suppose it is that occult foolishness of yours. You have not spoken a word in ages."

Without any hesitation, Elizabeth said, "I was considering the expansion of our kitchen garden to grow more herbs."

"The roses are in the way," Thea said. "We can't cut those down because they were Mama's."

"I have no intention of cutting down your mother's roses, my dear. I think they are beautiful and lovely, and perfect just where they are. No, I was considering that small patch up on the hill, where the sun hits for the entire day, would make an excellent strawberry bed with a thick barrier of herbs about them. What say you, Papa?"

The request caught Mr. Knight by surprise. "I suppose there is no harm, but that area is nothing but nettles and brambles, not to mention dead branches everywhere. I suspect it would take a week to clear it and dig the beds for your strawberries."

"But I wish to contribute to the improvement of the rectory property, and I think our own strawberry beds would be exciting."

Her father seemed dubious, so Elizabeth said, "I shall consider it more. May I speak to Mr. Crow about it? Perhaps he could recommend a sturdy lad or two to help prepare the area for me."

"Oh, I have no objection if you wish to add strawberries to our table. You will need to have a fence about the area, or else the pigs and chickens will get into the beds."

With that, Mr. Knight abruptly abandoned his sermons on female virtue and went to a deep and detailed discussion on strawberry production. By the time they arrived at Ashbrook House, their father had designed an entire strawberry industry running from the small hilly spot behind the rectory that could net them as much as ten pounds a season if they managed to get their crop to London.

They were already out of the carriage and partway up the steps to the front door before Mary arrived outside to greet them. She curtsied to her father and Elizabeth, and hugged Theodosia tightly.

"How exciting! Finally, coming out into society! Now, do not fret if you do not fetch a husband this first season. I was married by my second season," Mary said. "So do not let Eliza's bad luck with men to cause you worry."

Elizabeth rolled her eyes behind her sister's back.

"You should have seen the scene at the rectory, my dear Mary. A Mr. Grant from London came to visit us. He is your aunt

Spencer's attorney and a very respectable young man. He rode all the way from London simply to deliver Theodosia a shawl."

"Oh, did you get your coming out shawl? You must show it to me," Mary said, interrupting her father.

"Eliza made me pack it in my trunk so that I would not get it dirty," Thea complained.

Mr. Knight waved his hand to bring attention back to himself. "Never mind all that. Elizabeth did nothing to encourage him in the slightest. He left us the following day without any promise of his return."

"Oh, Papa!" Elizabeth turned to Mary. "Aunt Cass asked Mr. Grant to rush the shawl to Thea, as she did not know when we'd be leaving for Ashbrook. Mr. Grant agreed because he wanted a break from the heat in town. He wasn't here to find himself a wife. If he wished to do that, I'd recommend somewhere a bit livelier than here!"

"And what, pray, is in Bath or London that Bryden or Eastmore cannot offer a young man?" Mr. Knight demanded.

"A great many things, Papa," Elizabeth said.

Thankfully, they were saved from another argument by Mary's husband. Mr. Fitzharding was a gentleman in his early fifties and could be best described as being full of big smiles and physical intimacy. He clasped Elizabeth's hands in his own and squeezed them tightly. "My dear sister, it is good to have you with us once more."

"Good day, Mr. Fitzharding," Elizabeth said.

"James, sister! My name is James. I will not have my own family calling me mister, as if they were strangers."

"That is very good of you, Mr. Fitzharding. Very, very good of you," Mr. Knight said.

"Now, you must forgive the silence in the house. I told the children they were not allowed downstairs to see you until you have your trunks put into your bedchambers, had a change of clothes, and a cup of tea in you."

"My dear husband," Mary protested. "I told the children that Aunt Elizabeth would be up shortly upon her arrival to get them started on their studies."

"And, I told you, *my dear*," James Fitzharding said, "that *Elizabeth* is our guest and not our governess. We should allow her to at least have a cup of tea in her before you send her off into the schoolroom."

"That pelisse looks familiar, Elizabeth," Mary said.

"It was Mama's!" Thea exclaimed. "Miss Sims finished all of her work early, so she helped us alter some of Mama's old gowns."

Mary gave the outer garment an appraising look. "It is a bit shabby, don't you think?"

Elizabeth looked down at the blue silk pelisse she wore. The tie ends were a little frayed, but she'd planned to work on it while here at Ashbrook. The hem was slightly discoloured but that was nothing to signify and only someone staring to be critical would notice it. Which, Mary was doing.

"No, it doesn't look shabby at all," Elizabeth said.

Mary made a displeased sound. "No wonder we cannot get you married. Well, let us not have you influencing Theodosia unnecessarily."

"My dear wife, your poor sister has only just arrived. Shall we give her an opportunity to catch her breath before we begin the teasing, please?"

"You are always taking her side," Mary said. "Well, come along then. John, please have the footmen bring in their bags. Papa, will you be staying to dinner?"

"Alas, no, I need to be back at the rectory. However, I shall stay to tea and visit my grandchildren while the horses rest," Mr. Knight said. "Now, where are my grandchildren?"

Mr. Fitzharding called out for Nanny Rideout to bring the children to see their grandpapa. There was a commotion before the shouting and shrieking of tiny throats and tinier feet pounded through the house. They flung themselves at their grandpapa and their aunt, in one mass of bodies, while their mother berated poor little Miss Lucy for stepping on her aunt's gown.

"Mind yourself!" Mary scowled. "Look at you! You are filthy. What is all down your dress?"

Miss Lucy looked up at her mother and said, "Jam."

Mary looked at Miss Rideout and asked, "Why did she have jam?"

"She was very hungry, ma'am," the nanny said. "She could not wait until teatime. So we had a small treat of bread and jam from the kitchen."

"Take her away. She must be changed."

"Oh, there is no call for that," James said. He picked up his sticky daughter. "Your mama is quite the fussbucket, isn't she? Always wanting little girls to be perfect and never a speck of jam or mud on them."

"You are spoiling her!" Mary complained.

"And name a better person to spoil a daughter than her father?"

Elizabeth's mouth twitched with envy. She had no recollections of such an encounter with her own father.

"Now, now, Mary is right. We cannot spoil the girl," Mr. Knight said. "Girls are not like little boys."

"Nonsense!" James said as he swung little Lucy around in the air shouting, "We're flying like a bird!"

Lucy squealed and giggled until Mary's protestations won and she was put down. "If you keep spoiling her, no man will be good enough for her."

"I am going to marry my papa," Lucy said.

James smugly said, "There is no better man in England, my girl. You have chosen well for yourself."

Mary harrumphed but said nothing.

"Come, Mary can show her father to the drawing room. I shall escort you to your room, Miss Knight, and carry your...is that a writing desk?"

"I shall show her," Mary said.

"No, no, I wish to interrogate Elizabeth on her new furniture purchase," James said. "Tell me, which London shop did you purchase that from, because I know you did not find anything that exceptional in Eastmore. Oh, stop your fussing, Mary! Come, Elizabeth, before my wife stops us."

Thea followed behind them, with Mary shouting for the maid to take Thea to the garden room. Elizabeth had already turned down the corridor, toward the bedroom that overlooked the stables, and she smirked when Mary had confirmed it.

Once out of hearing of both the servants and his wife, James asked, "I hope you are not affronted that my wife gave you a view of the stables again. Though, I suppose you have already divined it with your occult ways for you'd turned down this particular hallway before I could even direct you."

Elizabeth laughed. "Indeed, no, I take no offence and am honestly very comfortable in that room. For one thing, the fireplace does not smoke. And, if I might be so bold, I would have thought Mary was scheming if she'd upgraded my room to one with a view. Allow Thea to have it. This is her special time and, if I recall, Cassie has that room whenever she visits. It is only fair that Thea have it now."

"Allow me to carry that. You carry too much. Which is heavier?" James took her writing box by the handles when she offered it to him. "My goodness, this is a rather robust box. Did you purchase it at Randall's in London?"

"Indeed! It has been an excellent purchase and well worth the investment. I can store several of my personal items under lock and key in it, and also it allows me to work no matter where I go."

"Ah, yes." James pointed to her room. She walked in first and he carried her desk in. He waited for her to set up her portable table. Once snapped into place, he placed the writing desk atop it. "Ingenious. Now, I conspired against my wife to escort you to give you a hint about your visit."

"Oh dear," Elizabeth said. "Is there anything truly the matter?"

"Oh, no. Just Mary's usual queer ways. But I wish to give you a hint, Elizabeth. Mary does not approve of the occult. Now, I do not care what you read or conjure from the depths of hell, but Mary does. She has been speaking to your father, and our local vicar, who is rather opposed to young ladies having any education of their own."

"Ah," Elizabeth said. "This comes as no surprise to me, but I thank you for the hint. I promise to be exceptionally discreet."

"Good. Good. Well, I shall leave you to change into something less dusty. And, pray, if it is possible, will you make some time for me this trip to tell me a little of your occult studies? I am so very fascinated by it all, but I can hardly write to you without Mary finding out. That woman has more spies than Napoleon."

Elizabeth laughed. "I would be happy to share it with you, though I do not know when such an opportunity will arise."

He waved vaguely about the room. "There is much planning to accomplish yet before the ball. I shall wager Mary will be dragging poor Miss Theodosia all about the countryside to the shops."

"Just as a hint for your own purse. Theodosia has spent all of her money to prepare for this ball. I have a few items to finish sewing for her, but they are trivial. She has no money of her own at present, so if Mary wishes to drag her about..."

"My accounts need to be open, I understand you perfectly." James smiled. "Never fear, my dear. I shall—"

"Husband! Hurry now. It does not take that long to show Elizabeth where her room is. My father awaits you!"

James Fitzharding sighed, but he gave Elizabeth a wink. "Never envy a married man, Miss Knight."

Elizabeth chuckled. "Oh, how you suffer, Mr. James Fitzharding, with your ten thousand pounds and a charming, doting wife who ensures you are always well cared for."

"You forgot the incessant nagging." In a louder voice, he called out, "Coming, dearest."

Elizabeth waited until he closed the door and then began to change. She slipped out of her pelisse, gloves, and hat, and placed those items over the railing of her bed for the maid to shake out later. She opened her trunk and pulled out the brown dress that had been Augusta's, the hem now completed. She hung Mrs. Egerton's locket about her neck and quickly began changing dresses.

"Mr. Fitzharding is an astonishingly gentleman-like man," Mrs. Egerton mused.

"I like him excessively. I do not believe he is a good match for Mary, but only in terms of personality and interests. However, he does seem amused enough with her antics. And he does love the children. Indeed, you will never find a more attentive father."

"Will you honour your sister's request of no occult studies in the household?"

"Of course not," Elizabeth said, wriggling into her brown gown. "I do as I please, and what would Mary do? Send me home? That does not sound like a bad punishment."

"But your father?"

Elizabeth re-pinned some of her loose strands of hair. "There is nothing I can do to satisfy my father, Mrs. Egerton. I can hardly start now."

"Is that a note of bitterness I detect, Miss Knight?"

Elizabeth unlocked her writing desk and pulled out Mrs. Egerton's book. There was a small shelf underneath her table that perfectly stored the ghost book. She emptied the bank notes and guineas from her reticule and wrapped those in a stocking before stuffing them deep into one of her travelling boots, pushing it straight to the toe. She placed the occult books she'd brought with her underneath her bed. Ditto her accounts book and her occult journal.

She placed the occult books she'd brought with her underneath her bed. Ditto her accounts book and her occult journal.

"Elizabeth! Hurry up!" Mary called out. "Do you need my maid to help you dress? Why are you putting on something that requires assistance? Elizabeth! Where are you?"

"I shall be right out," Elizabeth called out as she got on her hands and knees. She lifted the bed skirts and pushed all of the books between the ropes and her mattress bottom.

"Miss Knight, forgive my observation, but it appears you do not trust your sister."

"Indeed, I do not," Elizabeth said. "If she thinks I have no money, she will merely berate me and mock me. I can say I have left it at home, if pressed. I can live with that. If she sees me saving my money, she will call it hoarding and demand I spend it upon her children, Theodosia, the poor, and every other living soul in England not myself. I must save as much as I can because I do not know what the future holds. I need the independence it provides me, Mrs. Egerton. Surely, you understand that."

"You do not need to justify your actions to me," Mrs. Egerton said. "I would not have said anything if you chose to convert all of your money into jewelry."

"I have been tempted at times, I confess," Elizabeth said. "But I fear Mary would just steal it and claim it was our mother's."

A knock came to the door. Elizabeth managed to get to her feet in time before the maid walked in. She curtsied low and said, "Mrs. Fitzharding sent me to help you with your gown."

"I am already dressed. I was merely sorting my things."

"I can unpack your trunks, miss."

"Thank you. Pray, leave the writing desk where it is."

"Very good, miss."

Elizabeth locked the desk and put the key in her dress pocket. She'd only had time to sew one, as opposed to the usual pair, but she only needed the one for now. She shoved the key deep through a small slit in her gown and into the hidden pocket that was tied about her waist. Mary would never notice in any case. And, even if she did, she'd just tut at how unfashionable Elizabeth was with her secrets and be done with it.

With her desk key pressed safely against her hip, Elizabeth left to head downstairs. She could not risk bringing Mrs. Egerton's book around Mary, and she knew the spellworking upon the locket would fade as soon as she walked from the room. She needed to work harder to find a way to have the comfort of an impartial observer to assist her. Else, she'd be left to recount the entire day's events over and over, wasting valuable time.

Also, Elizabeth thought darkly, it was tiresome reliving all of the minor abuses Mary threw her way. It would be nice to simply skip them all and start at the end for a change.

"Elizabeth Knight! What are you wearing? Why, is that not Augusta's old gown for when she was ill? What is the meaning of this? Why are you wearing such an old thing to tea?"

Elizabeth smiled at the gathering, and accepted the offered cup of tea from Thea.

Three thousand pounds.

MR. KNIGHT'S VISIT was cut short after two hours. The coachman feared rain and the rectory lane often flooded, so Mr. Knight took the man's advice and said his goodbyes. With Mr. Knight's subduing influence departed, Mary and Thea began their schemes.

"Now, Theodosia, we must lay out all of your gowns that you brought so that I can help you decide which to wear. I have procured you three invitations to dinner parties, and I have purchased you a ticket to the public ball that is held in the village at the inn."

Thea was all delighted excitement. She begged to bring down her gowns to show Mary, and Mr. Fitzharding laughed and said he didn't mind any parade of silk and lace as long as he was permitted to finish his slice of cake, so Thea rushed off to gather her gowns. While that was happening, Mary began her schedule for Elizabeth.

"Now, we have a new governess, the niece of Mrs. Shipley, a Miss Shipley. She's a very sturdy girl and she lived in France and India most of her life. However, she came back to England because her father is now dead and she's been without a mother since childhood. She will be teaching the children French. However, three children are a lot for her, so if you could assist as much as possible, that would be very helpful."

"Of course, I will speak to Miss Shipley about it."

"No need, I already have laid out an excellent schedule for her to follow."

"My dear Mary," James said through a mouthful of cake, "pray let the governess dictate the children's schedule. After all, she is the expert here."

"There is no point for her to be worn out teaching three children when Elizabeth is right here."

"Elizabeth will be assisting with the ball, do not forget," Mr. Fitzharding said. "We cannot have her doing everything."

Mary's expression clearly said she had no idea why Elizabeth could not do everything, but she acquiesced without much fuss or grumbling. "If you say so, husband. I will be so busy with Theodosia arranging her outfits and taking her about to meet people that I will not be here for the hourly needs of preparing for a ball."

"I would be very happy to organize the servants for you, Mary, while you are out," Elizabeth said.

"If you had married, you could have had a house like this and thrown balls."

"If I did marry well, you would be forced to look after your own children," Elizabeth said and took a sip of her tea.

Mary's cup clattered against its saucer as she stared open-mouthed at her sister. Mr. Fitzharding turned away so that his wife could not see his expression of amusement. Thea had walked into the room just before Elizabeth had spoke, with her armful of gowns, and did not bother to hide her shocked expression.

"Thea! You are going to crease your dresses holding them like that!" Elizabeth and Mary said at the same time. They both glared at each other for daring to interrupt the other while chastising Thea.

Thea dutifully put the gowns down on a chair. "That is everything I have brought."

Mr. Fitzharding leaned over to take a better look. "My dear Miss Thea, are they all new?"

Thea nodded, but then she clarified. "Well, this one here Miss Sims altered from one of Mama's dresses. We decided, us girls, that it was time to pull out Mama's dresses."

"And no one thought to consult me." Mary said it as a statement, not a question.

"Well, Eliza said that..."

Elizabeth interrupted her younger sister before the other unleashed upon her. "I set aside Augusta's mink muff for you, along with the gold watch and chain that her grandfather gave her as a wedding gift. I felt those best suited your tastes, and I recall you, after her death, mentioning your worries about the girls ruining the muff. They are in one of Thea's trunks."

Mary settled into silence at that. She made several critical comments about the dresses, but mostly she found them very acceptable and was pleased by the total cost. "That is an excellent start. This shawl from Aunt Cassandra though. Strawberries? What was she thinking?"

"I love strawberries, they're so pretty," Thea said. "She must have remembered it from a letter I sent Elizabeth when she was visiting in the spring. Mr. Grant said she had two seamstresses working on it non-stop to have it ready in time."

Mary made another disapproving sound. "I would not have thought our aunt would support such frivolities as strawberries."

Elizabeth examined the sweets on offer before deciding to take a macaroon. "I recommend you spend more time with our aunt if you wish to understand what she does and does not support."

"Eliza!" Thea whispered.

Elizabeth grinned at her younger sister and sipped her tea. "What say you, Mr. Fitzharding? What is your position on embroidery and fruit?"

Mr. Fitzharding took one look at the three women staring at him and stood up. "I believe I shall go see what the children are up to."

"Husband, I asked you to stay," Mary said in a whisper. She gave a significant glance at Elizabeth, who pretended not to see it. "Because, I needed your assistance."

"I am quite confident in your ability to be left alone with your sisters without your husband there to hold your hand. The three of you can argue about strawberries and lace until dinner. Elizabeth? Miss Theodosia? Dinner is at five-thirty here at Ashbrook. I believe we are having mutton and pigeon."

At Thea's disappointed expression, Mary said, "Now, dear, we cannot have you wasting away."

"Pray, tell me, James. Will there be anything for Thea to eat at table? I do worry for her," Elizabeth said.

"Do not worry about such things. I have instructed cook to provide all of the best foods Ashbrook can provide. We have pigeons shot here right on the estate, mutton, tongue, pickled herring, potted lobster...Trust me, it will be an excellent table and especially for you. Why, look at you! You are so thin. No one will think you are a young lady if you do not put some meat upon your bones."

"I don't eat those things," Thea whispered.

"Foolishness. You will absolutely change your mind once you see it upon the table, and I can promise you that..."

"Mr. Fitzharding? James. Please, can you speak to the cook? Thea will need something to eat, lest she live off cake and buns."

"That is not his role," Mary said. "Husbands do not speak to the cook."

"I did before I married you, Mary," James said with a laugh. "Otherwise, I would have starved to death!"

Despite her discomfort, Thea snorted audibly and then followed up with a giggle at her mishap.

"Theodosia! Cover your mouth when you laugh. Goodness, you look like Jezebel with your teeth showing."

"And with that, I shall take my leave." Mr. Fitzharding didn't leave without taking another piece of plum cake. Then he and his cake left the room for the privacy of somewhere else that did not have two warring sisters.

At Thea's downcast expression, Mary sighed and said, "I shall speak to cook and ask her to make you something. Would an omelette and an herb pie be acceptable?"

"Very much, Mary. Thank you," Thea said, brightening.

Elizabeth gave Mary an, "I told you so" look, which only soured Mary's own expression.

"I shall take you to Ashbrook town tomorrow. They always have a small selection of ready-made clothes at the shop there. It's a little out of fashion, but his wife and eldest daughter do the repairs and updates. With modest adjustments, we can get you at least another gown or two with very little expense. And another spencer. Two is simply not enough for a young lady coming out. And perhaps they will have an excellent pelisse. Something made of silk for the summer months."

"I thank you, Mary, but I do not have any money left."

"Place it on my accounts," Mr. Fitzharding shouted from the next room.

Elizabeth laughed and said, "Mr. Fitzharding! Are you spying upon your wife?"

"No, my sister, I was not. I dropped my cake and was attempting to pick it up before Rocky gobbled it. But alas."

"Husband! Do not feed my dog cake!"

"My dear, do not berate me for how quickly your dog moves when there is cake upon the floor."

"That man is going to kill my dog, I swear it." Mary sighed. "Please step back into the drawing room, sir. I do not wish to shout between rooms like common servants."

Mr. Fitzharding poked his head back in through the door. "As you command, my wife."

Mary took a steadying breath. "We do not need to pay for the gowns, even if we can afford it with little notice whatsoever. However, my father said to rely upon Elizabeth for whatever trifling things Thea needs."

"No, Mary. The purchases will be upon my accounts and mine alone."

"But, sir, my father says..."

"It pains me to say this in front of your sisters, but you are Mary Fitzharding now, and not Mary Knight. I am the head of this household, at least for the present and as long as my health remains. So, while I go on as the head of Ashbrook, my word is final. Miss Theodosia, you are now in charge of ensuring all purchases are placed upon my accounts when you are at the shops. I trust you will be firm with your elder sister?"

"Thank you, Mr. Fitzharding."

"You are my sister! You must call me James."

"Sorry, right, I forgot. Mr. James, sir," she said with a big grin.

Mr. Fitzharding pondered on the name before nodding. "Miss Thea and Mr. James. Yes, I approve of this. Oh, do not scowl at me, Mary. I am unmoved. Now, I am stealing two pieces of cake because Rocky has stolen my one and I need another to fend him off."

"Husband, you are taking the last pieces of plum cake!"

"I am certain there is more cake somewhere in this house," Mr. Fitzharding said. "Ladies, pray attend. I only have ten thousand pounds per annum and I have an expensive wife to maintain. Kindly do not bankrupt me this week. The local town depends quite handsomely on my solvency, I assure you."

"Expensive wife," Mary muttered. "There are days I wonder why I married."

"I heard that, Mary Fitzharding."

"It is unchristian to eavesdrop, sir," Mary shot back.

Elizabeth took a long sip of her tea lest she enrage her sister with her smirk. Mr. Fitzharding and Mary were not well matched. If anything, he was more suited to her own temperament. However, the shocking age difference had made him ineligible in her eyes. And, he did always prefer Mary. Even now, after three children and her excessive expectations. He clearly still preferred her.

It made Elizabeth happy for her sister, but also sad for herself. She was always most lonely when she was around happy people.

"Does it not bother you to take money from my husband when you have your own riches?"

Elizabeth smiled at her sister. "I am not properly prepared for expenditures, as I had assumed I would be very busy with the servants."

Elizabeth felt the sting of telling her sister a lie, as she had all her money with her. Obviously, money could not be trusted at home. She did not trust either her father or Georgiana anywhere near her writing desk and any of the money within. And her father was not stupid. He might miss the back concealed compartment, especially since Miss Thorne's puzzle box provided an excellent distraction. However, her puzzle box contained enough money to fit her father up with a hired carriage at least once a week as he travelled to visit Mary and back. She would rather he not do that with her inheritance.

"How much money did you bring with you?"

Elizabeth did not wish to lie to her sister, but there was also no way she was going to answer that question directly.

"I have enough to cover my tips to my maid, to pay for the hairdresser for the ball, and a little extra to cover the odd expenses that spring up the night before a ball. I also have a small sum for gifts for the children, which I had hoped to task Thea with purchasing for me."

"You did not bring the children gifts with you? They will be very disappointed."

Elizabeth kept her serene countenance enough to say, "I did not have the time. I've had a great many things to do."

"What could you possibly have to do?" Mary asked.

"She was helping sew my dresses, Mary," Thea said. She held up the yellow silk gown. "Now, what do you think of this one?"

"It's lovely, and a good colour for your hair. Now, why was Elizabeth sewing when Miss Sims was there?"

Elizabeth went to answer but Thea let out a dramatic sigh and interrupted. "Miss Sims' eyesight is really bad. Everyone knows that, Mary. We needed one of her nieces to help in the kitchen because our cook is sick, and we don't have any servants living in the house now because she's gone, so we have two girls working in the kitchen. Now, I want to talk about my gown."

"Theodosia, watch your tone," Mary said.

Elizabeth raised an eyebrow at Thea who rolled her eyes. "I believe Thea does not wish to be in the middle of your criticisms of myself. Perhaps you could save those for when we are in private."

Thea spoke over Mary's rebuttals. "Mary, look! Isn't this dress lovely? Miss Sims made it in a similar style to Mrs. Thorne's new ballgown for London balls. I am thinner than Mrs. Thorne, so she cut the line in a different style so that it would hang better, but I think it's still excellent."

"It has short sleeves. I believe all of the fashionable people in town are wearing sleeves this season." Mary glanced at Elizabeth. "You'll be fashionable for once."

Thea cut in before Elizabeth could make her own remark. "Miss Sims mentioned that, but I prefer short sleeves, so I shall simply wear long gloves. Oh! And the shawl Mrs. Spencer gave me suits all of my everyday gowns, so that is perfect because I love the shawl so much."

Thea wrapped the strawberry-embroidered shawl about her shoulders and posed as if for a painting. "It is the most beautiful thing I have ever owned. I shall have to write to her soon to thank her."

"Thea!" Elizabeth exclaimed. "You have not written to her?"

"I wrote her a hasty note and gave it to Mr. Grant I assure you. I am not that heedless," Thea said. Then, a little more slyly, she said, "I just thought Mrs. Spencer would like to hear about me wearing it visiting and any compliments it receives, for I am certain it shall receive many. The embroidery work alone is the best I have ever seen. Don't you think, Mary? Even you cannot deny how extraordinary the work is."

"I cannot believe my aunt got you fruit, of all things." Mary shook her head.

"Our aunt wished to give Thea a gift that she would love, as opposed to something that my aunt wished for herself."

"Yes, Eliza, I understand how gift giving works," Mary said. "Now, I must say you did very well for only twelve pounds. That is a very good start indeed. Now, with Elizabeth's five pounds, we can..."

Elizabeth opened her mouth to protest, but Thea interrupted her. "I hate to contradict you, Mary, but I will not be spending Elizabeth's money. Mr. James said we were to charge our purchases to his accounts and I promised him most faithfully. I cannot go back on my word now. It would be unchristian of me."

Elizabeth turned her head away to hide her smirk. She picked up another macaroon. If this continued, she would not have room for dinner.

"I am too excited to argue with you, Theodosia. Though, I see Elizabeth has been a bad influence," Mary said.

Elizabeth said nothing, taking the opportunity to nibble at yet another sweet. "The macaroons are always exceptional here, Mary. Mrs. Cook never makes them because my aunt doesn't like them, so I rarely have the opportunity to eat them unless I come to Ashbrook. This is probably my favourite thing about coming here."

"Indeed, the macaroons? Pray, not my children? You are the most ungrateful—"

Thea dramatically sighed. "Mary, please. We have only just arrived. Now, why are you saying this is a good start? Is this not good enough? It was all we could afford but I believe Miss Sims did an excellent job making use of what we could purchase. And I love what she and Isabella did with Mama's dresses. I am very proud of her work."

There was hurt in Thea's voice that pained Elizabeth.

Mary made a dismissive gesture in the air. "My dear, I was not criticizing Miss Sims' skill. I would never stoop to such a thing. Indeed, Miss Sims is an excellent country seamstress. No, my objections are only for that I wish you to have more. After all, you are the sister of Mrs. Fitzharding and, with that, comes a responsibility to look a certain way."

"Mary, pray, don't scare the poor girl," Elizabeth chided. "Look at her. She's stone white now. She thinks you hate her gowns."

"I am not attempting to scare her, and her gowns are excellent. I've said so several times now. I only wish...what...why do you have string in your hair?"

Elizabeth sighed. She had hoped to tell Mary about it out of Thea's hearing so that she could bear the brunt of her critical eye. "There was a mishap and this is how we have repaired it until either Thea grows tired of it or the hair itself grows."

"At least a quarter of her hair was cut!" Mary exclaimed. "What happened?"

"It doesn't matter," Thea said. "Mary, please. I want to talk about my dresses."

Thankfully, they were interrupted by little children. They assaulted Elizabeth first by climbing over her lap and causing her to spill her tea. Thankfully, it was not scalding and Elizabeth only yelped from the surprise.

"Children!" Mary said. "Boys! You should be ashamed of yourselves for climbing over Aunt Elizabeth like that. And Lucy, that is not very ladylike, to be running with your brothers and jumping on people! Where are your manners?" Mary demanded.

The children protested that they wanted to know what gifts their aunt purchased them. Mary declared, "She brought you nothing because you are all horrible children. Now Miss Lucy. You have ruined Aunt Elizabeth's gown and she cannot simply afford new clothes whenever she wishes. She is not like us."

Elizabeth accepted a handkerchief from the footman who'd been standing by the doorway and he helped her to her feet. Tea ran down her legs but her shift and dress absorbed most of it, so she only left small drops on the floor. The sofa underneath her was not wet, thankfully. However, her dress was soaked through.

"I shall have to change my gown," Elizabeth announced. She did not bring quite enough to be changing several times a day for washing.

"Matthew, please inform Emma she is needed in Miss Knight's room to help her with her gown. We shall need that cleaned immediately or we shall never get the tea stains out. At least it is dark wool, but even so."

"Oh, please do not send this to the laundry for my sake," Elizabeth said. "I am certain it shall be fine."

Mary gave Elizabeth a smug look. "We have our own laundry maid living with us, Elizabeth."

Leave it to Mary to remind Elizabeth of the difference in their financial positions. No wonder their poor father was obsessed with things like a carriage; he wasn't attempting to keep up with his neighbours. He was attempting to keep up with his own daughter.

It was a brief moment, but Elizabeth felt sadness for her father.

"Now, Thea, I shall call my maid at once. Your hair simply looks a state and we need to hide that…whatever has happened to you before anyone sees it."

Chapter 14

THE LETTERS ARRIVED early the next morning, providing Elizabeth with something to do before breakfast that was not assisting with either child rearing or ball planning. The first letter was surprisingly from Charles, which had been sent directly there.

My dear sister,

Our father tells me you are leaving for Ashbrook soon, so I write to you directly there in hopes you can assist me with a small problem. I understand you and the girls have been sorting through my mother's things. Proper job of it, as I hear, and I am not complaining that you have done it without me at home. I certainly would not wish to touch her things, nor would I know what to do. However, there is something I had been meaning to ask, but was waiting for Mary to speak up. As she has not, I feel I must before my plans go awry.

There is a particular ring of my mother's that you will know as I describe it. It is a gold band with four pretty little white pearls in a cross, with the tiniest little red stones about the pearls. The band was very plain and fine. I would greatly wish to have this ring to save for my future wife. Now, do not excite yourself as ladies are so wont to do; I have no designs on any young woman at present. However, my mother often spoke of that being her grandmother's engagement gift and it has been passed down through the family. I would very much like to continue the tradition.

I have not spoken to anyone else in the family because I knew you would alone be discreet about the purpose. Truly, I do not have designs upon marriage at present. However, as Augusta's only son, I feel the ring should come to me. If necessary, please speak to the girls about it.

Sincerely,
Charles

"Shall you honour his request?" Mrs. Egerton asked. She was not manifested, but Elizabeth had reworked the spell as she did each morning so that the ghost could converse with her.

Elizabeth thought on the question. "Mary has not requested it, who was the most likely of us for it to suit, so I do believe the rightful owner should be Charles. However, I do worry about the temptation of such a jewel. What can be done? Ah, I believe I know the best approach. Mrs. Egerton, I do believe my father is right."

"Right, my dear?"

"Yes, right that the occult has been a very bad influence upon me."

Dearest Papa,

We are settled well at Ashbrook and Mary is threatening to empty all of the shops about the local town for every trifle she perceives Theodosia needs. I send you this warning now for when Theodosia return to Bryden with several new trunks. Mary asks that you not purchase a new hat; she said there is an excellent tricorn hat in just your style in the local shop that she plans to purchase for you, as she believes it will be a tolerable fit.

Now, I must get to the true purpose of this letter, as I am in need of your assistance. There is a ring of Augusta's that you will recall as soon as I describe it. It was her own grandmother's engagement gift ring—the one with the pearls and tiny red stones on a gold band.

Charles has written to me, requesting that it be set aside for when he marries. Now, pray, do not excite yourself with notions of Charles having a woman already in mind. He assures me this is merely a measure of good planning and nothing more. I have considered the request and I do feel that Augusta would have wanted Charles to have the ring for his future wife.

However, to the point of the matter. I worry about the delicate nature of the ring. Charles does not have the benefit of much space while at Oxford, and I worry that he will be forced to move from house to house as he searches for a stable curacy after his ordination. I fear, in fact, that it would risk theft by a gamester or another nefarious individual who might chance view a sight of it and find some manner to take it from Charles, either by trickery or outright housebreaking.

I know my worries are most likely just the normal worries of a young woman, but I would be much calmer if you took charge of the ring. Your desk can be locked from servants and labourers, and no gamesters are in our home to be tempted. This would give me great comfort to know Augusta's ring is safe and that her family tradition can carry on to the next generation when Charles marries.

I hope I am not being too bold, Papa, in making this request. I feel that, as the eldest child, this is my duty to ensure such matters are looked after. Also, I do not wish you to think I worry Charles would purposely lose the ring. It is merely that I know such items can prove too large of a *temptation to many a person. Also, I worry that Charles has enough upon his shoulders, both with his studies and being the only boy to carry all of the family's hopes, that having to also care for a ring of immense family value would be just added worries.*

Also, there is the general disposition of the ring itself. It is very delicate and small, if you recollect. I do fear it will not withstand being knocked about as Charles moves from lodgings to lodgings. Heavens! What if it were to fall out of a trunk and be lost?

What is your opinion on the matter? If you feel I am too hasty, perhaps we should allow the ring to go to Charles at Oxford where he can take charge of it. If you feel I am being prudent, the ring is in the large trunk of Augusta's that I had placed in the upper drawing room. Inside you will find a small wooden box, well sanded, with the letters AL etched into the top. I believe the box itself should go to Charles, as that is how the ring was presented to Augusta upon her engagement.

After Elizabeth read the letter aloud to Mrs. Egerton, the ghost said, "My dear Miss Knight, that is rather sneaky of you."

"Would you have preferred I have the ring sent to Charles so that he could lose it at the gambling table?"

"Oh, I believe you did the correct action. However, it is more devious than I had thought you capable."

Elizabeth chuckled as she sealed the letter. "I know my father, Mrs. Egerton. This will allow him to claim the credit, as I requested his opinion. Most likely, he will write Charles directly informing him of his grave and important decision. Charles will have nothing more to say on the subject, as not even the only son has that much sway in our home. Charles may suspect me and I shall receive one, perhaps two, irate letters. Then, it will be at an end since there is nothing else to be done."

She placed the addressed letter on its plate for the servant to take later. "I must confess that I did not like Augusta, but she was his mother. I will not allow her family heirloom to be lost through foolishness or heedlessness. My father refuses to see Charles for who he truly is, and I cannot unsee that knowledge. All I can do is remove as much temptation as possible. Perhaps with time in the world, he shall become the man his father thinks he already is."

"Do you believe he would gamble away his dead mother's ring?"

"I believe that a night of drinking and gaming has led many a man to do things he regrets in the sobriety of daylight," Elizabeth said. "I will not be a party to temptation for anyone, least of all my own brother. He might not respect me, but I will not reduce myself to his level."

Since her next letter was from the Ladies Occult Society in London, Elizabeth summoned Mrs. Egerton fully to better allow her to read the news itself.

My dearest Elizabeth,

We have been pondering your locket questions and it occurred to us that you would not have had enough thyme to do the working as many times as your last letter intimated, which lead us to consider that you would have used some from your own garden. We are both in agreement that we caused an issue of too many occultists in the kitchen, if you wish. We should have not purified the items for you, as you were the one to do the spellworking yourself. Indeed, we feel that is why your own working became stronger with each attempt, as you were having to purify and gather items yourself.

Would you consider purifying the locket and then retrying the spell? We hope that the removal of our own interference will assist your work further.

We have also received a letter from Miss Keats only this morning! She appears positively delightful, and we have sent her several pages of notes and issues we are having. I have taken the liberty to inquire about her family and have determined she is an unmarried woman of about thirty-five or so, with little inheritance to speak of and

177

totally under the control of her brother. I was fearful that our letters would overwhelm her family's good will. I have placed a shilling under her seal to help pay for the letters. Might I be so bold as to suggest you do the same? If you cannot, of course, do not think of it. I can happily take it upon myself.

I have included two spellworkings that we know will fail for Miss Gibbs, as we are still researching and studying how best to summon her. However, our hope is that you or Mrs. Egerton can see any flaws in this initial draft. That might give us a hint on how to proceed. Of course, try it. Who knows? Perhaps you may summon her on the first attempt. Wouldn't that be jolly?

Good luck at your sister's house. I hope Miss Thea enjoyed her shawl and it is silly enough for her tastes. Oh, Mrs. Spencer is giving me that look as I read out that last sentence aloud. Apparently, she believes me and Susan young ladies, too! Ha! We are nearly to where we need reading glasses, an imperious white hair cap, and a cane to thwack youngsters upon the shins when they get too rambunctious.

Pray write if you require anything from town. I am growing bored of the same shops, and long for some adventure. However, Susan (of which does not see this part of the letter) only wishes to spend her time at the Osborne bookshop. I believe love is in the air. If I do not have that girl married by Christmas, I shall be extremely disappointed.

Elizabeth laughed at her letter. "I would never have taken Alice as a romantic gossip, but I must learn not prejudge people."

"Is Mr. Osborne a good match for Miss Susan?"

"Oh, indeed. He comes from a very established family in trade, by way of a family grocer business. Mr. Osborne has turned his inheritance into a publishing business and bookstore. His mother helps with the running of the occult store, and they are well respected in the community. Indeed, I would not be surprised if he took an estate once he married and settled into a gentleman's life."

"That is great promise then," Mrs. Egerton said. "Miss Susan comes from more modest roots, though, does she not?"

"Indeed. Mostly servant class. Her parents did not have other children and so could afford to educate Susan and properly so. They saw education as the only means for her to rise to a better life."

"If she married her Mr. Osborne, she would still be a shopkeeper's wife," Mrs. Egerton said. "She would still be in the same class."

"A shopkeeper who is rumoured to make two thousand pounds a year, Mrs. Egerton." Elizabeth smiled.

"Two thousand pounds!"

"That is the rumour. I do not know the truth of it, of course, but he leads a noticeably more comfortable life than my father. And, I can see him being very smart to set aside savings. He lives very modesty, all things considered, when you look at Mary and you see the style in which she lives. Mr. Osborne, with luck and care, may indeed afford an estate for himself in his lifetime. To purchase outright, I mean. Not simply to lease."

"Do you think he'd marry her, then? Since she brings nothing to the table."

Elizabeth shrugged. "Another man, I would doubt it, but he seems very independent in his decisions. If he loved her, I suspect he would marry her and not give a fig what others thought."

"Miss Thorne would be an excellent match for him," Mrs. Egerton said. "Alas, she does not seem interested in marriage. What is it with young ladies these days?"

"There are not enough handsome, rich young men for us to marry, and we are all too polite to fight over them," Elizabeth said. "Now, shall we get started on attempting to see if you can spy upon the household in my locket?"

ELIZABETH SET OUT the items upon her writing desk, as there was no proper table of size in the room and she did not want Mary to catch her kneeling upon the floor. She went through the steps of the letter carefully. First, she removed all of the items in the locket and then purified each individual one, reciting the incantation words that the ladies had found in one of the basic books by Mrs. Egerton's society.

Then, Elizabeth worked through the necessary steps for each individual item, placing each back into the locket as she spoke the words of incantation that should bind Mrs. Egerton's essence when called upon.

Finally, she slipped the locket's glass back in place, repeating the entire process again. Then, when all items were in place, she did the spellworking that combined Mrs. Egerton's summoning with one to move her to the locket.

Mrs. Egerton disappeared from sight. Elizabeth hated each time that happened, for she feared the loss of the ghost. However, she also knew that the ghost had previously simply returned to her book when the working had failed, so she trusted Mrs. Egerton's wisdom on that score.

She left the ghost book in her bedchamber and made the walk down to the breakfast table. She was wearing her loose blue dress with a shawl, perfect for quiet meals at home. She entered the drawing room, where Mary always took breakfast. There was no one there, but the food was laid out on a sideboard.

She turned to the footman, Matthew, and asked, "Has everyone already eaten?"

The footman bowed and said, "Mrs. Fitzharding suffers a head pain this morning. I have been commanded to tell you and your sister to enjoy breakfast at your leisure and to not wait upon ceremony. Your youngest sister has yet to come down for breakfast."

Elizabeth thanked the servant and took a plate to help herself. Breakfasts at Ashbrook were always excellent, and they were about the only thing she looked forward to in her visits. They were casual affairs, as well, which was surprising given Mary had grown up with the more formal breakfasts of the rectory. However, perhaps it was the influence of Mr. Fitzharding there, encouraging her to be comfortable and relaxed for a quiet hour at home.

She helped herself to hot chocolate first, since the rectory did not have it now that Augusta was gone. Elizabeth was occasionally tempted to purchase some for the rectory, but she'd always worried her father would see it as an invitation for her to purchase it all of the time. At too many shillings per pound, she would soon be bankrupt if she were required to keep their entire household in chocolate, as she suspected G and Thea would happily drink a pot between them every morning.

Fortified with a sip from her small cup of hot delight, Elizabeth examined the rest of the offerings. This morning there was pound cake and plum cake, of which she took a slice from both. Of the cold and hot rolls, she decided to take a hot roll and added a little butter and jam to its middle. The brioche had a significant slice already missing, and she helped herself to one of the cut smaller pieces. There was regular milk for the tea and coffee, but also milk fortified with egg. That was a favourite of Mr. Fitzharding's, and Elizabeth found it was a welcomed addition the mornings she did not have much of an appetite. However, this was not that morning.

On the contrary, she found herself quite ravenous, so she helped herself to a boiled egg, ham, and snatched a strawberry from the fruit tower displaying Mary's hothouse offerings.

She sat down at the small table with her plate and cup, ready to tuck into a delightful meal, when Mr. Fitzharding walked in.

He was still in his dressing gown and was wearing his shirt and trousers from the previous night, though missing the cravat, jacket, and boots. He was smiling when he said, "I see you have found the food."

"Indeed, I have. And what an impressive display. I was just thinking to myself, in fact, I should have cold meat served at our own breakfast table more often. I believe it would sustain our father. He's been growing weary in the afternoons lately."

"Indeed, has he?" Mr. Fitzharding poured himself a cup of coffee and topped it up with the fortified milk. Then, he procured himself a plate to hold two cold rolls and a slice of ham. "Should we be concerned?"

"Oh, do not mention it to Mary, as it would only worry her. You know how she can be sometimes. I have merely noticed that he is not as robust after about two in the afternoon as he once was. He refuses to take much more than a small piece of ham before going out to visit in the parish. I have wondered if a heartier breakfast would do him good. What is your opinion on the matter?"

"Oh, I highly recommend it. How old is your father now?"

"He is fifty-five, sir," Elizabeth said.

"Now, see? Only three years older than myself. So, as an expert on being an old man," he chuckled when he said that, "I confess to you now, Elizabeth, that I have never felt younger than once I switched to eating a hearty breakfast. Mary prefers a light meal in the morning and then to have the same meal all over again at...oh what are the ladies calling it now? Luncheon? Noncheon? Some foolishness. Then, she eats a proper dinner and another proper supper."

"And you do not approve?" Elizabeth asked.

"I cannot eat a heavy supper now, for the burning sensation in my chest and throat is too much to bear. There are times I have had to sleep sitting up in my chair in front of the fire, and I am too old for that."

"Nonsense, I say! You are still very young. Look how robust you look this morning."

Mr. Fitzharding gestured at the spread of food. "It is the breakfast, I assure you. With your permission, I shall write to your father. I wished to discuss his plans for his new property in any case. However, I will make a quiet note about how you mentioned breakfasts are quite different at the rectory and I shall recommend cold pork and chicken in the morning for his own health. Would saying it help Mrs. Knight be of use?"

Elizabeth smiled and continued to smile until the first uncharitable comment left her mind. "If saying it is for Isabella's sake, then he would only make her follow your instructions. However, if you recommend it for him, it would be available for everyone else to try themselves."

"I take your meaning," Mr. Fitzharding said. He stood back up and said, "Well, I should bring my wife a little something to eat so that she feels well enough for visitors today."

"Oh, is she expecting someone? Mrs. Batstone perhaps? I did not see her on my last visit."

Mr. Fitzharding tapped his finger to his nose. "I am sworn to secrecy, I fear."

After Mr. Fitzharding left with a plate of food for his wife, Elizabeth went back to her own bedchamber. There, she summoned Mrs. Egerton. "Well?"

"Mr. Fitzharding is a very perplexing gentleman," Mrs. Egerton said. "He seems an excellent man, but how good is his judgment if he is married to such a woman?"

Elizabeth laughed, joyous that the work of the Ladies Occult Society had been a success.

~ Chapter 15 ~

ELIZABETH CALLED ON Betty, the upper chamber maid, to help lace up her stays. Betty helped Elizabeth into a comfortable white dress, and then the maid folded the blue dress carefully to be worn again the following morning at breakfast. Mary was still in bed with Thea now sitting with her, so Elizabeth took the opportunity to test the range on Mrs. Egerton's locket.

Elizabeth confirmed she could make it to the hothouse doors, but no further beyond inside. However, as nothing ever happened in the hothouse, Elizabeth was not bothered by this. The far more pressing concern was the ballroom, where Mrs. Egerton confirmed she could view in its entirety. The ghost expressed great excitement about seeing the changes in dance styles since her youthful days at a ball.

After spending most of the morning rambling about Ashbrook's gardens, Elizabeth returned to the drawing room to quietly work on a tiny dress for a doll. Soon, Mary arrived and joined her, along with Thea who was wearing one of her new dresses.

"Is that Mary's necklace?" Elizabeth asked.

"Indeed it is," Thea said. "I could never afford anything like it. What do you think?"

"It's a touch showy for the morning, is it not?" Elizabeth asked.

Thea rolled her eyes in that dramatic way that only young ladies could manage. "I am wearing my neckerchief."

"Yes, it's so thin I can see the necklace underneath it," Elizabeth said with a grin. Hers was not much thicker, but she had the addition of her muslin shawl if she felt the least immodest.

"Elizabeth, you are acting like an old maid," Mary said. "There is nothing improper about how she's dressed. Goodness, you have become rather prudish in your old age."

"Yes, I'm practically in the grave," Elizabeth said.

There was a commotion beyond the room to interrupt the sisterly harmony and Mary announced, "Oh! That must be him."

She didn't explain herself. Instead, she stuffed Thea's work back into the basket by the sofa. Elizabeth was too far away to easily snatch at, but Mary admonished her to hide her work. "Put that away, Elizabeth! We can't have him see you working."

"Him who, Mary? I have nearly finished this for Lucy and I'd made a promise." Elizabeth sewed several more backstitches into the blue garment. "I wish to make use of the light in this room before the sun moves behind the hothouse and I cannot see as well."

Footsteps sounded beyond. Elizabeth made no move to stop her sewing.

"He's here!" Mary exclaimed. "Elizabeth Knight, have you no compassion for what I wish?"

"Who is here?" Thea asked.

"I am certain whoever it is I have met them before and, therefore, will be completely understanding of me finishing a gown for Lucy's doll."

To Thea, Mary said, "It is such a surprise."

To Elizabeth, Mary said, "I should not have expected more, I dare say."

There was something in Mary's voice that Elizabeth did not like. A smugness, perhaps, that it announced satisfaction at knowing something Elizabeth did not. Elizabeth had no illusions that her father did not have favourites amongst his children, and she knew he told Mary and Charles far more than he told her.

"Well, do you not wish to know who it is?" Mary demanded. In a lowered voice, Elizabeth said, "By the sound of the boots upon the floor, I suspect I shall know within seconds."

She would not give Mary the satisfaction of seeing her interest in what was happening or who was arriving.

A rather handsome man walked into the room and bowed deeply. Elizabeth stood, amused at how quickly Thea rose to her feet at the sight of the man.

"Mr. Sinclair, ma'am," the footman announced.

Mary gave him a wide smile and said, "Welcome! Allow me to introduce to you two of my sisters. This is Miss Knight, my eldest sister, and one of my younger sisters, Miss Theodosia Knight. Girls, this is Mr. Sidney Sinclair."

Elizabeth had stood as soon as Mary did, and she bowed graciously at the stranger. She then sat back down a second before Mary, garnering a displeased sideways glance. "It is very good to meet you, Mr. Sinclair. Are you new to the area?"

Mr. Sinclair sat down on the far end of the sofa where Elizabeth was currently seated. "Indeed, I am, though I am only passing through for a few weeks before I arrive at the parsonage. Oh, did I interrupt your work, Miss Knight?"

Elizabeth showed Mr. Sinclair the dress. "It is for Lucy's doll. I promised her a proper ballgown for the toy, so you find me employed in my duty as an aunt."

"Then, pray, continue your work! You ladies can all sew and talk at the same time. I know my own sisters can, and I have no reason to believe you cannot."

Elizabeth smiled at him and asked, "You said you were arriving at a parsonage. Will you be taking up the curacy here in Ashbrook? I heard old Mr. Gardner was considering taking someone on."

"Oh, no. Though, I had heard of that news, as well. No, indeed. I will be taking up residency at Deane House, in Bryden."

Elizabeth stared at him. "Deane House? Why, that's for the curate for Bryden. Surely you must be mistaken. Our father is the rector there, you see, and..."

"There is no mistake," Mary said with no lack of triumphant glee. "That is the great surprise. Our father has employed a curate! Isn't it wonderful?"

ELIZABETH STARED AT her sister in sickening horror. This would be coming out of her reticule. Of course, it already had. The curacy position paid fifty pounds a year, and had been the reason her father had resisted the assistance of one in the past. Her father had managed to claw back thirty pounds from her purse. He had already slyly passed on some of Thea and G's expenses to her.

He'd said it was all for Isabella's nurse. She'd gone along with it all because it was for Isabella's nurse.

But no nurse had yet arrived. There had been plenty of talk, of course, but no such woman had yet moved into the rectory. It had all been for this upstart gentleman, with expensive boots well beyond his station.

"Why, Miss Knight, are you well?" Mr. Sinclair asked.

"Eliza, you've gone rather pale," Thea said.

"A curate?" Elizabeth managed to say.

"Yes, indeed!" Mr. Sinclair said. He attempted a cheerful demeanour, but each glance at Elizabeth showed great concern laced with confusion.

Mary made a laugh that sounded cruel somehow. "Oh, do not mind my eldest sister. Elizabeth loathes surprises. However, as my dear Theodosia loves them, I wagered Elizabeth would be very happy to endure this one so long as it made one of her sisters happy."

Elizabeth relaxed her clenching jaw so that she could offer a demure smile. Thankfully, she needed to make no reply, as Thea allowed her natural curiosity to take over.

"We had no idea! When are you to start? How long have you known?"

"I reached an agreement with Mr. Knight about a fortnight ago," Mr. Sinclair said. He glanced at Elizabeth and gave her an uneasy smile.

There was a significant amount of smiling happening in the room. Elizabeth added to it and asked, "And when do you arrive?"

"I take possession at the end of the month. Mrs. Fitzharding was very good to issue me an invitation to the ball. I shall leave for the parsonage that Saturday."

"The drawing room chimney smokes," Elizabeth said flatly. "My father lived there before moving into the rectory. He often mentions it. There are most likely birds' nests in the chimney, too."

"I have already sent my housekeeper and manservant to get the house ready for me," he said. At Elizabeth's surprised expression, one she could not hide, he said, "They are from my home in Bath. They will be moving to Bryden with me. It will be quite a change for them, but they requested to be allowed to make the move, and good servants are difficult to find, as my mother is fond of saying."

Elizabeth wondered how a man living off fifty pounds a year could afford two servants living with him, when Thea interrupted her thoughts with, "Bath? You live in Bath?"

"Indeed! I am one of the rare people who hail from Bath by birth, as opposed to for the social scene," Mr. Sinclair said. "My parents own a substantial property there and, as I am one of many sons, I went into the church. However, it seems that there are too many rectors already in England and, thus, I am to be a mere curate. I could have gone to the north of England, but I wished to remain closer to London and all of my friends."

"And where do you stay while in the neighbourhood?" Elizabeth asked. She attempted as much politeness as possible.

"My aunt is Mrs. Andrews of Baker House. Do you know her?" Mr. Sinclair asked.

Mary interrupted Elizabeth. "Thea is just out in society, but I assure you, my dear sister, Mrs. Andrews is an excellent woman of the highest order."

Elizabeth found Mrs. Andrews to be a snobbish bore who offered no conversation beyond polite chitchat concerning the state of her children, her roses, and her husband's gout.

"Isn't she, Elizabeth?" Mary asked.

"She's very elegant," Elizabeth said dryly. To Mr. Sinclair, she said, "So, you will be working with my father as curate?"

"Indeed. Pray, did you have not a hint of it? I feel that I am imposing this news upon you, but your father said in his last letter that his eldest daughter was very excited about the news." Mr. Sinclair looked between the Knight ladies. "Just to clarify, Miss Knight you are the eldest, correct? And not Mrs. Fitzharding?"

Elizabeth clenched her jaw until she was certain the first hot reply that came to her mind would not be said aloud. When the moment passed, she gave Mr. Sinclair a smile and said, "My father occasionally forgets that the rules of precedence does not change actual birth dates."

With that, Elizabeth picked up her work to finish Lucy's gift.

"Elizabeth, for the love of God, put that down. We have a guest," Mary said. She offered Mr. Sinclair a beatific smile, before turning a scowl back to her sister. "Mr. Sinclair does not need to see a lady at work."

Elizabeth did not look up from her work. "As I said to you, I require the light to finish this gown for Lucy, which I promised to give to her before dinner. I shall not be tardy in my commitment, and I am certain Mr. Sinclair will back me up that a promise broken is a sin."

"Well...I..." Mr. Sinclair said.

"And, as Mr. Sinclair shall be frequently at the rectory here soon enough, he must see for himself the industry that will be taking place most days at Bryden Rectory."

Mr. Sinclair chuckled nervously. "There must be a great amount of sewing and mending in a house of...how many girls is it again?"

Mary interrupted Thea. "There is also Charles, but he is away at Oxford. He is also assisting a friend of our father's there, as well, so that he can pay for most of his way. My husband, of course, offered his assistance, but Charles wished to earn some of his keep. However, between our father's help and my dear husband's generous assistance, Charles wants for nothing."

"Why did he put it off so long?" Mr. Sinclair laughed. "I suppose, it's for the best, though, or I'd have lost my position."

Mary laughed along with him and said something about young men being of minds of their own. Elizabeth, however, offered a more reasonable explanation. "Our brother took ill with a serious infection nearly two years ago. With God's grace, he recovered, but the illness sapped his strength for some time. It was many months before he was strong enough to resume his studies, as there was always the fear of a recurrence of illness especially when one is weakened. It was my father's hope that Charles will take over the curacy here at Ashbrook, when he receives his ordination next Easter."

"Ah! That explains much," Mr. Sinclair said. "When I inquired into the curacy vacancies in this neighbourhood, Mr. Fitzharding said unfortunately they were all taken or promised. Yet, I had seen no evidence of any such curate and was concerned I was being politely shuffled off elsewhere."

Mr. Sinclair leaned forward toward Elizabeth and said, "However, to tell the truth of it, I would not want to live so close to my aunt for any longer than necessary."

"Sidney Sinclair!" Mary exclaimed.

Elizabeth forced a small coughing fit in hopes of covering up the snort that escaped her. Since her marriage, Mary turned overnight into an elderly matron who felt obliged to use the Christian name of anyone under the age of fifty if they acted a hair's length beyond propriety's rules.

"Oh, quit coughing, Eliza. We all know the snort came from you."

Elizabeth glanced a little guiltily at Mr. Sinclair. "Mary, Mr. Sinclair will learn soon enough the high spirits of the rectory, and I should not like to give him false hope that it will be a place of high decorum."

Mary sighed. "It would be if you took your task as eldest daughter seriously."

Elizabeth accepted a cup of tea from Thea and winked. "My dear Mary, I thought you were the eldest daughter now. It's so hard to keep these things straight. Now, Mr. Sinclair, I see you trying to hide your laughter behind your cup. There is no need. I promise to behave from this point forward, lest I aggravate my sister so severely that she develops one of her headaches."

"Have you tried plain coffee and cold mutton for your headaches?" Mr. Sinclair asked.

"Plain coffee?" Elizabeth and Mary asked at the same time.

"Indeed. My own sister gets terrible ones that send her frequently to her bed, at times, for days. Some have blinded her.

Temporarily, thankfully, but they are truly terrible. However, when she suffers them too often, she only eats mutton that has been boiled in plain water with nothing but potatoes and carrots, and coffee with nothing added to it. After a day or two of that, she feels completely recovered."

Mary nodded. "You know, Mr. Sinclair, I have taken a great liking to plain coffee myself and I find it does not give me the same headache as tea with sugar and milk."

"There you go, Mrs. Fitzharding. You may suffer the same affliction as my sister. If you wish, I can write to her by way of an introduction and perhaps the two of you can become acquainted. She had found it very isolating that so few people understand her condition and it irritates her whenever the physicians say it's a nervous complaint."

"I feel the exact same way!" Mary exclaimed. "I would love to correspond with someone who truly understands."

Elizabeth had her own theories on the matter. In her experience, too often the headaches manifested themselves when Mary was unable to get her own way. However, Elizabeth knew that was not entirely charitable, as Mary had suffered the affliction even before her marriage, when Augusta pampered her night and day.

Once Mary and Mr. Sinclair settled upon the details of the introductory letters, Elizabeth asked, "Mr. Sinclair, you mention a sister. Do you have other siblings?"

Mary answered for him. "Mr. Sinclair is the eighth son of Sir William Brookbank of Bath. He has a baronetcy, does he not?"

"Indeed, though fifteen children would be a strain on anyone in this nation, even the king," Mr. Sinclair quipped.

"Fifteen!" Thea declared.

He leaned forward to speak to Thea in a conspiratorial tone. "Three sets of twins."

"Your poor mother," Elizabeth said.

"Yes, and she reminds us of it at every interval, I assure you," Mr. Sinclair said.

"Mr. Sinclair! I have met your dear mother and found her to be a very proper and kind lady who loves to discuss her children."

Mr. Sinclair tipped his cup at Mary. "As Miss Knight was good to point out, not every home is what they present to visitors. I assure you, I am very well educated on how horrible the experience of fifteen children has been for my mother. Thus, I am moving to Bryden in the middle of nowhere, as opposed to Bath."

ᴀ❧ Chapter 16 ❧ᴀ

MR. SIDNEY SINCLAIR and his expensive boots left an hour later. He found a ready audience in Theodosia, who hung on his every word. Elizabeth found him entertaining enough if a bit showy for her tastes. His collars were too high, for one thing. He looked like a London dandy, not a country curate living off fifty pounds a year.

Of course, if what Mary said was true and Elizabeth had no doubts on the subject, Mr. Sinclair was not going to be a typical country curate.

Elizabeth's letters arrived, prompting Mary to complain that her sister received more letters than she did, and she the mistress of the house. Elizabeth ignored her as best as she could, instead directing her to various concerns of Thea's. In particular, they had not left yet for the town, due to Mr. Sinclair's visit, and there was still much shopping to be done.

> *My dearest Miss Knight,*
>
> *I hope this letter finds you well and that your time at your sister's has been pleasant and mostly uneventful. As I recall the entire purpose for this particular visit is for a ball, I cannot wish for completely uneventful time. Mrs. Spencer*

frequently comments her hopes of marrying you off one day. Do not worry; I always inform her that there are no worthy men left in England.

With Miss Keats' assistance, we are working through Miss Gibbs' summoning. I have included several more possible directions to take with summoning. Oh, how I wish you could be in London right now! This would be so much faster and infinitely more fun. If you are parted from us much longer, I shall have to come down with a terrible illness that requires your assistance to bring me back to health. Then, we can all have fun without your father interfering.

Susan sends her love. She says she will write you tomorrow, as she is simply too busy today to spare you a drop of her ink. She is busy writing recipes for Mrs. Osborne. Oh, now she is upbraiding me for giving the hint that she cares more for her duties as a writer of recipes than a lady occultist. If I continue this line of writing, however, Susan threatens to write to you with all of my own gossip. Well, I shan't wait to hear that myself, since I have nothing of use to tell. My life, at present, is without event and exactly how I wish it to be.

I bought a new hat yesterday. Mrs. Spencer is convinced it is the most hideous thing she has ever laid her eyes upon, but I shall wait for Mr. Osborne's opinion today at dinner, since he lives with us now. I read that sentence aloud to Susan who has now declared I am doing nothing but telling falsehoods. A shocking claim! However, even Mrs. Spencer confesses Mr. Osborne had never set foot in this house before all of this book business, and now it seems he is here nearly every night. Not that we are complaining, of course. In fact, we all find it delightful. Well, perhaps Susan finds him the most delightful, as is only right and proper.

I still plan to have her married off by Christmas, my dear Elizabeth. Mark my words upon your journal, for I shall have my way.

Write back at your leisure with all of the details of Miss Gibbs.

Your affectionate friend,
Miss A. Thorne

"What is your letter about that it is so amusing?" Mary demanded.

Elizabeth carefully folded it and placed it in her apron pocket. Then, she went back to putting the final touches on the dress for Lucy's toy gown. "It is from one of the ladies in London."

"I find it very distressing that you have given so much of your time to these complete strangers, when your family needs you," Mary said.

Elizabeth ignored her sister's sermon on the importance of an aunt's influence in the raising of children, and how it was cruel that Elizabeth—without children of her own and, therefore, without any responsibilities whatsoever—would leave the task of child-rearing solely at Mary's door, when it was simply too difficult to manage three young children by herself, with only a governess and a nanny to offer help.

"The boys will soon need a proper tutor before we send them off to school, I suppose," Mary said. She sighed and said, "That will be such a hardship on me."

"I thought it would be a relief."

"How dare you say such a thing! You act as though I do not care one lick for my own children. I swear, Elizabeth, you have grown very strange since you have been involved with the occult."

Three thousand pounds.

Elizabeth said nothing, acutely aware her behaviour *had* changed. They had assumed it was the occult's influence on her. They had assumed incorrectly.

The occult had no true influence upon her unless Mrs. Egerton's witticisms were contagious. No, it had been the temptation of independence that made her bold. She was sensible

195

enough to know society, nor her family, would never allow her to live on her own in delicious solitude, but there were plenty of widowed women in need of companionship and a little extra income to purchase tea. Many were relations of hers, even if distant in both geography and the family connections.

Her inheritance would not make her a burden upon any poor relation. Indeed, her fifty pounds per annum would be a welcome addition, as she could assist with household chores and economies.

The sale of the precious occult book would mean the addition of over a hundred pounds a year on top of her own income. Her presence would be welcome in most circles.

Of course, Aunt Cass would never allow Elizabeth to live with distant relations, far away in some retired village that no one had ever heard of. But one could never predict the future well-being of even the healthy, and she was not guaranteed the luxury of having a safe place to fall. No, a sensible woman in her situation would make many plans, for she must be ready for anything.

"I suppose you're thinking about your next...whatever it is you do with the occult," Mary said.

"I was thinking upon my books, actually," Elizabeth said. "I wish to have a steel box with a lock made to fit four books in total, along with a small trunk for the steel box to be stored in."

"Why on earth would you wish a steel box? They are just books, Elizabeth."

Elizabeth ignored the question and said, "I shall write to Maria and ask her to enlist Mr. Thorne's help. He would be very happy to oblige, I think. The man loves to be useful to ladies, and that would have him venturing to Eastmore, for certain, which would give Maria her own excuse to go shopping."

"You should stay away from Mr. Henry Thorne, Elizabeth. People are already talking," Mary said.

Elizabeth laughed. "Whatever do you mean?"

"It is no secret that you spent a lot of time with Mr. Thorne in London." Mary's voice was rather smug. "It has made some tongues idle with gossip."

"And I trust my sister was very supportive and assured everyone that Mr. Thorne was only assisting with the selling of my inheritance?" Elizabeth asked sweetly.

Mary's guilty expression answered the question.

Elizabeth ignored it, and Mary went back to stabbing at her own small piece of needlework. The ball was to happen eight days hence and there was both an excessive amount of work left to do and very little to do at present. Most of the tasks, such as flower arrangements, could not be done until the very day. Other tasks, such as the polishing of the silverware, had already begun by both the coachman and the footmen, and the maids had begun pulling out all of the silver serving ware for polishing.

Thea had eaten too much cake during Mr. Sinclair's visit and asked to be excused to lie down. Mary gave her consent, and instructed Thea that they had an appointment with her personal seamstress at ten in the morning sharp, so her sister was welcome to sleep until then.

That left the two eldest Knight sisters alone, a situation rarely allowed or welcomed. The air grew thick with the silence, and it physically pained Elizabeth to take each breath. They had once been closer than G and Thea.

Not any longer.

Finally, Mary sighed and asked, "What does Thea actually need? Not what she wants, of course, I shall see to that. However, I wish to ensure she has all of the basics as well."

"I would have preferred her to have one more pair of gloves, but I could not find anything suitable in the shops before I left, and did not have the time to commission Aunt Cass or my friends in London to find something appropriate."

Mary nodded. "I shall see to it tomorrow, then. We will be gone most of the day, so I will instruct the servants to bring you nuncheon."

"I can wait until you return," Elizabeth said. "We do not eat in the middle of the day at the rectory."

"Still?" Mary shook her head. "I would have supposed Isabella's situation would have allowed for the habit to finally take hold with our father."

"Alas, no," Elizabeth said.

Several more minutes past before Mary tried starting a conversation again. "What is your opinion of Mr. Sinclair?"

"He seems a good enough sort of man, I assume. What is your opinion of him?"

"You seemed very dismissive of him when he visited."

Elizabeth sighed. She shook out the little doll's dress and was satisfied with her work. "Finally, that is done. I did not intend to be dismissive, and I am wholly sorry if Mr. Sinclair came away with that impression. I was merely taken aback by our father having hired a curate, considering how he has been worried about money as of late, with Isabella needing a nurse."

Mary shook her head. "Oh, I talked Papa out of that. Isabella will be fine without a nurse, and a curate would be of more help. After all, Papa can look after Isabella."

Elizabeth stared in shock at her sister. "You should not have interfered."

"Why ever not? Someone needs to offer good advice to our father."

"Mary. What have you done?"

Mary's smirk flickered away. She seemed to consider her words before asking, "What is it that you know that I do not? You forget that Isabella is my closest friend in the world. I know her situation and perhaps better than you, for I have, too, been with child three times and have endured the indignity and worries of the event."

"Mary," Elizabeth said again with all of the patience and fortitude she could rally. "You have not visited the rectory since Christmas. You do not understand what life is like for Isabella right now."

"Papa has told me all about it, do not fret. I know all about you refusing to do anything and..."

"Mary," Elizabeth interrupted. "Our father has talked about how he is planning for the arrival of his *fourth* wife."

Mary gasped. She stared at Elizabeth, and mouthed several words before finally saying, "You must have misunderstood. Our father would never say such a thing. He is a man of God, for heaven's sake! He would never say that."

"Ask Thea about it tomorrow on your carriage ride to the seamstress. Our father yelled loud enough for the kitchen servants to hear him. He has not been a kind support during her ordeal and has been the cause of most of the household strife he complains of. It has been a difficult time for all of us, and now without a nurse, it will only be worse because our father will be about the house more because of Mr. Sinclair."

"He cannot be that bad, Eliza," Mary said. Her laugh sounded hollow.

Elizabeth looked at her sister, and said the one thing that only the two of them knew. The one secret that tied them together.

"Recall why you married the first man who looked at you."

Mary made no further attempts at conversation.

THE KNOWLEDGE SHE had not behaved without reproach weighed heavily on Mary's mind, for she was stricken with one of her headaches and was unable to come down for dinner. Instructions were sent down for Elizabeth to have the preliminary menu for the ball's supper sent up to Mary, as well as to inspect the silverware polishing.

Elizabeth consulted with the housekeeper concerning the polishing. Mrs. Webb was a stern and proud woman, who took great pride in Ashbrook. She assured Miss Knight that she had a tight rein on the maids and that they were working from dawn to dusk on the silverware.

Mrs. Webb had one concern, however. There were not enough candles in the storeroom, but Mrs. Fitzharding had not requested if the four-hour or the six-hour candles were to be used. Mrs. Webb did not wish to bother the ill Mrs. Fitzharding.

Elizabeth took it upon herself to send a note up to Mary via Matthew, the footman who was usually about the drawing room. Matthew returned moments later with instructions that the six-hour candles should be used and with permission for Mrs. Webb to purchase as many as necessary for the ball.

With that, Elizabeth checked in with the cook, a Mr. LeBlanc who still had the accent of his native Normandy. He passed Elizabeth a list of the current menu items and circled the substitutions that had been made since Mary had last seen the list.

"Alas, there is only so much to be purchased this time of the year," he'd said, but promised her that the supper would be splendid.

Elizabeth assured him she believed him, and went off in search of Matthew to bring the note to Mary. She'd only had enough time to sit in front of the fire and asked Bartholomew to call for tea for herself before another note from Mary arrived. This time, it instructed her to go to Mr. LeBlanc and ask for the addition of dropped plum cakes and rout-drop cakes, both made as small as possible.

Mr. LeBlanc thought about it, looked about his kitchen, and nodded that this was satisfactory and achievable. Elizabeth sent the news back up to Mary, and the letters stopped.

Elizabeth had a quiet dinner with Mr. Fitzharding and Thea, and a plate was sent up to Mary by way of Matthew. The dinners at Ashbrook were always outstanding, though Mr. Fitzharding lamented this was only a single course.

"With all of the ball preparations, and the dinner guests we shall have traipsing through the house at all hours to see our Miss Theodosia, our poor cook asked if we would be willing to have simpler dinners the nights we did not have guests." Mr. Fitzharding gave Thea a wink. "Family does not count as guests!"

Thea giggled heartily and even Elizabeth smiled. She glanced at Thea and asked, "Is the food acceptable?"

"Of course it is! Look at it!" Thea exclaimed.

"Alas, you see your dinner before you," Mr. Fitzharding said, signalling there would be no other courses.

"I am grateful for that, for I suspect we shall be eating this for the rest of our visit!" Elizabeth said with a laugh.

A large dish was filled with stewed beef. Another was piled high with lamb steaks and potatoes. There was currant jelly, rolls, and plenty of sauces and pickles. The Oxford Dumplings were made with butter, instead of suet, in consideration of Thea, and the girl had eight of the fried delights upon her plate, smothered in parsley butter and pickled mushrooms. Mr. Fitzharding laughed and encouraged her to take more; he did not want his young charge to pass out from hunger at her upcoming ball.

"Pray, let us see if she can even eat those first, sir," Elizabeth said.

Thea did, in fact, eat all of her dumplings, as well as some stewed celery and the rest of the pickled mushrooms. She even found room for two rolls in all of that. It took an hour, but Thea finally declared herself stuffed full. Mr. Fitzharding laughed and was greatly entertained by this, but Elizabeth worried that her sister was not eating enough at home. Their father's tastes and preferences dominated the dinner table and Elizabeth feared that, as long as Thea lived there, she would go hungry.

James said he would take an evening walk to his neighbour's house, a mere mile away, to aid his digestion. Soon after, Mary soon sent down a note for Thea to join her in her bedchamber for tea, so Elizabeth decided to take an early evening in her own room to work on her studies.

Once in the safety of her room, she summoned Mrs. Egerton from the locket and into view. The studies were delayed somewhat due to the ghost's blistering appraisal of Mary, Thea's peculiar eating habits, and Mr. Fitzharding's inability to control his wife.

Elizabeth quietly endured the ghost's biting tongue and took the opportunity to change from her dinner gown into her comfortable gown, the dark one that the children had spilled tea upon. The laundry maid, who Elizabeth had yet to meet, had done an excellent job and returned the gown. She also took the opportunity to let out the lacing on her stays.

In time, Mrs. Egerton's ghostly spleen had been appropriately vented. The ladies got to work.

June 21, 1810
This is an account of the attempts to summon Miss Gibbs.

Attempt One.
Used purified wheat seeds and chaff. Spoke the exact words upon her page. No noticeable reaction.
Attempt Two.
Used purified carrots and peas. Spoke the exact words upon her page. No noticeable reaction.

Two hours later and in great agitation, Elizabeth wrote:

Attempt Eighteen.
Angrily said her words upon the page and said I wished
her very much to appear. Possibly heard a soft giggle.

"Mrs. Egerton, what is your opinion, for you knew Miss Gibbs in life. I fear I have missed the most obvious thing imaginable, and yet I cannot think what it might be. Do you agree that Miss Gibbs just reacted to my spellworking?"

"I believe so, for it was not I who giggled." Mrs. Egerton lifted her chin. "I have never giggled a day in my life."

Elizabeth thought for a moment. "Is it possible she is aware of my attempts to summon her?"

"Undoubtedly."

"Then, I know not how to proceed from here."

Mrs. Egerton shook her head. "Knowing Miss Gibbs as I do, I suspect we are missing something cheerful and gay. She was, as I've said, aggressively cheerful."

"Shall I tie ribbons in my hair?" Elizabeth asked. She was exhausted, and her own head was beginning to throb behind her eyes.

Before Mrs. Egerton could offer a witty comeback, Elizabeth's door flung open and in marched Mary all in high dungeon. She took one look at Elizabeth's organized chaos, and said, "I forbade you from working your occult nonsense under my roof."

As Mrs. Egerton was standing behind Mary, she disappeared from view. However, Elizabeth's gaze moved to the ghost, and it caught Mary's attention. She turned and looked about her, demanding, "With whom have you been speaking? Demons? The devil?"

"Mary," Elizabeth said as she put down her quill. She stood next to her desk and said in the calmest voice she could muster, "You cannot ban me from doing my work."

"Your work? Your work?" Mary was shouting now. "Your job is to care for your niece and nephews, to make my life easier."

Elizabeth attempted to moderate her voice. "I am not your servant, Mary."

"You will do as I say!"

"You are not my father!" Elizabeth shouted back.

Mary feigned mock shock. "How dare you raise your voice to me in my own home?"

Elizabeth glared at her sister, but did attempt to moderate her tone as best as possible for her own sake, and not Mary's. "Is it not enough that you command my very moments and can summon me to Ashbrook at a moment's whim?"

Mary walked over to the desk and began to move the books and journals about. "This is what is more important than your own nephews and niece?"

Elizabeth resisted the urge to push Mary away from her things. "What is it you want from me, Mary?"

"I want you to do your duty."

"Me?" Elizabeth declared, and she could not help but laugh bitterly. "It is bad enough that you purposely keep secrets from me about my own family so that you can embarrass me in company. You abuse our father's affection for you by turning me into one of your servants. And, if that was not enough, you steal my things that you could afford to purchase a hundred times over and not even notice the expenditure at the end of the year."

"The necklace was mine!" Mary roared.

"It was left to me!" Elizabeth shouted back. "Mrs. Egerton was right about you. You are an awful human being and I am ashamed to call you my sister! To think we had once been friends!"

"Who is Mrs. Egerton?"

Horror filled Elizabeth with the realization she had revealed Mrs. Egerton to Mary of all people. She had never meant to reveal the ghost's existence to anyone outside of her tiny occult circle, and now in a fit of unchecked emotions, she risked everything. Mary was powerful enough, through her husband, to have Elizabeth locked away for hysteria. She'd heard the stories, of course, of Bedlam and its poor, wretched inmates chained to walls while screaming into the night.

Her dealings with the Royal Occult Society meant none of them would defend her. They would watch the young lady who dared display independence of thought be punished as a lesson to others.

And she had just handed Mary such a weapon.

Elizabeth remained silent until Mary picked up Mrs. Egerton's autograph book.

"What is this?" Mary demanded.

"Put that down, Mary Knight."

Mary's smirk was dangerous and signalled that she had sniffed out something of personal value to her sister. She flipped through the pages. A cold breeze blew through the room, so fierce that it disturbed the curtains and blew out one of the candles. Mary glanced about the room and then back down at the book. "And this is what our uncle left you? Utter foolishness."

And then Mary threw the book into the lit fireplace.

Elizabeth shrieked in horror as she threw herself at the fireplace. She plunged her hands into the engulfing flames. Smoke billowed forth, choking Elizabeth, and the searing pain in her hands caused her to instinctively pull away. Steam and smoke filled the room and both ladies coughed violently.

"Now maybe you will focus on the rest of us instead of yourself!" Mary attempted to shout the words, but the smoke made her voice little more than a rasp by the end.

Now weeping, Elizabeth grabbed the book from the smoldering ash. Miraculously, the flames were gone and now it was only the hot ash and steam. She pulled out the book, ignoring the heat upon her hands as best as she could, and her incoherent sobs of half-muttered words all meant the same thing in the end: *No*.

Elizabeth did not listen to Mary's rantings, which seemed to only infuriate her sister further.

Elizabeth brushed her hand over the ash-covered leather cover. She carefully turned the pages, ready to find burnt edges and smoke damage. There was nothing but a little ash dust.

"You deserved this," Mary said in a self-satisfied tone. No, it was triumphant. Mary had finally found a way to hurt Elizabeth so thoroughly, so completely, that she celebrated openly. "Remember this when you defy my commands."

Elizabeth clutched the book to her chest, tears welling up in her eyes from both the ache in her heart and the physical pain of her burns. She pushed herself to her feet and squared her shoulders. "It is not my fault that you are unhappy, Mary. How sad your life must be that you want to destroy everything that makes me happy."

"I demand you give up the occult. I demand you obey me!" Mary was shrieking now. Smoke from the curiously smoldering fireplace curled its way around Mary, choking off her words. "Cease attacking me with this smoke!"

"I do not control the smoke, Mary," Elizabeth said. Though, she did wonder why the smoke was only curling around her sister.

"Someone is making the smoke do this and I believe it is you and your damned occult!"

That was when Mrs. Egerton solidified in front of Mary and slapped her across the face with her fan. "It is I, madam, who is assaulting you with this smoke. I will do all that is in my power to protect both myself and my book's owner. You will learn to hold your tongue, or I shall find a way to remove it."

Elizabeth was too shocked to speak. Mary cried out when the fan struck her, pressing her hand against her face to see if there was blood.

"What...who...what..."

And then Mary fainted.

Chapter 17

ELIZABETH RUBBED THE bridge of her nose. At her feet was the crumpled, unconscious form of her sister. Mr. Fitzharding and Thea both rushed into the room before Mary could regain her sense.

"What in the devil is going on in here?" Mr. Fitzharding exclaimed. "What have you done with my wife? And who is this woman?"

Elizabeth closed her eyes. She had wanted to keep Mrs. Egerton a secret from her family, but here she was, standing in front of two more family members in all her glory.

Mrs. Egerton, for her part, did little to help the situation by saying, "I do not speak to men. Begone with you and take this foul wife of yours."

"Mrs. Egerton, please. Not now," Elizabeth said. "Mr. Fitzharding, James, please. Just...*please*."

Mary was roused, and fainted, twice more before she finally rallied herself enough to endure no longer being the centre of attention in the room. Mrs. Egerton disappeared from view, but kept taunting and insulting from the air, and rudely mocked Mary's continuous struggles to regain consciousness.

"You were fighting so loudly that the servants in the drawing room could hear you both plain as day," Mr. Fitzharding complained. "You had scared the children."

"Why would Mrs. Fitzharding care?" Mrs. Egerton's voice was laced with scorn. "She expects Miss Knight to be their mother, since she cannot be bothered to muster her courage to do the duty."

It took significant coaxing on Elizabeth's part, but Mrs. Egerton finally reappeared, wearing a severe green dress with an imperious hat. She glared at the roused Mary before turning to Mr. Fitzharding. "Your wife assaulted my very person and the property of Miss Knight. You will instruct her to apologize at once."

"Remarkable," Mr. Fitzharding said. "She actually believes she is real."

"I am real," Mrs. Egerton said coldly. "Your wife is a jealous thief and I demand you behave like a man and control her."

"How dare you," Mary snapped.

"Now, Mary, we must be calm," Mr. Fitzharding said.

"James! Do you not see there is a ghost in our house, standing here, demanding we follow her edicts, lest she rip out my very tongue! Those were her words. And Elizabeth simply stands there and allows it. This is demonic, it is! Demonic! This is the devil sent to lead us..."

"Mary, enough!" Elizabeth shouted. "If it was not for Mrs. Egerton, I would have lost her book forever. Because of you, I might have lost any chance to revitalize women in the occult."

"Why would I care about that?" Mary snapped.

Thea, in a very low, very timid voice, said, "Because it is important to Elizabeth."

"And what does that matter to me?" Mary demanded.

In that same voice again, Thea said, "It matters because she is our sister."

Silence filled the room for several beats of Elizabeth's heart. Finally, it was Mrs. Egerton to break the silence, as ever. "Which one are you again, dear?"

"Miss Theodosia, ma'am. It is a pleasure to meet you. I have never met a ghost before."

"Miss Theodosia. You are a very sensible girl when pressed to be one. Once the vigour of youth wears off, I believe you will be the most sensible of all the Knight girls, save perhaps Miss Knight," Mrs. Egerton suggested.

Elizabeth smiled at Thea's beaming expression. She was so rarely told anything good about her future self, and it must have given her such hope to be declared to, one day, be sensible.

"You will not address my sister," Mary said.

"I shall do as I please," Mrs. Egerton countered. She turned back to Mr. Fitzharding. "As a rule, I do not speak to men, for you are all beneath my notice. However, given these extraordinary circumstances, I shall make this one exception for my delightful young friend. Your sister-in-law is not free labour and it is wrong for you to treat her as such. Her father steals from her purse to pay for God only knows what, and the two of you demanding she come here and look after your horrible children—"

"Mrs. Egerton!" Elizabeth exclaimed. "I must protest. I have never once said that about the children."

"No indeed. I am, however, saying those words, since it is clear Mrs. Fitzharding considers her children thusly, or else she would not wish to avoid them whenever possible. Miss Knight is not your servant nor your governess, sir. Kindly stop treating her as one. And, pray, remember that she is poorer than you, and deserving of your protection, not your contempt. Perhaps with that consideration your wife will stop stealing what is not hers."

Mr. Fitzharding turned to his wife and asked, "My dear, what is the ghost speaking of?"

"Nothing that concerns you, my dear."

"On the contrary," Mr. Fitzharding said, and for the first time, Elizabeth heard the anger in his voice. "I believe this concerns me greatly since it affects my home and family. Elizabeth, is it true that my wife attempted to steal your property?"

"Yes," Elizabeth said simply.

"That is a lie," Mary said.

"More than once," Thea added helpfully. "You tried to steal her necklace from her mother."

"That necklace is mine," Mary snapped.

"But Mary did not take the necklace, yes? So all is well."

Elizabeth lowered her head, but said nothing.

Thea said, "Mary broke the necklace. The knots around the pearls had worn enough that most went flying everywhere. Several of the pearls were lost. We all tried to find them, but they're so small. Elizabeth had to buy more of the pearls in London with her own money to have the necklace restrung."

At Elizabeth's surprised expression, Thea said, "I overheard you talking to Mrs. Thorne in the drawing room."

"Miss Theodosia Knight, it is not polite to eavesdrop on private conversations," Elizabeth said.

"It is the only way I am told anything of consequence that is happening in our family." In a lower, sullen voice, Thea said, "No one tells me anything."

"Alas, that is the plight of all younger sisters, my dear," Mrs. Egerton said. "Now, you are all wasting valuable study time. Will I have your assurance, sir, that I will not be assaulted nor will Miss Elizabeth's property threatened while we are in this house?"

Mr. Fitzharding squared his shoulders and bowed. "Mrs. Egerton, please accept my profound apologies for what has happened, and I assure you that, while you are under my roof, you will be accorded all of the rights and privileges of any guest of mine, living or otherwise. I can only profess my sincerest regret that this misunderstanding and childish tiff between sisters threatened you in any manner."

Mrs. Egerton gave a sharp nod of her head.

"But, husband!" Mary protested.

"Enough, Mary. I have tolerated your moods and whimsies long enough. How dare you throw your sister's book upon the fire? What were you thinking?" James lowered his voice into a harsh whisper. "She is poor. For the love of God, woman, have some mercy on her."

A tinge of guilt struck Elizabeth at the expression on Mary's face. She'd seen it often enough, back when Mary lived at the rectory. The expression that was the reason she agreed to marry a man she did not love. The reason she fled with the first man who turned his attentions to her.

"Yes, sir," Mary whispered. Elizabeth recognized the defeated voice.

"I must defend Mary and say it was as much my fault as any, Mr. Fitzharding," Elizabeth said. With a smile, she corrected, "James."

Mr. Fitzharding's angry expression turned confused. "What have you done in this matter to make you think it was your fault?"

Elizabeth looked at her sister's downtrodden expression and said, "We are sisters, sir. There is much between us and, though I believe we love each other deep within our hearts, we find ourselves steeped in years of resentments that have not been spoken aloud. It is the way of sisters in the Knight family, I suppose. Isn't it, Thea?"

Thea flushed. "Yes, Elizabeth."

Mary's eyes filled with tears when she looked at Elizabeth. She was very quiet now. With her husband's verbal prompting, Mary managed to say, "It was an old argument that got out of hand. I am very sorry, Elizabeth."

"I am sorry, too, Mary," Elizabeth said.

She wasn't certain for which part, but she was sorry that this divide existed between them. She and Mary had once been tighter than Thea and G. Now, they were worlds apart and unable to bridge the resentments and jealousies of neither being fully in command of their own lives.

Mary had married into wealth and consequence. She would, most likely, be a young rich widow soon. That had been Mary's goal in marrying a man her own father's age. However, her husband's health was robust and showed no hint of slowing down. So, Mary had to continue in a marriage to someone she did not love.

Oh, Mr. James Fitzharding was an excellent man and the very definition of a gentleman, but there was a difference between a very good man and a man who was better than all others. Mr. Fitzharding was not that man for Mary. Henry Thorne had been that man for a time, but he had not shown Mary any interest whatsoever. And he'd have not been a good match for Mary in any case.

Elizabeth sighed and spoke aloud, mostly to pull herself from her own mind. "I believe Mary is still exhausted from her headache, and this will only bring on an episode if we linger here any longer."

Mary nodded weakly. "It has already returned."

"Thea, please take Mary to her bed. Fetch her plain coffee and ask Mr. Leblanc for boiled mutton. If there is none, pray send instructions that I have advised the remedy as soon as it is possible to obtain. Is that clear?" Elizabeth said.

Mr. Fitzharding interrupted. "I shall take on that task myself. Miss Theodosia, if you would be so kind as to escort my wife, I shall arrange the remedy for her. Now, what about her laudanum? Mr. Slade swears it is the only cure."

Mary gave Elizabeth a pleading look that Elizabeth understood. "Laudanum has never agreed with Mary. She should not be given it."

"But Mr. Slade insists that it is..."

"The best remedy for others. Not Mary," Elizabeth said sternly. "James, you must accept that your wife knows her own wishes more than the local apothecary, no matter how excellent he may be."

Mr. Fitzharding opened his mouth to protest, but Mary said, "It is true, husband."

"Then why did you never speak up before?"

Mary glanced at Elizabeth, pleading for assistance. Elizabeth obliged.

"It is difficult for a woman currently suffering to explain adequately to a man of medicine that his remedy will not work. But, you must trust me, and promise me, that you will not allow her to be given it for her headaches. It only makes them worse upon waking."

"Now that we have settled Mrs. Fitzharding's head pains," Mrs. Egerton said loudly, "might you all vacate the room so that Miss Knight and I can continue our work in silent peace?"

Mr. Fitzharding cleared his throat and said, "I am not used to being spoken to in such a manner, madam."

Mrs. Egerton snorted. She actually snorted out loud. On purpose. Like a common worker. "Sir, you pretend to think I consider your feelings on the subject. I assure you, I do not."

"Mrs. Egerton, perhaps tact would be best employed here," Elizabeth said.

"When has tact gotten us anywhere?"

With that, Mrs. Egerton shooed the Fitzhardings about in their own home. And, perhaps more surprising, they let her.

~✧ Chapter 18 ✧~

IT WOULD BE a grave understatement to say that Ashbrook was subdued for the next two days. Mary took all of her meals in her bedchamber, and only stepped beyond its threshold to take Thea visiting or shopping. Mr. Fitzharding found two dinner invitations rather quickly and was out of doors riding and visiting his companions for the rest of the time. Even the servants were speaking in whispers.

Elizabeth was not avoiding Mary as a rule, but the sisters did not see each other for those two days. Thea attempted to spread her time evenly between the sisters, but Elizabeth advised her that Mary needed the company more than she did, and that she had her studies to occupy her.

"And Mrs. Egerton," Thea had said.

Elizabeth chuckled and asked, "You did not seem surprised by her appearance."

"I'd heard voices in your bedchamber late one night and was worried it had been an intruder. I spied through the keyhole and saw a rather grand lady standing in your room. I opened the door, just a crack, and I saw her disappear and reappear. I nearly fainted! The lady saw me, winked, and that is when I made my escape."

"Why did you not say anything?"

"I did not want to get you into any trouble. If our father finds out…" Thea shrugged. "He will make you live in Cornwall."

Elizabeth squeezed her sister's arm. "No, dearest. He will do nothing of the kind to me. Do not fret on my accord."

Despite the mood at Ashbrook, Mr. Sinclair was due for dinner and the invitation was not to be put off. Mary descended the stairs in an exquisite gown of blue silk and a necklace of sapphires and diamonds. She looked refreshed, without a hint of the ill-temper that had plagued the household for days.

She did not meet Elizabeth's eyes, however.

While the ladies and gentlemen separated after dinner, Thea asked permission to run to her room to fix a pin in her hair that was hurting her. Mary gave her consent, leaving the two older Knight sisters alone. Elizabeth would have been content to sit politely and stare at the fire until the gentlemen decided to grace them with their presence. However, Mary had other plans.

"What is your true opinion of Mr. Sinclair?" Mary asked.

The question startled Elizabeth and she stumbled over an answer. "I do not know him well enough to offer a true opinion. He appears gentlemanly enough, excepting that his attire is too fashionable and expensive for his income. My father cannot be able to pay him more than fifty pounds. Sixty, at the very most."

Mary gave Elizabeth a confused expression. "Oh, did Thea not tell you? Eliza, he has twelve hundred pounds per annum and is assumed to inherit more eventually. He even owns his own carriage."

"Then why work as a curate of all things?

Mary glanced behind her to ensure the men were not near the drawing room entrance. "As I understand from his aunt, Mr. Sinclair bores easily. His family has placed a great deal of pressure on him to be something important or grand. And, if he cannot achieve that, then marry accordingly."

"I do not see how a curacy in a retired country parish will suit their schemes for him."

Mary nodded. "Very true. However, they are also a pious family, and none of their other children went into the church. Gaining his ordination and taking a curacy has meant he has some independence from family expectation."

Elizabeth considered that. "Then, I say my opinion of him has changed slightly. I cannot support a man of means stealing a living from a young man who would need the living. And, yet, I intimately understand the longing to be one's own person, independent of family pressure."

Mary rolled her eyes. "Do not injure yourself complimenting him."

"I believe I shall continue to give your Mr. Sinclair the benefit of my good opinion, until as such time as I am confident to make a declaration. Why do you ask?"

"I believe he would be an excellent match for Cassandra. What say you?"

Elizabeth smiled. "Mary, leave the poor man alone!"

"Be serious, Eliza." Mary glanced over her shoulder again, but there was no sign of Thea nor the gentlemen. "Consider the situation. Cassandra is shy, yes, but she is not without wit or accomplishments. What is more, she is sensible, and resourceful, and I have no doubt she could take an income such as his and make it stretch. I know that his personality is more aligned with Thea's, and she is already in love with him I can plainly see, but she would be a terrible wife for him. Please, consider the comfort it would give all of us to see Cassie married to a man of twelve hundred pounds, with far more destined to come his way. Not just for my benefit, either. Think of yours, too. With Cassie married, you could...you could live with her when our father dies. That would be better than living with Charles."

Elizabeth heard the unspoken "or with me" plainly enough. "Have they even met? For all we know, she might hate him."

Mary did not answer and her shoulders slumped a little.

Elizabeth sighed. "I am no matchmaker if that is where your hopes lay. I am as likely to cause them both to never marry as it is for me to do any good in the matter."

"I am not asking you to arrange a marriage between them. All I am asking if you believe Cassandra should be pushed into his direction or not."

"I suppose it would not be the worst match in the world. She would be comfortable and protected, and I do not believe he would be cruel to her. She might enjoy the challenge of stretching an income without having to be concerned with true poverty. However, he is to be our father's curate. It will be difficult to arrange for them to see anything of each other without it being obvious that I am attempting a match."

"Nonsense. Invite him to dinner twice a week."

Elizabeth snorted, and she covered her mouth instinctively in embarrassment. Mrs. Egerton was indeed a terrible influence. "Mary, our father is not going to allow me to feed another mouth twice a week. It was hard enough to convince him to let poor Julia Cooper live at the rectory and her mother is upon her death bed."

"Has he been truly so tight with money? Answer truthfully." Mary sighed. "I spoke with Thea and, granted, the girl knows more than she pretends, but I was not convinced. I have attempted to coax even a hint of it out of Isabella, but she has become rather tight lipped as of late."

"I tell you truthfully and without no embellishment, it has been a very difficult year, and my inheritance has not improved matters for us. I have taken charge of paying for my gowns, and he has cut off my pin money all together. I had to give G some pin money from my own because Papa refused. And, well, Thea. I've taken to purchasing her fruit at the market whenever possible because he will not accept any change in our table, no matter how small to accommodate her."

"I had hoped she would grow out of it with time."

"It is as likely she will become more entrenched, not less."

"He should not have served her up her favourite cow so soon after Augusta's death," Mary said with a sigh. "It is easy to forget how difficult it was when it is behind you."

"It was always easier for you. He prefers you to the rest of us." Elizabeth attempted a smile, but it was sad. "You, at least, get a name. The rest of us are not afforded that luxury."

Mary seemed to struggle, but finally she said simply, "Should I write to encourage him to invite Mr. Sinclair over? One assumes he would be on his best behaviour with company about the house."

"I will also make a hint of it." Elizabeth sighed. Thea was purposely taking too long with her hair, of that Elizabeth was certain. "And, I shall write to you with my honest opinion after observing them for a time."

They fell quiet as Thea entered the room. "Are the gentlemen not back yet? The pin was very painful against my skin, but I have fixed it."

"Does Miss Theodosia miss our presence already?" Mr. Sinclair asked as the two gentlemen walked into the room.

Elizabeth smirked at how Thea's face lit up at the sight of Mr. Sinclair. For a curate, he was very well dressed. Not too fashionable to make him appear foppish, though Elizabeth felt his collar was too high for good sense.

And, if she were to care to notice—which she did not—he was a rather handsome young man. About her age, she suspected, with the slightest dimple in his chin that was not distracting enough to make Thea stare gap-mouthed at him. His light hair bordered upon blond, the dirty kind that labourers developed when outside in the muck. His eyes were grey, though, and quite animated whenever he spoke.

"Miss Knight. Your gaze is piercing. What do you stare at so intently? Have I spilled the soup upon my vest?" Mr. Sinclair asked as he took a seat.

Elizabeth gave him a smile and said, "I was thinking that the collar of your shirt is too high for a country curate."

"Elizabeth!" Mary scolded.

That only made Mr. Sinclair laugh harder. "I solemnly promise that I rarely wear such foppery, but it is always good to have a fashionable shirt or two in one's trunk for elegant dinner parties such as this."

"I don't know, sir," Elizabeth said, still smiling. "I fear the residents of Bryden will judge you severely by that collar alone."

"Never mind how he ties his cravat," Thea said with a giggle.

"And what is wrong with my cravat, pray, Miss Theodosia Knight?" Mr. Sinclair demanded, though his jovial expression signalled he was only teasing.

"It is very fashionable," Thea said, her cheeks flushed now and bowing her head to avoid Mary's glare.

"I believe what my sister is attempting to say, Mr. Sinclair, is that it looks as though your servant took a great deal of care dressing you today," Elizabeth said. "Which you will find that, in Bryden, will often be teased."

"Poor Mr. Thorne often complains that Bryden has no sense of taste," Thea said with an enthusiastic nod.

"Then, Miss Thea, I do not know how to proceed. I had planned to ask you for the first two dances at Mrs. Fitzharding's ball, but now I worry that my collar will offend you all."

Mr. Sinclair's delivery produced the desired effect. Thea exclaimed that she loved his collar and cravat and begged him to tie it exactly so for the ball. He declared he would and just for her private enjoyment.

Elizabeth admittedly felt the smallest prick of nostalgia. She did not care that Mr. Sinclair had asked Thea to dance; she had no expectations on that account. No, instead her sadness came from how she was long past the time when she'd have been the one to ask for the first two dances. But, approaching twenty-nine years of age and poor, she had finally been passed over and no man would look seriously in her direction again.

She gave her sister an encouraging smile. But for her small disappointments, she had very few regrets.

"Miss Knight smirks!" Mr. Sinclair said.

"Oh, ignore Elizabeth," Mary said. "She's always inventing some sort of mischief quietly to herself. After growing up with her, you learn to ignore it."

"Well, please, Miss Knight, share your thoughts with the room," Mr. Sinclair said.

"Oh, I could not, Mr. Sinclair," Elizabeth said with a grin. "To do that would reveal my mischief and I am ever so good at keeping it quiet."

Thea and James Fitzharding both choked on their tea.

Mary closed her eyes as she sucked in a breath to avoid bickering.

Matthew, the footman, coughed.

Mr. Sinclair's face twitched as he clearly attempted not to laugh at the scene, which would have been very impolite to inquire further. Elizabeth looked him directly in his fine, grey eyes and smiled delicately. Mr. Sinclair raised his teacup to her in a salute before taking a sip.

She was still not convinced he'd been a good match for Cassie. He would probably terrify the poor girl. However, she was starting to see what Mary saw.

They had a delightful tea and conversation. Soon, several other guests arrived who'd been invited for the supper party and cards. They gathered about the room and were engaged in conversation when there was a commotion at the door. Footsteps could be heard hurrying through the house. Even Mary turned to ask the footman, Bartholomew, what was the matter. He was about to leave the drawing room to inquire down below when Mr. Thorne stormed into the room.

He looked as though he was called from his bed to come there. He did not wear a cravat, nor a dinner jacket. He had his greatcoat over his shirt and trousers, and he wore his riding boots.

"My apologies, everyone. Miss Knight? For you. News from Bryden. It is most urgent. Mrs. Fitzharding? Please, is there a place we can speak in private?"

Chapter 19

ELIZABETH EXCUSED HERSELF and went back into the dining room. Thea, Mary, Mr. James, and Henry Thorne all gathered as Elizabeth read her letters aloud:

> *My dearest Elizabeth,*
>
> *I wish this letter could begin with the usual salutations of health, but alas I cannot. It is upon my pen to share with you the dreadful news from Bryden today. Isabella has been brought to bed with a stillborn son.*
> *Mrs. Green assures us that, for now, there are no signs of infection or, to use her language, other worries. She would not detail those for my letter, as Papa felt I should not know the particulars. I can tell you that Isabella is very weak and I have called on Maria Thorne to assist me. She has brought her own maid, who is assisting me with keeping our house from falling apart.*
> *The apothecary and the midwife advise us that the danger is the first night, and then the following week. We are doing all within our power to ensure she survives this*

night. She is very weak, but she took a little broth and had three spoons of the thinnest gruel just now. The Thornes' cook has been sending instructions for Julia and Alice, but as you can imagine, it is difficult without experience in the kitchen.

If you require any excuse to leave Ashbrook, pray, use this one. However, if you fear Thea cannot be left to her own devices, stay where you are, and we shall endure without you. I have asked Maria to write, too, in hopes to share additional thoughts on Isabella's condition.

Cassandra

My dearest Elizabeth,

I am writing this letter now from the rectory drawing room, at Cassie's request. I have been upstairs to visit Mrs. Knight and, while she is indeed weak and low in spirits, she appears surprisingly robust. She is neither hot with fever, nor pale with blood loss. I have spoken at length with the midwife—for your father would not hear of the details being given to your sisters—and I feel confident in saying that Mrs. Knight's prospects of recovery are as excellent as any of our sex can hope to accomplish given the extraordinary circumstances of her situation.

As for if you are needed at home, I have come to stay, along with my maid who is an excellent woman, and we are providing assistance until we are no longer needed. *However, if you require an excuse to return home, by all means do so. However, if you are having a gay time, please remain.* I or Cassandra will write with updates, and we'll have one of our footman ride back and forth as necessary to ease your mind. I will send this letter now with Henry,

221

however, who wishes to be of use.

Maria

"Well? What does it say?" Mary demanded. She snatched the letters from Elizabeth and began to read sections aloud, including the underlined bits that Elizabeth had delicately concealed. "Why would you need an excuse to leave Ashbrook? What on earth is Cassandra talking of?"

Elizabeth put her hand on her chest. She closed her eyes and attempted to steady the shock to her system.

Thea remained surprisingly silent throughout this exchange. Finally, when prompted by Elizabeth, she said, "I am glad she did not die."

"As am I. Pray, tell me, Mr. Thorne, is the situation at Bryden as poorly as I seem to be reading in Cassandra's letter?"

Mr. Thorne answered, though he was grave. "Mrs. Green cannot stay because Mrs. Fletcher's time has come and now there is talk that she might be bringing forth three, not twins."

Elizabeth seemed to understand what Mr. Thorne danced about: she was needed at home. "Mr. Thorne, did you come by carriage?"

"Indeed, Miss Knight. I am ready at your disposal."

Elizabeth nodded. "Then, I shall fetch a few of my things and, would you be so kind as to return tomorrow so that I can gather the rest of my things?"

"Yes, of course. Anything to assist," Mr. Thorne said.

"What are you saying?" Thea asked. "You cannot leave now. The ball is on Thursday. If you leave now, you won't be back. Papa won't let you."

"Thea, my love, I cannot have poor Cassie there all alone. I'm certain G is not being useful in any sense of the word, and Isabella will need support."

"You cannot leave before the ball!" Mary exclaimed. "You're needed here."

"You promised you'd go to the ball with me," Thea said.

Elizabeth sighed and said, "Mr. Thorne? Mr. Fitzharding? Would you kindly allow me a moment alone with my sisters?"

James Fitzharding did not correct Elizabeth on the formal use of his name. He simply nodded and said, "Thorne? Come with me. Let us get some hot tea into you. Is it still raining out there? By the state of your boots, it appears so."

"That would be most welcome."

Once the gentlemen had left them alone, Elizabeth turned to her sisters. "Ladies, I am needed in two places at the same time. What solution can you offer me?"

"I need you for the ball," Mary said.

"All of the preparations are done, excepting that the bedrooms are not made up for the overnight guests, which will be happening over the next few days. What else is there for me to do?"

"Who will help Theodosia with her hair? Or her gown?" Mary asked.

"The maid, of course," Elizabeth said. "Just like the maid will help me with my hair."

"But you promised you'd be there!" Thea said.

"You will do fine," Elizabeth countered. "I am needed at home."

"You are needed here!" Thea said.

Elizabeth glanced at Mary, who said, in a very gentle voice, "Thea, kindly watch your tone when you speak to your eldest sister. This isn't how a young lady behaves."

"She is always choosing someone over me!"

"That is completely unfair, Thea. For heaven's sake, I came here with you, didn't I? It isn't like I had the time to leave Bryden and my studies or my duties there, but I came with you because you asked. It is not my fault, or yours, or even Isabella's that this happened."

"She didn't have to marry our papa," Thea said.

"This isn't the time for that argument," Mary countered.

Elizabeth said, "I know that you have never approved of Isabella's arrival in our home. You must remember that we cannot control the actions of others. We can only control ourselves. And you must govern yourself accordingly."

"I shall send Letitia with Mr. Thorne tonight," Mary announced.

Elizabeth did not wish to send a stranger to the rectory, to add to more of the servant gossip about their household. She should go and...

"Yes, I believe this is our plan. My nursemaid is very experienced, and she has helped me recover after my three children. No offence to Mrs. Thorne, who I have nothing but the highest opinion, but she has never laid in before. To be very honest with you, Eliza, neither have you. We must have someone who is experienced in these matters. Letitia will be an excellent choice."

"But surely the children need her here," Elizabeth countered. "Poor Nanny Rideout cannot be expected to care for them all day long. And Miss Shipley has only just begun her employment here. Lucy is too young to be mindful of a governess's instructions."

"Miss Shipley will get along well enough. I shall make inquiries in the village for a nurse to help here at Ashbrook for the present."

"I would prefer to be at the rectory in case I am needed," Elizabeth said.

"And you can be at the rectory in a matter of hours if you are needed, as we can send you in our own carriage. However, there is no point to fuss and worry, and you'll only be in the way there. Yes, this is settled. Elizabeth will remain here at Ashbrook and I shall..."

"Mary, we never agreed..."

Mary was already half out of the room. "I shall be right back. I must let Letitia know she is needed at Bryden."

"But Mary..."

It was too late, and Elizabeth sighed. Once Mary had come upon a decision, there was nothing any mortal could do to stop her. Elizabeth folded up her letters and began the process of squaring her shoulders to go face a room full of strangers all too eager to see her falling apart.

"It's not fair," Thea whispered.

"I'm sorry?"

"I said it is not fair," Thea said louder.

"What is not fair?"

"That you keep breaking your promises to me. You promised to be here, but when the others need you, you were ready to rush off and help them as opposed to be here and keep your promise."

Elizabeth looked at her younger sister and struggled to find the right amount of compassion. Unable to find it, she finally said, "Then, I recommend you put on your best smiles and flattery. For if you do not attract a husband, you will spend your life having others tell you what they wish of you. You will be unable to make the simplest of decisions for yourself because you will be required in three different places at once. And, if I might be so bold, Isabella's life is more important to me than a ball."

Elizabeth did stop by the door and said, "Thea, I realize this ball is the moment you've been waiting for your entire life thus far. However, there will be other balls, and other parties. It is natural to be disappointed. It is not acceptable to be sullen to the point of making life difficult for others. Govern your feelings or not, I cannot make you do either. However, the rest of us do not need to endure your moods and complaints in silence."

With that, Elizabeth walked out of the room, head high, and went in search of Mr. Thorne. She would not be brow-beat into guilt right now.

MARY'S SUPPER GUESTS were enthralled with the details of a stillborn babe and were all quite gleeful to share their own grisly misadventures and mishaps. Elizabeth used the shock of the terrible news to excuse herself from the card party and escaped to the silence of her room. She decided to attempt summoning Miss Gibbs. For if ever there was a time for the advice of a healer, now was that time. She brought Mrs. Egerton forward, reviewed her journal, and began where they left off.

She continued her notes for both her journal and the London ladies, but the most she could produce was a soft giggle. Frustrated, Elizabeth said aloud, "Miss Gibbs, I know you are able to hear me. Would you kindly come forth for no other reason than to prove Mrs. Egerton incorrect about you?"

With that, Miss Gibbs appeared with a big smile and even bigger hair. She was shockingly short for a woman, with a face fatter than what matched her figure. Still, she was smiling and laughing and said, "My dearest Sarah! What year is it?"

Mrs. Egerton let out a long sigh that was rather shockingly rude.

"1810, madam," Elizabeth said. She curtsied and said, "I am Miss Knight. It is a great honour to meet you."

⚜ Chapter 20 ⚜

MISS GIBBS EYED Elizabeth's outfit, as well as Mrs. Egerton's, and said, "Is this representative of the latest fashions?"

"I am perhaps more simply dressed than you will find in the higher ranks of society, but this was in fashion two years ago," Elizabeth said.

Miss Gibbs gave Mrs. Egerton an appraising eye. "Look at you, Sarah. Pink and brown stripes. Well, I cannot have that myself, though I do love the style. Goodness, look how flimsy this gown is. I'd be afraid we could see your legs with a candle behind you. What about yellow? Is that an acceptable colour in...1810 you say? My goodness, has it taken that long to summon me? I do not recall any such summoning until your attempts. Well, no matter, for I am here now and you shall tell me all, I am certain. But of course, I must update my gown. Now, do I recall how to do this? Goodness, I have been dead for some time now. How strange indeed."

Elizabeth attempted, and failed, to get a word in while Miss Gibbs fussed through eight different outfits before receiving Mrs. Egerton's begrudging consent. Finally, Miss Gibbs settled on a smart dress of mustard yellow, a yellow and black hat adorned with black feathers, and a white cotton shawl.

"Now that I am properly attired for this introduction, shall I make the assumption that I am needed to solve a matter of someone being sick?" She grinned at Elizabeth. "Perhaps you are sick?"

"No, indeed. My stepmother has been very ill with her first child. We had hoped to summon you before it was too late."

"Oh dear. Is she dead then?" Miss Gibbs asked. Cheerily.

"She lost the babe this morning," Mrs. Egerton supplied.

"Ah. Then I am not needed. Oh, that is a shame. I do love to teach how healing magic works after all! Alas, it is back to my book page for me. Perhaps the next young lady to summon me will be wearing nothing at all and be as naked as the day she came into the world. Wouldn't that be a laugh! Given how the gowns are going, I suspect naked breasts will be all of the..."

"Miss Gibbs," Elizabeth said, interrupting the new ghost's opinions on fashion, "I would still like to know more about healing magic. It is my hope to learn more to share with the Ladies Occult Society. We are, um, a small collection of ladies who are attempting with work with the occult."

"Women are not allowed to use the occult in this time," Mrs. Egerton supplied. "The men took over."

"Have they? How ghastly. What does a man know about midwifery healing? Why, he might think he does with his medical forceps and his dirty hands and miasma simply oozing off his dirty clothes, but I tell you that he knows nothing."

Elizabeth waited several more minutes of Miss Gibbs' cheery dismissal of just about everything before she found an excellent place to interject. "Miss Gibbs, thank you for appearing for me. I wish to learn more about the healing side of the occult. I am a hard worker, and will do all that I can with the limited resources that I have."

"Then, who do you wish to kill?"

"No one!" Elizabeth exclaimed. Laughing at herself, she said, "I believe you misunderstood me. I wish to heal someone."

"Yes, I heard you. To do that, you will most likely kill someone. Who should we kill? Mrs. Egerton, you've been here longer than myself. Who should be our sacrifice?"

Elizabeth's rising panic was dissuaded by Mrs. Egerton's dramatic sigh and eye roll. "Ah, you are teasing me, ma'am."

Miss Gibbs' grin showed rather excellent teeth. "The most important lesson of the healing art is that it is unpredictable. You cannot remove the illness. You can only move it. Depending upon the severity, you may be choosing who lives or dies. At all times, you must remember that, my dear young lady."

"Then an occultist chooses where the illness goes?" Elizabeth asked.

"No." Miss Gibbs' grin returned. "Unless she chooses herself. She can always choose that. Now, the issue will be if she is able to move the condition to herself. It is not always possible."

"So, I could not take on my stepmother's ailments as she recovers from a stillbirth?"

"Exactly. However, you could make her condition go to another. You will have no choice in the matter, but sometimes it is easy enough to predict. If there is only one woman lately laying in, then it stands to reason she would endure the suffering."

Mrs. Egerton said, "This is why healing arts are so dangerous, my dear."

"Everything is dangerous, my dear Mrs. Egerton." Miss Gibbs smiled. "After all, perhaps you have the occult to thank for making you a widow."

Mrs. Egerton rolled her eyes at Elizabeth's gasp. "He was a sick, old man who dropped dead from eating too much meat and port. It is the entire reason I married him."

"That and his money, of course."

"Of course. A woman must make her own way in the world. It is easier with an inheritance."

Elizabeth was unsure what to think of this conversation and made several attempts to speak. Mrs. Egerton answered Miss Gibb's quizzical gaze.

"In this time, they believe in love *before* the marriage ceremony."

"Good god. How vulgar."

Elizabeth said, "I must defend my sex in this. Some women do not wish to marry simply for a comfortable home. We wish to like the man we are to spend the rest of our lives with."

Mrs. Egerton and Miss Gibbs looked at her as if she were speaking a foreign tongue. Elizabeth sighed and asked, "Would you be so kind as to share a list of books for myself and the other ladies to research? Even if we do not wish to engage in such risky enterprise, it would be excellent to have the knowledge."

Miss Gibbs clapped her hands together and said, "Let us begin."

❧ Chapter 21 ❧

June 25, 1810

My dear Miss Keats,

I wish health to all of your family. I must apologize for my delay in responding to your lengthy and informative letter. We have had a distressing bit of news at the rectory and I have been visiting my sister at Ashbrook when all of this took place. Now, I must be alarming you so pray allow me to explain the situation.

Mrs. Knight has been brought to bed with a stillborn son. At present, she remains out of danger, and we pray constantly for her continued health. She has not developed the typical infections or fevers yet, thank God.

I an unable to leave Ashbrook at present, but my dear friend, Mrs. Thorne, is assisting, and my sister Mary has sent her nursemaid to help at the rectory so that I can remain here. Thankfully, there are no other illnesses or even so much as a headache to report. Well, my sister Mary's headaches *continue, but she has suffered those since we were girls. She was also excellent friends with the current Mrs. Knight long before her marriage to our father, so the worry is most likely causing this new wave of pains to plague her.*

My sister has been given a new remedy to try: plain boiled mutton and plain coffee to drink. She has tried it just last night, desperate for any relief that was not a draft of laudanum, and she reported her headache was gone by this very morning upon waking, which she has never experienced in her life. She is very pleased with this advice. I pass it along in case you yourself suffer from any headaches. This has been most miraculous for her quick recovery, especially given we have our ball in only three days. She vows not to stray from this menu for anything, as she wishes to be in her finest form. Though, she also confesses she misses cake with her tea.

I wish to share with you the exciting news: we have successfully summoned a Miss Gibbs! She is a ghost of amazing healing knowledge. She has agreed to share with me—and, therefore, all of you—her knowledge on healing arts. Her first lesson, as ever, is more study. I provide a list of books we already own, and its current location. As well, I have included a list of books I do not own. Could you write back to indicate if you own any of them? I shall then write to Mr. Osborne in London for assistance finding the others.

Now, I have written to our dear friends in London already with this list that follows on its own page, so do not feel obligated to re-write them this list. Oh, for us to all live in the same village so that we could simply walk to each other's home every morning. One of us must marry very well so that we can all live merrily together. I suppose no sensible man would take us silly women all on at once. Alas, I worry we shall have to rely upon the excellent letter service.

Sincerely,
E. Knight

Books in our possession:
Instruction in Occult Uses of Common Plants for Healing Purposes (Bryden)
On the Forgotten History of Female Occultists (Bryden)
First Forays into the Study of Occult Flora (Bryden)
A Complete Guide to Occult Uses of Common Kitchen Foods, with Recipes by Women of Experience. (London)

Books we do not own:
A Complete and Thorough Introduction to Occult Uses of Plants Native to England and Wales for the Direction of Healing Arts, with Careful Considerations
The History of Occult Healing in England, Including Stories by Occultists from Ireland and France.

June 25, 1810

My dearest Isabella,

First, I must apologize for my handwriting. I have some small blisters upon the tips of my fingers that burst today. Do not be alarmed; Mary accidentally dropped something into the fireplace and, without thinking, I plunged my hand in to rescue it. The blisters themselves are of a trivial size and nature and will most likely be gone in a day. However, I confess they sting this morning as if they were the size of my entire hand.

Thank you ever so much for your letter this morning. I am relieved to discover you so much improved that you have taken a turn about your bedchamber. Pray, however, please heed the instructions of both Mr. Collins and Mrs. Green. Please do it for my nerves if not for yourself. I worry every moment of the day about your health. If you need me there, please do not stand on ceremony. I shall abandon Thea and Mary to their ball and return home as quickly as I can convince Mr. Fitzharding to ready the horses.

With regards to the ball, there is little for me to do except keep Thea from purchasing everything in Ashbrook's shops. She has already purchased three new pairs of gloves, another pair of shoes, and three ready-made dresses that have already been fitted up to her size, which I confess was extraordinary luck. Apparently, the shop owners have a daughter about Thea's size, so they always keep a selection of gowns on display in the case of dire emergencies. It required almost no additional work whatsoever to make the gowns fit Thea.

And you know Mary well enough to know that Thea only having two everyday gowns was a Mrs. Fitzharding emergency of the gravest sort. Nay, only a full invasion of England not seen since the days of Hastings would have account for more of a fuss. Mary made the shopkeeper and his wife, a seamstress of exceptional skill that nearly rivals Miss Sims, very happy with the purchases, according to Thea.

Pray, do not make yourself uneasy that my father promised you to secrecy with regards to the new curate. I understand all too well that there must be secrets between a man and his wife, and I cannot expect exceptions to be made in my own family. Mr. Sinclair is a good sort of man, from what I can tell, and I believe he will offer the levity we desperately need at the rectory. Mary is already matchmaking, however, so pray be upon your guard when she writes to you of her plans.

Please write with frequent updates so that I do not worry. I shall, of course, worry in any case, but I would prefer to be silly about it and it be all in vain.

My full affection,
Elizabeth

⁂

My dearest niece,

I have just received the news about poor Mrs. Knight and I am writing to offer you my support. How dreadful for you all to have such terrible news. I am relieved that she survived the ordeal, however, and that the last word I received was just this morning from Mrs. Thorne who reports that Mrs. Knight is out of danger now. I pray this is true.

I trust all is going well at Ashbrook. What a terrible time for you to be away from home. It is moments like these that I feel I should move to the country. Though, I must also think of poor Miss Susan, who I am certain you have heard all of the details concerning. However, I do not believe Miss Thorne has had the opportunity yet this morning to write to you about dinner last night, so allow me to share my side of things.

Elizabeth laughed as she read the letter aloud to Mrs. Egerton, which detailed a shocking amount of flirtation between Mr. Osborne and Miss Susan Markson, and ended with a declaration that Mr. Osborne had better make a proposal of marriage soon lest Miss Thorne abduct them both and drag them to Gretna Green in a hired carriage.

"I have heard of young people running off together, but this is ridiculous," Mrs. Egerton said.

"When people are married themselves, they have nothing better to do than marry off everyone else," Elizabeth said. "Though, I confess Miss Thorne has no interest in marriage at present. However, if Miss Markson manages to catch the delightful Mr. Osborne, then I fear poor Miss Thorne will not escape the matchmakers."

❧ Chapter 22 ❧

AT LENGTH, THE day of the ball was finally upon them. Youthful vigour caused Thea to roam the halls at five in the morning and the servants took it upon themselves to wake the housekeeper for assistance. When Elizabeth rose at the luxurious hour of nine in the morning, Mrs. Webb informed her that she'd ushered the girl back to bed.

Elizabeth smiled and asked how she managed such a feat on the day of a ball.

"I reminded her that Mrs. Fitzharding's balls are famous for carrying on through the night until dawn's light." Mrs. Webb smirked. "Then I informed her that, no matter how excited she felt upon rising, she could not feel thus at midnight after having been up since five in the morning. The young miss saw it my way and retreated back to her bed."

Elizabeth thanked the housekeeper for the quick assistance. "Quite a similar intervention was needed for me at that age."

"I am certain many a young lady has needed the help of her elders on such a morning," Mrs. Webb assured Elizabeth. "Now, as I understand, Mrs. Fitzharding will be taking her breakfast in her bedchamber, as she normally does before a ball. However, please help yourself to what is laid out in the drawing room."

The breakfast was, as usual, hearty and Elizabeth helped herself to a full plate. With the ball preparations, there would not be much to eat until around very late that night, when the ball's supper would be served, and she did not wish to feel faint all day.

Elizabeth was tasked with cutting the hothouse flowers for Mary to make an arrangement for the entry hall, so she took to that assignment after her meal. Several letters arrived for her in the course of the morning. She only opened the one from Maria announcing that Isabella's health had improved so much that she took breakfast in the dinner room the previous day. Maria was still travelling back and forth daily, with her maid sleeping at the rectory, and Elizabeth was happier than ever for Mrs. Taylor's previous foresight in preparing the attic rooms.

After cutting the flowers and having the maid place them in water until Mary could do the arrangement, there was little for Elizabeth to do. The servants knew their tasks well enough that they were bustling about with their day already planned; offering assistance would only get in their way.

Elizabeth retreated to her room to inspect her ballgown. The maid had hung it upon a hook in the closet to shake out the creases. The yellow silk gown was two years old now, but was still in excellent shape. Miss Sims had provided a lovely textured blue ribbon for under the bodice, which lent a very fashionable edge to the simple gown. The sleeves were short and puffed just a touch at the shoulders, with the improvement of the blue ribbon also added in a narrow strip from the cuff to the shoulder. All in all, the small improvements suggested by Miss Sims had refurbished a basic ballgown into something that looked rather new and fashionable.

A knock came at the door followed by Mary and her maid. She took one look at the gown and asked, "When did you get a new gown? You said nothing of it."

"This is not new at all. It's my old yellow dress," Elizabeth said.

Mary stepped over to investigate. "The plain yellow silk gown? My goodness. It looks completely new. Oh, it is the ribbon. My, what expensive ribbon this is. I purchased something quite similar in Eastmore, when I was there last Christmas, and it cost me a shilling for three yards! How on earth did you manage to afford this? Elizabeth Knight, you are going to be poorer than a church mouse if you keep spending like this."

"I purchased it from Miss Sims. I assure you, she was not charging those prices or I could not have afforded it."

"Oh, yes, she has her trunk of wonders. Yes, Theodosia was telling me of it. Well, very good then, if she can make her money off selling the fabric of others."

"Mary! That isn't what happened at all. She offers the cut ends back, and if no one wishes them, she keeps them. A small cost to improve an old gown is very agreeable, and nothing goes to waste." In her best imitation of her father, Elizabeth said, "Waste is a sin, Mary Knight."

"I did not mean anything harmful by my words. Indeed, I think it is very resourceful," Mary said, rather defensively. "Now, I have arranged for my hairdresser to arrive at one, and I suspect he will be with Thea for most of the day to fix whatever Georgiana has done to it. I am so vexed with her at this moment. We may have to resort to faux curls to correct it!"

"Mary, it is not yet eleven in the morning."

"I have no notion of how long it will take Mr. Price to do her hair. It will need to have enough cut so that my maid can glue it to some ribbon. Then, it will need to be curled. This will take the entire day, I am certain, to ensure she does not look like a boy."

"For pity's sake, keep your voice down," Elizabeth scolded. "She doesn't need to hear that, not hours before a ball. Have some compassion."

Mary appraised Elizabeth's braided hair. "Your hair has grown too long on top. You look like a sheepdog."

"Why, thank you, Mary. I adore a sheepdog. So fluffy. So soft. With such kind, unjudgmental hearts." At her sister's growing annoyance, Elizabeth said, "Yes, send in your hairdresser first. I would like my top cut a little."

"I assume you shall wear a ribbon in your hair?" Mary asked.

"No. Do you recall that old white band of Augusta's? She stopped wearing it because she'd dropped it in the mud? G wrapped it in the blue ribbon from my gown and it looks rather striking, I believe."

Mary nodded that she did remember the piece well and asked to see it. Elizabeth dug it out of her trunk and showed it to her sister. Mary inspected it and made several sounds that showed she was pleased with the work, but would not say so. "Georgiana's craftsmanship improves. I assume she still cannot sew for her supper?"

Elizabeth laughed, and for the first time in a very long time it wasn't forced. "She is still an appalling seamstress. But give her ribbon and a pot of glue, and she can work wonders. Her and Thea could open a milliner's shop tomorrow and be the most successful businesswomen in all of England."

Mary's eyes grew sad, and Elizabeth understood all too well what her sister was feeling. There was a time when Elizabeth and Mary were that close. Closer, even, for they had the maturity of circumstance and situations to discuss. G and Thea did not spend a night in bed together under the blankets, to muffle the sound of their voices, as Mary announced she wished to marry Mr. Fitzharding to escape their father. How Mary said a rich husband she did not love was better than her father's penny-pinching and beratements.

And how Elizabeth attempted to discourage her, saying marrying without love was not an escape. How they'd argued that night. How Elizabeth's good opinion of her sister faded when Mary announced her engagement. How jealousy overtook her when her father declared Mary the best of his daughters. How jealousy overtook Mary when Elizabeth seemingly continued to thrive under her father's thumb.

Elizabeth realized the maid was no longer in the room. Somewhere in the conversation, and the subsequent silence that followed, the maid quietly escaped and had closed the door. Bryden servants were likely to stand around the door and listen in to share the gossip later about the village. Ashbrook's servants understood the family and the quirks of sisters, it seemed. The maid had the good sense to leave the ladies alone to work out whatever it was that stood between them.

"I hope you are not upset that Mr. Sinclair asked Thea to dance," Mary finally said, breaking the silence.

"Not at all. This is her coming out ball. I am long past such things."

"You could choose to marry," Mary said. She hastily raised a hand, to stop Elizabeth's protests. "Please understand me. I am not suggesting that you must or should marry just for society's sake. I simply mean you could make that choice for yourself. You are still young enough that a man of good sense would not be appalled by your age."

Elizabeth chuckled. "Indeed, Mary, you make it sound as though I have one foot upon the grave."

"I did not mean that. You always take what I say and twist it to tease me."

"Mary, I am nearly twenty-nine years of age. No man wishes to marry me as poor as I am."

"You are not so poor as you once were and consider Aunt Cassandra's estate. We all know you will inherit much from it, no matter what you may say."

Elizabeth shook her head. "Do not forget that Cousin David expects all of her lands and property. As for Aunt Cass, we have never spoken on the subject."

Mary waved a hand. "David will inherit the London house. That is not ready cash, and you have no need for a house in town. You also forget Aunt Cass has the estate in Derbyshire that she lets out and, as I understand it, at a very handsome sum. She still earns all of her income from the lands there, too. Indeed, Elizabeth, I suspect whatever ready money she can give you, she will."

"Our dear aunt isn't even fifty yet," Elizabeth said. "It is my hope she is still alive when I am fifty. No man is going to marry me upon the hope that my aunt eventually drops dead and that my cousin does not produce little ones that my aunt immediately falls in love with."

They were silent.

"James married me."

"You married the only man in England willing to take a poor wife." Elizabeth smiled. "It is unfortunate he does not have an unmarried brother."

"You would no doubt find fault with him." Mary's eyes fell upon Mrs. Egerton's ghost book. "Did I damage your book terribly?"

Elizabeth shook her head. "No. There is some staining from the ash, but I have been using a brush to clean as much as I dare."

"Then I am sorry for that," Mary said. She sighed and said, "And I am sorry for Mama's necklace."

"I know you are," Elizabeth said quietly.

Tears filled Mary's eyes. "James is an excellent man and has been the best husband a woman could ask for."

"I know," Elizabeth said.

"I have been unable to read the letters you sent me, from Mama to Uncle Edward."

Elizabeth thought about reaching out to touch her sister, but did not. She was not ready for that. The distance seemed too far, as if she were to reach across the ocean. Instead, she said, "They were not meant to distress you, but rather for you to know she loved you."

Mary's jaw trembled, but she said nothing.

The silence stretched between them. It was Elizabeth who broke it. "I shall get dressed so that the hairdresser does not see me in my dressing gown and shift."

"Would you like me to send in the maid?"

"Please," Elizabeth said.

Without another word, Mary left and the maid returned. Elizabeth's spirits sank as her heart ached for companionship.

﹊❦ Chapter 23 ❧﹍

NO MATTER ONE'S opinion of Mary, there was no denying her ability to throw a private ball. Her "intimate affair" comprised of sixty-three guests, including sixteen single young men of good breeding who would be encouraged to dance with Thea until dawn the next morning. Elizabeth had been excused from the receiving line at the front, thankfully, under the guise of greeting guests inside, and making any attempts to direct single young men toward Thea's arm. Elizabeth took the task with good humour.

The first two dances with Mr. Sinclair went rather smoothly. Thea's nerves were visible, of course, but her face was radiant and her shoulders straight. Her hair was exceptionally arranged. Thick curls lined the front of her head and were framed by one of Mary's tiaras. Then, more curls and swirls were pinned into place with borrowed pearl-tipped pins.

Theodosia Knight did not look like a boy.

Mr. Thorne approached her and said, "Miss Knight? Might I interrupt your private delights and request this dance?"

"I would be delighted, Mr. Thorne!"

They took their position in the set. There were enough dancing couples that required the formation of two lines down the room, which delighted Mary to no end and could be seen grinning and clapping off to the side to the first notes of the music.

"Your sister seems very pleased with the ball," Mr. Thorne said.

Elizabeth laughed. "Which sister, pray? Both look very pleased with themselves indeed."

"How fares Miss Thea?"

They stepped apart and Mr. Sinclair appeared in the set, grinned at Elizabeth as they danced their steps, and then she was returned to Mr. Thorne. "I will consider the ball a success if she does not run off to Gretna Green by the morning."

Mr. Thorne laughed at that. "Maria sends her regrets on not attending. She did not want to leave Mrs. Knight's side."

"How is Isabella? I received a letter this morning from her own hand. She sounds much improved, but I do not know how faithful her account is."

Mr. Thorne was happy to share that Isabella was in excellent health and was declared out of all danger. "She still has to recover her strength, but Mr. Collins believes she shall be at her best within a fortnight."

"A fortnight!" Elizabeth exclaimed. "Goodness, that is ambitious."

"Indeed. Mrs. Green believes it will be several months before Isabella has recovered her strength..."

They parted again and Mr. Sinclair was once again her partner. They chatted and did their turn together before Mr. Thorne reappeared. "However all of the worries, Mrs. Green believes Isabella will be her full self by Christmas."

That was excellent news indeed and brightened Elizabeth's spirits considerably. She finished the set with Mr. Thorne, who asked if she thought he should ask Miss Thea for a dance. Elizabeth looked over at Thea who was red-faced and glowing while talking rather close to a young man she didn't know.

"She looks rather occupied at the moment," Elizabeth said with a grin.

Mr. Thorne laughed at that and said, "Then I shall inflict myself upon another young lady."

A Mr. Finch from London, down visiting his country relations, asked Elizabeth to dance. He wasn't a great dancer, but he was funny, and she enjoyed the half hour standing up with him.

She kept an eye out for Thea, however, and noticed the girl was being accosted by a young man. Elizabeth walked toward them, attempting to be casual and not make a scene for either of her sisters. She eavesdropped with her back partially turned to them.

"Isn't this affair dull, though?" the young man was asking.

"No, indeed, sir! I protest. I am having a grand time." Thea's voice was light and airy, but Elizabeth knew the anticipation of hoping an invitation to dance was in the future.

"I believe I shall take a turn in the walk outside. Why don't you accompany me, Miss Knight? I could show you the hothouse."

At Thea's awkward giggle, Elizabeth intervened. "Theodosia! There you are, my dear. Pray, who is your friend? We are not introduced."

"Oh, this is Mr. Stone. He is visiting his aunt and uncle in the country," Thea said. The girl was still smiling, though she also had a look of mild embarrassment. As if the girl had been caught nearly accepting an invitation to be alone with a strange man to tour the hothouse of her own sister's estate. "Mr. Stone, this is my eldest sister, Miss Knight."

Elizabeth curtsied the bare minimum as required by etiquette. Mr. Stone's bow was one of a man wanting to flee.

"Mr. Stone, how are you enjoying the ball?"

"Very well, Miss Knight," he said. He was glancing about the ballroom now, no doubt looking for an acquaintance to help him escape.

"Who is next to be on your arm, Thea? The music will be starting up soon again," Elizabeth asked.

"Um, well, um, Mr. Stone was asking about Mary's hothouse."

"Indeed! Are you a botanist by trade or by hobby, sir?"

Mr. Stone cleared his throat and flashed what he no doubt believed was a disarming smile. "Well, by hobby. I have heard a great many things about the Fitzharding hothouses."

"Then, pray, you should visit tomorrow. I would be happy to take you on a tour of them."

Confusion came across Mr. Stone's face. "Oh, are you staying here with Mrs. Fitzharding?"

"I am her eldest sister," Elizabeth said. Her smile did not fade. "Miss Thea, here, is Mrs. Fitzharding's second youngest sister."

"Oh," Mr. Stone said. His disappointment only faltered for a moment before he said, "Oh, I see my aunt is attempting to catch my attention. Ladies, if you will excuse me, I shall go attend her."

"With pleasure, sir," Elizabeth said.

When Mr. Stone walked out of hearing range, Elizabeth said, "In future, invent an excuse to escape such a man."

"It was just a walk, Eliza," Thea said with a nervous laugh.

"A walk with a strange man you only just met for him to show you your own sister's hothouse of all things?" Elizabeth frowned. "My dear girl, there are many dangers. Some are from charming men."

"You always overreact," Thea whispered. "I wasn't going to run off to Gretna Green with him."

Elizabeth realized she had not prepared her sisters—any of them—on why they needed to heed their reputations so tightly. Their father lectured constantly about the behaviour of young ladies, but never once did he explain why they needed to be protected from men.

Thea sighed at Elizabeth's silence. "I wouldn't have left the ball with him. I trust I have better sense than that."

Elizabeth was tempted to begin a lecture, but stopped herself. Instead, she called out to Mr. Thorne and said, "My dear Mr. Thorne. My sister appears to be without a partner for this dance, and I recall you expressing interest."

Mr. Thorne asked for Thea's hand to dance, and they joined the set just as the couples formed up. Elizabeth would speak to Mary about it. Perhaps she could approach the subject with more sisterly compassion and less the edicts of an elder sister.

Elizabeth did not have a partner for the dance before supper, causing her to enter the dining room alone. The supper was elegant, of course, but she expected nothing less from Mary or the Ashbrook staff. Elizabeth was seated next to Mr. Finch again, with Mr. Sinclair, Mr. Thorne, and Thea nearby.

Elizabeth joked that she was well-positioned at the supper table, for she was near the macaroni and stewed endive, as well as the sweetmeats and cheesecakes. Elizabeth ate happily and drank Mary's excellent wine.

The table conversation soon turned to the others speaking amongst themselves and she grew more isolated from the discussions as the supper went on. Eventually, she excused herself from the table under the pretense of checking on the card players to see if they wanted for anything, as she noticed several faces missing from the dining room.

She eventually made her way to one of the balconies, away from the guests, and soaked in the quiet of it all. Soon, the music started up again, signalling yet more dancing. She had enjoyed dancing in her youth, and still, for she was not so old as to abandon the amusement all together.

Yet, it was also a reminder at times that she had not found a man who thought her better than any other creature.

She cupped her hand around her locket for just a moment.

"How can I be in a room so full of people and yet be so alone?" she asked aloud.

"I believe I know the answer to that question."

Elizabeth spun around to find Mr. Sinclair standing there with his hands behind his back. He bowed and said, "Forgive the intrusion. Your sister tasked me with finding you and said you would be here."

Elizabeth turned to look back outside at the torches below in the courtyard. "Did she?"

"Well, she might have mentioned something about how this is where you always hide from her guests."

"Does Mary need me to clear the supper dishes?" She caught herself too late and said, "I apologize. That was uncharitable."

Mr. Sinclair approached her, but not too close. "I have enough siblings, Miss Knight, to know that it is not possible to be charitable at all times."

"If a clergyman cannot maintain domestic bless, what hope is there for the rest of us laypeople?" Elizabeth asked.

"I recommend tithing more."

Elizabeth chuckled, though she was struck with a realization that she had not tithed a single shilling of her money. As the daughter of the rector, no one expected her to contribute to the running of the church or the rectory itself. Still, it had not even occurred to her to tithe.

"Shall we step back into the ballroom before some local gossip finds us together huddled in moonlight and then we shall have to marry?" Mr. Sinclair asked.

"I would not call this huddled, Mr. Sinclair," Elizabeth said. But then, with a dramatic sigh that would have done Mrs. Egerton proud, she said, "But I suppose marrying you would be such a disgrace. Indeed, a mere country curate! The scandal!"

Mr. Sinclair laughed heartily and asked, "Tell me, Miss Knight. Do you fear anyone?"

Her smile did not flicker. "Should I fear you?"

Mr. Sinclair bowed deeply. "My dear madam, I can assure you that you have nothing to fear from me."

"Then no, I fear no one. Now, let us find you a worthy dance partner."

ELIZABETH AND MR. Sinclair discovered the room where the coats and outdoor footwear were being stored offered an excellent view of the dance floor. Elizabeth pushed the door back into their room so that they could see more clearly.

"So, which of these young ladies should I ask to dance?" He grinned. "After all, if Bryden is as dull as you say, I might never have the opportunity again."

"As shocking as it may sound, we occasionally dance in the country," Elizabeth muttered. She gave him a smile to signal she was not offended. "Now, let me see. Who here is worthy of Mr. Sidney Sinclair with twelve-hundred and fifty a year."

"And fifty?"

"Is that not the going rate for a curacy in the country?"

Mr. Sinclair nodded. "Fair enough."

"Ah, I spy one of the Miss Arnolds over there, though I cannot recall her Christian name. There must be fifteen daughters between the three Arnold brothers. However, I have heard she is an excellent creature. Oh, what is her name." Elizabeth shook her head. "I can ask Mary if you wish an introduction. She knows everyone."

Mr. Sinclair made an uninterested sound. "She is a little plain."

"Mr. Sinclair, I will not allow you to abuse Miss Arnold, or anyone, to me. Lydia Arnold! I knew I would remember it. That is Miss Lydia Arnold, second daughter of Mr. Eli Arnold of Manydown Abbey, who has a dowry of six thousand pounds."

"I must say, Miss Knight, her features do improve upon second reflection."

"Yes, I suspected she would grow in beauty. Would you like an introduction?"

Mr. Sinclair made a show of thinking and pondering, and so Mary caught them in the closet.

"What are the two of you doing huddled together in the closet of all places? Here, in the view of everyone in the ballroom?" Mary demanded.

"Would we call this huddled, Mrs. Fitzharding?" Mr. Sinclair asked.

"Mary, you make it sound so nefarious. The door is open in plain sight of everyone," Elizabeth said with a laugh. "I am merely attempting to find him a young lady to dance with."

"She recommended a Miss Lydia Arnold, and I do find her six thousand pounds brings out the light in her eyes."

"Miss Lydia Arnold does not mean to dance this evening," Mary said with disgust. "Why even bother attending a ball if you have no interest in dancing? Even I have danced thrice tonight, despite how it brings on my headaches."

"Perhaps she did not wish to offend you by refusing the invitation," Elizabeth said.

Mary looked shocked. "Me? Offended? Why would I be offended?"

"Ah! What about that young lady there? With the white feather in her hair. She is very beautiful, in a country sort of way."

"Oh, Mr. Sinclair, you are abominable," Elizabeth declared.

"Blame my town manners."

Mary shook her head. "I beg you both. Kindly step out into the ballroom proper. There. Was that so difficult? Now, close the door, Mr. Sinclair, if you please. I do not want my guests to see their muddy boots. What is the point of having a closet to hide things away if your guests keep opening the doors to the room?"

"Mary, that isn't a closet. It's the drawing room we normally take breakfast in," Elizabeth said. "It's big enough for a dozen card tables!"

"Do not contradict me," Mary said. She waved at someone further down the crowded room. "I must go. Pray, make Mr. Sinclair dance with someone."

"I shall do my best, Mary," Elizabeth said. Turning to Mr. Sinclair, she said, "Now, what lady will be good enough for your snobbish town manners?"

ELIZABETH WAS ASKED to dance by the Arnold twins. She knew Emanuel had the large mole on his jaw (which was why he wore his sideburns thicker than was sensible) and that Eli had the full beard (due to the terrible skin pimples that plagued him). However, she pretended not to tell them apart, and the two young men delighted in teasing her. And, she got to dance two dances because of it, so she was very pleased with herself.

She was enjoying a glass of wine near her drawing room door once more, or as Mary called it, the closet. Thea bounced her way over to her. "I declare, I have never had more fun in my life."

Elizabeth smirked when her sister grabbed the wine glass from her hand and took a rather indelicate gulp. She carefully took the glass back and said, "Perhaps go easy on the wine, my dear. You do not wish to end up fatigued and too dizzy to dance."

"Not able to dance!" Thea declared. "It is impossible not to dance! The young men won't let me sit down, not once. They are all fighting each other to have a chance to take my arm and I cannot remember the last time I have had such fun. This is the best day of my life."

"Then, I recommend you do not waste it with me and go enjoy yourself. Oh, there is Mr. Neil Arnold. Mr. Arnold! Have you come this way to meet my sister?"

Elizabeth made introductions and Mr. Neil Arnold quickly asked for Thea's hand for the next dance that was just forming up.

Thea fluttered off, a significant bounce in her step, no doubt fuelled by too much cake and even more wine.

A pang of nostalgia hit Elizabeth once more. Oh, how she remembered her first ball. She had been the centre of attention, too. All of the young men asked her to dance. No one would let her sit out a dance. For the entire year, in fact, they kept her busy. Then, the next year she was not as busy with partners. And the year after, she was only thought of when there were no other new and fresh faces.

Now, she was rarely thought of as a dance partner, except when someone wished to dance and was desperate for any willing lady to take upon the task.

She refused to allow herself to sink in melancholic reflections. She was not yet an old maid, even if she sometimes wore a white cap about the house so that she would not need to do her hair beyond a braid. And at least she was not so old yet as to need to sit down between the dances to rest her feet or her sore back.

Though, she laughed to herself, her feet did, in fact, ache, from all of the standing about.

Mr. Sinclair returned to her side a moment later and asked, "What amuses you so much? I had to come to ask. I saw you laughing to yourself."

Elizabeth flashed her fan in front of her face and said, "Why, a lady never tells."

She was unable to maintain the joke, however, for she started laughing. She covered her mouth with her now-closed fan until she could bring some deportment to her expression.

"So, tell me. Are there balls in Bryden?"

"No public balls, though the Thornes and Baldwins usually have a private ball every winter near Christmas. They invite most of the local young people, which is very good of them both. The Thornes were considering hosting a ball for Thea, too, for her coming out. However, with Mrs. Knight's current condition, I suppose planning will be put off for some time."

"Is there any news of Mrs. Knight?"

"A servant from Vane Park was dispatched to me this morning with a letter to let us know there was no change in Mrs.

Knight's condition, and that Mrs. Green was very pleased. Mr. Collins, as well, feels she is nearly out of the worst of the danger. Mr. Thorne let me know that she is exceedingly well, considering her ordeal. However, we must be cautious and continue to pray for the best."

"I shall keep her in my own prayers, then, if it would please you," Mr. Sinclair asked.

"It would, sir. Thank you."

They were silent for a moment, watching the dancing unfold. "What about Eastmore? Are there public balls there?"

"During the summer months and into the autumn when the roads are mostly dry. They normally have a ball every fortnight starting in June. However, they had to do repairs to the floor. It was becoming too old to properly dance upon. If I recall, however, they plan to restart at the end of this month. Will you be in Bryden by then?"

"Yes, indeed. I must purchase myself a pass, as I plan to attend all of the balls." He gave Elizabeth a smile. "In fact, if I might be so bold, I plan to cause endless trouble with the hearts of all the young ladies."

"Then, I shall write to all of the young ladies in the county warning them to protect their hearts from you." She made a show of thinking. "Though, I suppose some will not listen, as there is always that percentage of young ladies who insist upon playing with candle flames, but I shall know that I had warned them. That will give me great comfort."

"That you warned them?"

She smiled at him. "That I was right about you."

Mr. Sinclair's laugh was so loud that it drew the scolding expressions of the older ladies about them. They went back to whispering, now no doubt about Mr. Sinclair and that old maid Miss Knight from Bryden. Elizabeth found she did not care. She did when she was Thea's age. That was only sensible. Even now, sometimes she did not want to rouse the notice of the old gossips; they would still make life difficult for her. Nevertheless, it was not she who had laughed like a common sailor; it had been Mr. Sinclair. Let them blame his relations.

"As everyone knows, Miss Knight, it is not the men who break hearts. It is always the ladies. This is known."

Elizabeth scoffed. "Pray, by whom is it known. I have never heard such a thing in my life, and I do believe I am older than you, if the rumours are true."

"Do you mean that I have been spending my time with an older lady? Good heavens. The gossip! The news!" Mr. Sinclair said. He was smiling, though, to let her know he was not offended. "As for my intelligence, I lean upon all that I have ever been taught or read. Women toy with the hearts of honest men and we poor men have to endure their abuse and teasing."

"Perhaps, Mr. Sinclair, you might wish to spend less time reading men's opinions of women."

Mr. Sinclair put his hand over his heart. "You are a harsh critic, Miss Knight."

"I speak as I find," Elizabeth said. Not wishing to continue the conversation further, especially not in the midst of a ballroom, she said, "Now, pray, confess to me the truth. Do you require assistance finding another partner? The candles have not yet burned down, so there are at least two more dances left if I am any judge. Now, do you see Miss Harris over there? She is seated and wearing a blue dress. She has not danced the last two dances. She is very shy and is too often overlooked. I believe it would mean the world to her to have your attention for a dance."

"I would be happy to make this young lady happy. May I request your assistance with an introduction?"

"Of course. Though, I must ask, if Mary inquires, pray tell her this was your request. I do not wish to stir her anger."

Mr. Sinclair frowned. "Does Mrs. Fitzharding not like this Harris family?"

"Oh, on the contrary. Her family is from reduced circumstances, but still very good and Mary would never dream of not including them. Apparently, Mr. Harris and Mr. Fitzharding were school fellows, but of course fortunes took very different turns for them. Mr. Harris owns Abbey Farms, which is a small property, so the girls are not as rich as many of the others here. And, if I must confess, it vexes me greatly that Miss Harris is so often overlooked because of her lack of a good dowry and her shyness. There is more to a woman than her dowry or her ability to flatter a man."

Mr. Sinclair made a thoughtful sound. "You must confess, however, that the only thing a man loves more than a dowry is a lady who will endlessly flatter him."

Elizabeth snorted, but she made no other comment. They walked toward Miss Harris, dodging dancers and servants carrying wine. When pressed for a comment, Elizabeth said, "A young woman like Miss Harris would know the value of a shilling more than any woman with a twenty-thousand pound dowry and, in my limited experience, a woman who can stretch fifty pounds to eighty or even ninety pounds is far more useful than one who only knows how to spend money."

Elizabeth did not mean for her words to be as harsh as she had delivered them, but she realized too quickly that she had taken the ball room's slight of Miss Harris more personally than perhaps she should have. After all, she was bringing Miss Harris a young man of wealth and consequence to dance with her; no one did that for Elizabeth.

Aware of Mr. Sinclair's silence, she said, "I suppose, however, that a young woman with ten thousand pounds would not need to make fifty pounds stretch."

He shrugged and his expression relaxed somewhat. "I do not plan to marry a woman with less than fifteen thousand pounds to her name. That way, I shall never have to worry about something so vulgar as paying creditors."

Elizabeth laughed. "You are impossible!"

"Nonsense. I will still dance with your Miss Harris, even without her lack of fortune. However, if I break her heart, Miss Knight, it will be entirely your own doing."

Elizabeth shook her head, but curtsied when she approached Miss Harris. She offered up the introductions and watched Mr. Sinclair ask her for the next two dances.

Miss Harris' pale face turned as red as a boiled beet, but she nodded. She mouthed a thank you at Elizabeth when Mr. Sinclair's back was turned slightly.

The world might too easily forget about the Miss Knights and the Miss Harrises, but she would not. And, for all of his bluster and silliness, Mr. Sinclair was dancing the last two dances of the ball with the shyest girl in the room. And he could talk enough for both of them.

Elizabeth smiled.

Chapter 24

ELIZABETH DOUBLED-CHECKED all of her hiding places about her room before she was convinced she had packed everything. She kept the ghost book with her, as was her habit, though she did not attempt to hide it from Mary's view now. Thea elected to stay behind with Mary, under the guise of helping organize the clean up. Elizabeth knew it was because Thea had drunk too much wine for the first time in her life and was no doubt suffering the most grievous of afternoons.

Mr. Fitzharding offered to escort her back to Bryden Rectory, but Elizabeth only laughed him off. Surely she was safe travelling six miles in a carriage with her sister's very own servants. Mary was too tired to protest properly, and Elizabeth was granted the rare luxury of travel completely alone.

She pulled down the shades inside the carriage as soon as they had pulled into the lane leading away from Ashbrook. She summoned Mrs. Egerton and Miss Gibbs.

"My dear girl, I would have thought you'd want to spend the journey in silence," Mrs. Egerton said. She glanced at her ghostly companion. "Not with endless nattering."

"How did you enjoy your ball, Miss Knight?" Miss Gibbs asked.

"She did not dance enough," Mrs. Egerton complained. "And she wasted too much time with that Mr. Sinclair."

Elizabeth was about to protest, but Miss Gibbs interjected. "My dear Sarah! Mr. Sinclair is about to be her father's curate. She must at least pretend to be delighted to him, lest he make her life uncomfortable."

"I was only being polite and showing him the proper attention as due my father's curate, Mrs. Egerton," Elizabeth protested. "After all, as Miss Gibbs has pointed out, he shall be living within view of the rectory."

"A long view," Mrs. Egerton muttered.

"Nevertheless, still within view. I would like to get to know him a little better before my sisters were faced with yet more surprises."

The next hour of the journey was filled with the endless bickering of two ghosts that sounded more like an old married couple than any two friends Elizabeth had known. For certain, she and Maria never bickered like this.

Elizabeth listened to the old ghostly friends bicker about the weather and the condition of the roads, and if the improvements of this era's roads were vastly different to their own, and she made a decision. It would be so tempting to use healing magic. To open up an occult book, find an incantation, and simply do whatever she wished without consideration to the consequences of her actions.

However, that was not Elizabeth Knight. She was a cautious, methodical woman who considered each and every action as carefully as possible to ensure others were not harmed. Miss Gibbs' had clued her into a piece, however: the occultist could always take on the sickness. The burden could be shared.

"I have come to a decision, if you ladies would be interested in hearing it," Elizabeth announced to the carriage. When she had the attention of both ghosts, she said, "From a practical sense, I wish to learn the basics of healing, for no other reason than my curiosity. However, I believe, if possible and with your approval, of course, I would wish to learn how to heal by taking upon myself the affliction. While I have no intention of bringing myself to harm, I believe I would be remiss in not knowing in case of extraordinary circumstances."

Mrs. Egerton gave Miss Gibbs a knowing look. "My dear, you must understand that even the knowledge of such a spellworking may take you many years to learn."

"The temptation to use it will be very great," Miss Gibbs warned. She laughed, in a manner that Elizabeth felt was inappropriate given the subject matter, and added, "I knew a girl who caught the plague because she was trying to heal her beau of it. She died."

"Did the young man live?" Elizabeth asked.

"No, indeed. He knew what she had done and took his life so that he would not have to bear the burden of her having lost hers for him," Miss Gibbs said with a laugh. "Oh, love. This is why I do not approve of it before marriage. It never leads to anything good or wholesome."

"I believe Miss Knight will be unmoved," Mrs. Egerton said.

Elizabeth made an airy gesture. "Honestly, us lady occultists are so busy that I do not see how any of us will have time for marriage."

"I wonder who this Mr. Sinclair will marry," Mrs. Egerton said thoughtfully. "I do like Miss Theodosia, though I find myself in agreement with Mrs. Fitzharding that they would be a terrible match."

"That reminds me. I am to ensure he is invited to dinner often, at least twice a week."

Miss Gibbs glanced between them. "Whatever for?"

"Mary wishes Mr. Sinclair to turn his attentions to my sister, Cassandra." Elizabeth shook her head. "I do not see how such a match would even happen, let alone be a happy one. Their tempers are nothing alike. Cassandra is shy and so serious. Mr. Sinclair wears his shirt collars too high and does not know the meaning of serious. They would not be a happy couple."

"Then why encourage the match?" Mrs. Egerton asked.

Elizabeth made a displeased sound. "No one wishes Mary's wrath upon them. Hopefully, Mr. Sinclair will turn his attentions to another young lady, or better yet, his family will find him a partner that meets with his approval and she could be brought here to Bryden. Then, there will be an end to it, and Mary can howl at his relations for all I care."

"I sense there is great uneasiness between you and your sister," Miss Gibbs said. She snorted and said, "Perhaps I will teach you how to transfer minor afflictions so that she catches every single sore throat in the neighbourhood."

"Do not tempt me, Miss Gibbs." Elizabeth smiled. "Oh, I beg you. Do not tempt me."

ELIZABETH PULLED HER chair close to Isabella and inquired into her health. Isabella was sitting up, and did not look feverish. She was exhausted though, and her body was still swollen and appeared uncomfortable from the pregnancy.

"Mrs. Green says the worst is over. In another day, provided no fever presents itself, I shall be allowed to walk about the hallways. I am not yet allowed outdoors, but she feels I will soon be ready for a little exercise. Oh, how I long for an open window, but Mr. Collins says we cannot risk me catching my death."

Elizabeth wished she'd brought her fan with her. The room was stuffy and overheated, and desperately needed a little fresh air to cleanse the room's miasma. However, one must never interfere with medical advice, so she resisted doing what her sense told her would help.

"I am very sorry you lost the baby," Elizabeth said finally.

Isabella nodded her head. She didn't cry. She simply looked exhausted. "Mr. Knight is very upset at the loss of another son. However, it has encouraged him that I can produce one for him in time."

Elizabeth bit down on the hot retort that came to her mind and successful planted a smile upon her face. "We must think of your health first, of course. After all, what good is a son if there is no mother to raise him properly?"

Isabella attempted her own smile, but it flickered. "Tell me, how was your ball?"

"Oh, Thea drank too much and danced every dance, and had a wonderful evening."

"I am relieved. How did her hair fare?"

"Mary brought in a hairdresser. He charged a shocking sum of money. Ten shillings! For each of us. I wish Mary would simply pay him out of her own pin money, but I know better than to dwell upon that fruitless hope. At least he put it up into pins and a very nice band and arranged my curls all around it. I could not have done that myself. And he trimmed Thea's hair in such a manner that the join is not nearly as noticeable. He was able to pull it all up in such a lovely style. Also, he said that short hair is very much fashionable in London at the moment, so Thea is considering cutting it shorter in the autumn when she goes to London."

"Your father will not approve," Isabella warned.

"I said as much, but she plans to concoct some scheme," Elizabeth said. She shrugged. "You cannot tell Thea anything once she has her mind made up. Best to let the idea leave her head on its own accord, or else she will simply dig in as stubbornly as any mule."

The ladies chatted on like that for a bit when Mr. Knight swung the door open without knocking. "Ah, there you are, Elizabeth. I had heard the carriage, but you did not come to see me."

"I wished to check on Isabella first," Elizabeth said.

"Yes, yes, your mother is well. Mark my words. You shall have a brother by next year this time."

"I hope I have a brother by next summer, sir, since I would be very grieved to lose Charles," Elizabeth said.

"I mean a new arrival, of course. After all, we cannot be remiss in our duty," Mr. Knight said. He gave the room a sniff. "The air is foul in here. Pray, why has no one opened the window? The heat is unbearable."

"Mr. Collins' instructions, for fear of a chill."

Mr. Knight scoffed that there was no possible way to gain a chill in the summer heat and pulled back the curtains. Even Elizabeth winced from the sudden brightness illuminating the room. He opened the window enough to shove the wooden block underneath.

"There. Not even the full length. Surely, my dear, you are ready to get up and about. There are a great many things to do, especially now that Mrs. Thorne had to return to Vane Park."

"I was wondering where Maria had gone."

Isabella gave Elizabeth a tight smile. "She had wished to stay for your arrival, but Mr. Knight assured her that I could manage on my own now and sent her away."

"I did not send her away. I merely informed her that we did not need a nurse any longer, especially now with Mary's nursemaid here about the house eating all of our bread." Mr. Knight made a disgusted sound. "You should have seen her, Elizabeth! She must eat three slices of our best bread in the mornings. And with butter!"

"I am certain we can afford to give a servant a little butter, sir," Elizabeth said flatly.

Mr. Knight glared at her, and in a rather surprisingly sharp tone, said, "It appears life at Ashbrook has made you forget your place."

"No, sir. I find myself well-informed on my place. Excuse me. I must speak with my sisters now that I am home."

ᕙᕋ Chapter 25 ᕚᕜ

IT TOOK ANOTHER two weeks before Elizabeth finally lost her patience. G and Cassandra got into a raging row that could be heard by any passing carriage on the lane. Elizabeth had been attempting to write a letter to Miss Keats about the importance of purifying herbs in any healing working. Unfortunately, the fighting had grown to such a pitch that she could not hear herself think.

Elizabeth walked into Cassandra's room, where G was draped across the bed wailing and Cassie was holding up a bonnet with determination written across her face. Theodosia was, unusually, seated in the corner and telling both to stop fighting.

"What is the matter?" Elizabeth demanded.

All of the girls began talking over one another and Elizabeth held up a hand. "Actually, girls, I find that I do not care. It is apparent to me that I have been remiss in the raising of all of you. I had hoped that advising our father to allow you some freedoms would put an end to this discord. However, it is clear to me now that none of you are ready for that independence. Do not give me that look, Theodosia Knight. You could not even get through your first ball without drinking and eating so much as to make yourself sick the entire next day. I leave you now to speak with our father and Isabella. And whatever happens, know that you alone brought it upon yourselves."

Elizabeth knocked on her father's study, with the cries of her sisters from the upper floor begging her to reconsider. He invited her inside and she found Isabella seated there with him.

"Should I assume you are here to complain about the girls?" Mr. Knight asked.

"No, sir. I am here to discuss myself."

Mr. Knight put down his pen. "What do you want?"

"Well, sir, to be very blunt, I wish more time to dedicate to my studies."

"Pray, what is stopping you?"

She blinked at his absurd question, but continued. "Neither I, nor Isabella, have the time to cater to the girls non-stop all day long. Cassie hasn't been demanding about needing our time, I admit, but she has been purposely leaving home far too much and avoiding her own tasks here to get away from G and Thea. They, in turn, are consuming all of my waking hours with their foolishness."

"What are you suggesting, Elizabeth?" Isabella asked.

"I believe it's time that the girls start learning how to properly run a household. There are five women living under this roof and I believe it is time the work is shared."

Mr. Knight looked at his wife. "What is your opinion on this? Are they of an age? I know nothing about what's proper for young ladies. I do not even know if it is proper for the girls to be helping about the rectory."

Isabella smiled at her husband and said, "I believe they are very much of the age to take on more responsibilities about the house. Further, I believe it will help keep Georgiana and Theodosia out of mischief."

Mr. Knight scratched at his beard. "Will I be expected to hand Georgiana her own twelve guineas to commission herself gowns?"

"I still hold firm that her birthday is when she should be allowed to come out, and not a day before," Elizabeth said.

"She turns sixteen in September, does she not? That does not give me much time to save for the expense."

"August, Sir. My birthday is in September."

Mr. Knight made a sound that said he heard her, but did not care to respond.

"Oh! The Eastmore assemblies are to start up again in August, as their repairs are to be done by then, so it will be perfect for Georgiana and Theodosia!" Isabella declared. "Yes, that will be perfect indeed."

"And how much is the ticket prices for each of the girls? Since I shall have to buy one for all of you, I suppose," Mr. Knight complained.

"I shall inquire personally," Isabella said.

"You will need your own ticket, Papa. Mr. Sinclair told me at Ashbrook that he plans to attend every public ball in the neighbourhood."

"That is very good for Mr. Sinclair, but let me assure you, everyone in the village knows where to find me if they wish to visit. I do not require a noisy ball to see people who are perfectly capable of finding the rectory." Mr. Knight pondered for a moment. "Perhaps Mr. Sinclair will be willing to share his carriage space with the girls. There isn't enough room for everyone, but surely between him and the Thornes, we can stuff everyone inside!"

"He has his own carriage?" Isabella asked Elizabeth incredulously.

"Indeed! He told me himself."

Mr. Knight shook his head. "I thought it was merely a rumour, but Elizabeth says it is so. I knew he came from an excellent family, but I had no notion he was already making an excellent income from his inheritances. Plural! Inheritances."

"Then why is he working as a curate? Surely his family must be appalled."

"Apparently," Elizabeth said in a conspiratorial tone, happy to put the conversation on an easy footing to make her father more agreeable, "he bores easily and his mother, annoyed by his boredom, is willing to accept him doing any task to keep him out of her bonnet."

"I do not understand it myself," Mr. Knight said. "But he is only going to cost me fifty pounds per annum, and the parsonage is as fitted up as it is going to be for a single man. Then, I shall turn my focus toward the new lands and perhaps we can finally have some comforts of life here about the rectory."

Elizabeth gave Isabella a desperate glance when Mr. Knight began his plans for the new property.

"My good sir, we have forgotten why Elizabeth has come in here in the first place. Now, I do believe she makes an excellent point. It is time for the girls to take a more active role in learning how to manage the household. Otherwise, they will never be any good to a husband, and no man wishes to marry a silly girl who seems to make fifty pounds turn into ten guineas!"

Mr. Knight nodded, seemingly convinced of his wife's opinion. "Well, if you say so, my dear. I do not understand all of these things. I cannot see why girls do not just sit reading and doing their needlework, but I suppose that is why men rule the important things."

"Indeed, sir," Isabella said, with a glancing smile at Elizabeth. "Also, as we have discussed, and has Mary written to you about, Elizabeth does need time for her studies. Even Mary has come around."

Elizabeth seemed surprised by this, as she still had the vivid memory of Mary throwing her book upon the fire. "She has written about this?"

"Indeed she has," Mr. Knight said. "It was most extraordinary, honestly, given her previous opinions on the subject. However, Mary is now convinced that your studies in the occult may help you find a husband who is also interested in the occult, and therefore would not have the same revulsion to you that another man might have."

The corners of Elizabeth's mouth twitched, but she managed to keep the laughter from her voice. Mostly. "I hope to never be considered repulsive by any man. I am pleased Mary has hope of me marrying yet."

"I have given up on the hope myself," Mr. Knight said. He sighed, the signal he'd lost the battle. "I suppose you wish me to break it to your sisters they shall be doing more of the work about the rectory."

"Indeed, not, sir," Isabella said. She stood and said, "I shall."

"Oh, Isabella, I believe I should..."

"I believe," Isabella said with gentle rebuke in her voice, "That I am mistress of this house, and not you. Now, go work on your studies. I shall have a schedule of tasks drawn up by the morning's end."

Isabella marched out of the room. Elizabeth looked back at her father who shrugged. "Do not look at me, Elizabeth. I wouldn't have wanted to do that task, not for a thousand pounds."

"I don't know, sir. I'd have done it for a thousand pounds per annum."

With that, father and daughter shared a rare moment of laughter. It felt good to Elizabeth's lonely soul.

Epilogue

"HE'S COMING!" THEA shrieked. "Hurry! He is coming!"

Thea had already finished her breakfast and had been seated at the window gawking at the lane in case anyone interesting rode by.

"Pray, who is coming? It had better be someone with a ten pound note." Mr. Knight looked at his pocket watch. "It is only nine-twenty in the morning. Who in their right minds visits a man at nine in the morning?"

"Men bearing ten pound notes?" Elizabeth inquired.

Mr. Knight made a dismissive sound. "That will be the day."

"Never mind all that! He is coming! Oh goodness. Cassie? How is my hair? Oh goodness, I am not even properly dressed!" Thea exclaimed.

"Ah," Elizabeth said. "Though I cannot see, Papa, I do believe Mr. Sinclair is about to grace us with his presence. We are honoured."

"You think so?" Thea's face lit up. It was adorable.

Elizabeth made a thoughtful sound. "Well, he believes we are honoured, so that is good enough for me."

Thea's groans were as dramatic as Elizabeth hoped.

"Oh, speaking of Mr. Sinclair, Elizabeth, when will you be hinting that he should be dining with us twice a week?"

Elizabeth chuckled. "I see Mary could not wait for me to choose the proper time to initiate her plan. I had wanted Mr. Sinclair to settle into the parsonage first and go through the dozens of dinner invitations that a new arrival must certainly attract."

"Never mind all that!" Thea declared. "He is coming up the walk! I am not even properly tied up!"

"For heaven's sake, Thea!" her father declared. "No one wishes to hear about that at the breakfast table."

"Take my shawl," Isabella said, passing her thick, woollen shawl across the table.

Thea snatched it and draped it so that it covered her chest. She looked down. "Oh, but Mary said I had a lovely neck and now it's covered."

Elizabeth pushed herself up from the table, even as Mr. Sinclair was knocking and calling out to them from the now opening front door. She quickly wrapped the shawl to visibly display Thea's swan neck but hide the fact that she'd not bothered properly lacing her stays under her pale pink dress this morning.

Neither had Elizabeth, but she was wearing her thick brown dress, for she believed mornings were for comfort not fashion.

"Hello! I did not realize you were such late diners!" Mr. Sinclair said. He bowed to Mr. Knight. "Pray, forgive my interruption. I was out for my morning stroll and saw Miss Thea at the window, so assumed the family was up and ready for company."

Mr. Knight motioned at the table. "Pull up a chair, sir, and join us. Elizabeth and I were just discussing extending a weekly invitation to dine with us. At least two nights. What say you?"

"Oh, no thank you for breakfast. I already ate. However, I will happily accept any dinner invitation. Standing or otherwise!"

"How are you finding the parsonage?" Elizabeth asked. She'd moved aside to allow Thea more room to display her figure proudly.

"The chimney smokes a little, but that is a small complaint."

"And are you settling in well?" Isabella asked.

"Very well. I have two servants with me. They have been old

servants of my parents, but they have a son living in Eastmore now. So they came with me to be closer to their son, and the impending announcement of their first grandchild."

"Oh, how exciting for them! To have the chance to move closer to their son."

"Indeed. However, it does need a lady's touch. Or so Mrs. Thorne said when she came by yesterday."

"Oh dear!" Elizabeth laughed. "What did Maria say?"
"Well, I confess it was a very bracing conversation! Would you like to take a walk about the park to see?" He nodded at Mr. Knight. "With your permission to steal your breakfast guests, of course."

Mr. Knight waved enthusiastically. "Pray, take them all away! I can't get anything done with them in the house."

Elizabeth glanced at Thea who was wide-eyed and grasping her shawl tighter. "Mr. Sinclair, would you mind giving us a few moments to change into gowns more appropriate for the mud? I fear my sister's pink gown would not survive the dirt."

Mr. Sinclair laughed and said, "By all means! I shall discuss farming with your father in your absence."

Elizabeth sat down to finish her tea and take the last couple of bites of toast. A thudding sound of footsteps rushing through the upstairs and then hitting the back stairs shook the house. Giggles were soon followed by high-pitched squeals of delight.

Her father shouted, "Girls! Propriety!"
"I'm more worried about them coming through the ceiling," Elizabeth said. "Excuse me, Mr. Sinclair. It seems an adult is needed."

With that, Elizabeth excused herself from the table to go upstairs and assist three very silly girls with their stays and thin dresses.

"This is why I wear dark wool at the breakfast table," Elizabeth muttered to herself. But she was smiling.

Author's Note

PERHAPS THE BEST part about writing this book is that I got to really indulge in dressmaking descriptions. Rarely can an author get away with so much ribbon and lace, and I packed in as much as I possibly could. During the editing process, my editor asked if I was certain all of the readers would actually know what I was talking about. Reticules. Fichus. Pelisse. It was a good question and, as it happens, I had not written this author's note as of that moment, so decided it was the perfect subject to cover some of the more uncommon terms I've used.

Reticule: A small lady's handbag on a drawstring. These could be beaded or embroidered, or even knitted. It could carry any number of items, including a handkerchief or a small coin purse (called a "sovereign purse").

Fichu: Basically, this is a piece of fabric worn about the shoulders and sometimes pinned in front to cover up your cleavage during the day.

Spencer: This is a cropped coat that sat just under a woman's breasts. It was cut very close to the body.

Pelisse: This is a coat that's cut very similar to the dress itself, and is almost as long as the dress. They could be made of various fabrics – from silk to fur-lined wool.

Shirts: It surprised several of my early readers that the Knight ladies were in charge of sewing Charles' shirts. They could understand their father, certainly, but Charles? It always surprised me, too, but even Jane Austen's own letters talks about her sewing up shirts for all of her various brothers. Men's shirts were very basic, and would be a waste of money for a family like the Knights to purchase from a tailor.

If you'd love to learn more about fashion in the Regency era, I highly recommend the book, *Dress in the Age of Jane Austen* by Hilary Davidson.

And, of course, if you want to learn more about the Regency era and all of the various jobs of the servants and workers in this book, check out *Hustlers, Harlots, and Heroes*.

All the Other Stuff

IF YOU ENJOYED this story, please consider taking a moment to review it or to recommend it to your friends. Reviews help small authors like me. Even the bad reviews help!

Sign up for the New Release Alerts so that you have first news on releases and sales. I send out the newsletter twice a month: http://kristadball.com.

Did you like my conversation style? If so, check out my other non-fiction books. **What Kings Ate and Wizards Drank** tends to appeal to those who are interested in how food worked before electricity. **Hustlers, Harlots, and Heroes** is more than just a Jane Austen and Victorian history book. It's about how everyday urban people got by in a world without a social safety net.

I also have a Patreon account! That's where, for as little as $1/month, I share recipes, animal stories, history topics of interest, and snippets of my work. I even do historical recipe recreations. https://www.patreon.com/kristadb1

Interested in trying out my fiction? There's a lot to choose from. Need a lighter romance, with lots of quirky neighbours? **Spirit Caller** is for you. Need swashbuckling wish fulfilment? **Blaze** is for you. Heads up, though! There is an on-page sexual assault scene in the first book. It isn't against the main character, but it does happen. In case you need that warning.

If you are interested in politics, meetings, bickering, and broody heroes, well, **The Demons We See** is what you should read. There are also hats and extensive descriptions about food and clothing. Did I mention the hats?

If you want space opera about redemption and forgiveness, and don't mind a dark read, then **Traitor** is where you need to go next.

❧ About the Author ❧

KRISTA D. BALL WAS BORN and raised in Deer Lake, Newfoundland, where she learned how to use a chainsaw, chop wood,and make raspberry jam. After obtaining a B.A. in British History from Mount Allison University, Krista moved to Edmonton, AB where she currently lives.

Somehow, she's picked up an engineer, two kids, six cats, and two very understanding corgis off ebay. Her credit card has been since taken away.

Like any good writer, Krista has had an eclectic array of jobs throughout her life, including strawberry picker, pub bathroom cleaner, oil spill cleaner upper and soupkitchen coordinator. These days, when Krista isn't software testing, she writes in her messy office.

Also by Krista D. Ball

Ladies Occult Society
A Magical Inheritance
A Ghostly Reqest
In the Society of Women (*forthcoming*)

Collaborator
Traitor
Fugitive
Rebel

Tales of Tranquility Series
Blaze
Grief
Interlude (short story collection)
Fury
Schemes
Liberate
Ambush

The Dark Abyss of Our Sins
The Demons We See
The Nightmare We Know
The Sins We Seek (*forthcoming*)

Spirit Caller Series
Spirits Rising
Dark Whispers
Knight Shift
Mystery Night
Dead Living
Blood Family

Nonfiction
What Kings Ate and Wizards Drank
Hustlers, Harlots, and Heroes
Appropriately Aggressive

As Dinah Lewis
First Impressions
Love in the Spotlight